The Island Decides

The Maui Trilogy, Volume 1

Jill Engledow

Published by Maui Island Press, 2022.

In memory of Joelle Davis Rudin

1967-2013

Chapter One

Carrie Ann leaned forward to watch a young couple, smiling and holding hands as they strode up Haight Street. Their brand-new bell bottoms and shiny faces marked them as newcomers. Didn't they know that Haight-Ashbury was no longer the hip, happy place they had read about in *Life* magazine? The Summer of Love was over. The season of hard reality had long since set in.

Clutching the phone, she sank back into the overstuffed chair next to the window overlooking Haight Street and answered Kathryn's question about her weekend.

"Oh, it was okay, I guess. Glenn's nice, and he has a really cute house," she said, stroking the chair's worn velvet upholstery. "But he didn't say anything about getting together again."

"Honey, it's just a matter of time," Kathryn said. "You need an old man, and somewhere out there some lonely dude needs you. You just haven't found the right one yet, but you will."

Carrie Ann sighed and examined her well-chewed thumbnail. "I suppose. So how was the Sacramento concert, anyway?"

"It was great—the audience loved the band. You have to come with us next time. Duke is setting up a gig in Santa Cruz next month. You and Rorie could drive down with us in the van. Hey, what about Rorie? How did she like her first camping trip?"

"I don't know. I went over to Willie's to pick her up, and they weren't back yet."

"Well, that's weird. I'm sure I saw that Daisy person Willie works with at the bus stop right outside The Beadnik this morning when I was getting ready to open up. She went with them, didn't she?"

"Yeah, I think so. It was her, Willie, and some other people he knows from school and work."

"Maybe Daisy came home early. Or maybe Willie took Rorie someplace else on the way home. Probably stopped for an ice cream or something; you know how Uncle Willie likes to spoil that child. Oh, somebody's here—a customer! What a novelty! Guess I better get off and see if I can sell her some beads. You call me later, okay, and let me talk to Rorie. Can't wait to hear her camping stories."

"Okay, Kathryn. Thanks for calling." Carrie Ann hung up, feeling a little uneasy. Should she call El Paso House? Glenn had dropped her off there an hour ago, and there'd been no sign of Willie and Rorie. The doorbell had wakened Willie's cranky roommate, Jason, and if she called now she'd probably wake him again and get him even more pissed off at her.

Jason was such a prick. If not for him, she and Rorie might still be living at El Paso house. But Jason was the oldest resident in this house, the first of the El Paso "family" to have made it to San Francisco, and he had a lot of say about who lived there. Jason just couldn't deal with having a baby around. Willie had tried to intercede for her. He and Carrie Ann had known each other since sixth grade and had come to San Francisco together when Carrie Ann quit her first semester of college to chase after her boyfriend, Jack. They'd all lived at El Paso House, a crumbling mansion with six bedrooms, until Jack got his draft notice and fled to Canada. Soon after, Carrie Ann learned she was pregnant, and Willie had been the first person she told. He was like a brother to her and an uncle to Rorie. But, sweet as he was, Willie was no match for Jason, and Jason's name was on the lease. Carrie Ann ended up moving from place to place for the first year of her child's life. Thank God she'd finally met Mimi, who needed a roommate, and had been able to settle down in as much peace as the single mother of a toddler could expect. The two roommates often laughed about how different they were—Miriam "Mimi" Levinson, an East Coast girl with a straight job as a legal secretary, and Carrie Ann Emerson, a Texas-born hippie mom on welfare—but somehow they had hit it off.

Carrie Ann drained the last of her coffee. It was only a little after eleven; she could wait a while, and if Willie didn't call, she would. Meanwhile, she needed to get her room in order.

She sighed, looking around at all the junk left scattered during the rush to get Rorie ready to go camping and herself ready to spend a weekend with Glenn. Back to real life. She began to pick up Rorie's toys, tossing teddy bears and building blocks into the old wicker basket next to Rorie's bed. She collected scraps Rorie had dropped while cutting out paper dolls and began to corral the dirty laundry. There was almost enough for a trip to the Laundromat, just from what was on the floor, and her welfare check should be in the mailbox today, so she'd have cash for the washers.

Thinking about washing clothes brought Glenn to mind. His tiny but exquisite Sausalito A-frame even had its own washer, with a clothesline in the small backyard She loved the stained glass in his windows, the leather couch, the silk-fringed lampshades, but the mother in her would love even more to have a washer right in her own house. Too bad there seemed to be no chance of Glenn asking her back. For reasons she didn't understand, their farewell this morning had felt final.

She had done her best—cooked her famous enchiladas, given him a backrub, brushed his long wavy hair. But the anxious feeling in her chest told her that whatever she'd done had not been enough to make this man want her to stay.

Carrie Ann didn't get it. She knew she was pretty, with a slender body and thick honey-gold hair halfway to her waist. She thought her eyes were her best feature—big and hazel-green, rimmed with dark lashes. She could cook, keep house, and sew well enough that she earned a little side money making fancy shirts for rock-and-roll musicians.

But she just couldn't find a man. She'd had no steady boyfriend since Jack split to Canada. Was it her personality? Or was it because she had a kid? Not many guys wanted to take on someone else's child.

She glanced at the clock. Noon; she'd better call El Paso House again. She counted twenty rings before she hung up. Now what? She tried to remember whether Willie had classes today or whether he had to work at the coffee shop. She called the coffee shop, but no one had heard from him. She looked up the number of one of the guys who had gone camping; no one answered. Now she was really starting to worry. Where the hell were Willie and Rorie, and why were they not back yet from camping in Big Sur? Frustrated, she called The Beadnik. Kathryn's husband answered. "Tell you what," Duke said. "I'll come get you, and we'll drive around and see if we can find anybody who knows anything. Kathryn said she saw Daisy this morning. Maybe we can find her."

Relieved, she threw on her jacket and headed out to the street to wait for Duke's blue Volkswagen van. Duke knew everybody in the Haight. He was one of the last of the hip community leaders to remain after the degradation of a perfectly good scene brought on by the media-inspired Summer of Love. Carrie Ann considered herself lucky to know Kathryn and her husband, who managed a moderately successful rock band. With Duke in charge, Carrie Ann knew they would have this mystery solved in no time. Her confidence in his knowledge of the neighborhood was confirmed when, after half an hour of cruising, they spotted Daisy's cascade of blonde ringlets.

"There she is." Duke pulled up to the sidewalk outside the Haight Street supermarket that had fed the neighborhood since long before the hippies arrived. He stuck his head out the open window. "Hey, Daisy!" The chick Carrie Ann knew only as an acquaintance from Willie's workplace turned from her conversation with someone lounging in the shade of the supermarket's entrance, then came over to the truck.

"Hey man, did you hear about Willie?" Daisy bent to peer into the truck. "He got sick, man, and he's down in San Luis Obispo, in the hospital."

Dumbstruck, Carrie Ann listened as Duke questioned Daisy. It took a few minutes to sort the whole thing out, but the bottom line was that Daisy had no idea where Rorie had gone.

"This friend of Willie's— her name is Paula—she said she would take care of Rorie. Don't worry, Carrie Ann. She's really cool, and I'm sure everything is fine. They're probably just taking their time coming back up—she was with Fred, you know the dude that works with us? This other guy, Raven, drove Willie to the hospital. We thought maybe he took some bad dope, but Raven came back up later that night and said it was appendicitis. I guess Willie's going to call somebody to come and get him. He didn't call yet?"

"Not that we know of," Duke said. "So, you don't know anything else about this chick Paula? Just that she was with Fred?"

Who were all these people? Suddenly a list of unfamiliar names had taken on tremendous importance in Carrie Ann's life. She found her voice at last. "When was the last time you saw Rorie? And why didn't you come and tell somebody about this? Willie's sick somewhere, and I have no idea where my child is."

"Well, hey, don't get uptight, lady," Daisy replied. "Since when am I in charge of your kid? She was just fine when I saw her last night. I caught a ride up with Raven when he came back from taking Willie to the hospital, and she was all tucked in and sound asleep when we split."

"And what about Willie's car?" Duke asked. "What happened to his car?"

Daisy shrugged. "It's still down there, I guess, parked off to the side by the campgrounds."

Duke shook his head. "Shit, what a mess."

"Yeah, too bad. I guess Willie just has some weird kind of karma. Well, good luck, I gotta get going." Daisy straightened, turned to wave at her friend outside the supermarket, and headed across Stanyan toward Golden Gate Park.

Duke and Carrie Ann sat for a moment, watching her leave. Carrie Ann's stomach hurt. Tears rose to her eyes.

"Duke, what do we do? I have to find my baby."

"Yeah, and I guess we better find out what's going on with Willie. Maybe we should go back to El Paso House and see if they've heard anything."

"But what if they bring Rorie back to my place? Maybe I should go home."

"How would they know where you live? Does Rorie know the address?"

"Well. . . no. . . and of course she doesn't know the phone number. Oh God, Duke, she's barely four years old. I don't think she even knows her last name. And she probably thinks my name is Mommy."

Duke stroked his beard, frowning. "Okay, here's a plan. I'll drop you off at your house just in case someone shows up there. Maybe we better pick up Kathryn. She can close The Beadnik and hang out with you. I'll stop by the coffee shop and find out how to get hold of this guy Fred. He can tell us how to find Paula. And then we'll figure out what to do after that. I'll call you as soon as I know anything."

Unable to speak, Carrie Ann nodded and used her sleeve to wipe the tears from her cheeks.

An hour later, Kathryn and Carrie Ann sat staring at the phone, drinking cups of hot chamomile tea; Kathryn said it would help them deal with the stress.

At last, the phone rang.

"I'm not getting anywhere on finding Rorie, Carrie Ann," Duke reported. "I did find out that Willie is still in the hospital, but there's no phone in his room, and I guess he's still kinda groggy. His appendix burst, and he's pretty sick. They said I could come get him in a few days, so we'll have to work on that, pick up his car somehow. But I still don't know about Rorie. The coffee shop said Fred is off until Wednesday. They gave me his home number, but he doesn't answer. So I'm gonna go find his house and see if he's there, maybe leave him a note. You just stay there with Kathryn."

Mimi came home from work, buzzing in with her usual grin, hip-length mane of hair flying, eager to share stories about the weekend's adventures. Apparently, the expression on Carrie Ann's face was enough to tell her something had gone wrong, for Mimi's grin faded and she sank into a chair and clutched her roommate's hand. Eyes wide, she listened as Carrie Ann sobbed her way through the story, then hugged her, sleek brown hair draping over both their shoulders as they embraced.

"Don't you worry, Kid, we'll find her. Duke's probably on his way with little Sweet Pea right now," Mimi said. But Duke arrived carrying nothing but ingredients for dinner. Carrie Ann watched as Kathryn and Mimi boiled spaghetti and chopped tomatoes. She was incapable of helping, and not interested in eating anyway, but between them, her two friends produced a meal, and they all sat down to eat and figure out what to do next.

Duke did most of the talking, working out a plan to drive down, pick up Willie's car and then Willie, while stopping along the way at various friends' houses to see if anyone had run into Paula, Fred, or Rorie. Duke had rock-and-roll connections all along the California coast and said he would start calling them tonight to get the word out.

7

Thank God for these friends, Carrie Ann thought, looking around the table. What would she do without them? It was all she could do now to suppress the panic filling her chest, let alone think coherently about ways to find Rorie. These friends, her San Francisco family, were an anchor to hold onto. Duke with his long hair and beard, looking like a skinny Jesus in striped bell bottoms. Mimi, with her big Kewpie-doll eyes, wasn't eating much more than Carrie Ann. And finally, sitting next to Carrie Ann, Kathryn, nervously twisted her long brown braid. Childless herself, Kathryn had done more than anyone to help Carrie Ann cope with motherhood.

This adopted family felt closer to her than her own mother and father ever had. The only ones missing were Rorie and Willie. Where was Rorie? What was happening to her?

It was all Carrie Ann's fault, she thought, pushing cold spaghetti around her plate. She never should have let Rorie go on that camping trip. If only she could go back in time and change that one decision, say "no" when she asked Willie to babysit, and he said he wanted to take Rorie camping. It had all been useless anyway—the weekend with Glenn had been a failure, and she had ended up with neither man nor child.

A bitter voice sounded somewhere in her head. *Does that mean it would have been a fair trade if you had lost the child but gained the man?* Carrie Ann groaned. Conversation stopped; everyone turned to look at her.

Kathryn dropped her fork and put both arms around Carrie Ann. "It's okay, honey, we'll find her."

Duke chimed in. "Yeah, Carrie Ann, I'll get right on the phone and start calling around. Somebody has to have seen them."

"Do you think we should call the police?" Mimi asked.

Duke frowned. "Shit, I hate to call in the heat."

Kathryn shook her head. "I don't know, Duke, we might have to. This is pretty serious—no, no, Carrie Ann, calm down. We'll find her. I tell you what. Let's give ourselves a deadline. We'll call around, and Duke can go look for this guy Fred again, and maybe we can get something out of Willie on the phone tomorrow morning. Then if we don't come up with anything by, say, noon, I think we better call the cops."

"Yeah, they could have all the patrol cars looking for her," Mimi said.

Duke pushed back his chair. "Okay, I'm going to hit it. I have to get back home. All my phone numbers are in my desk, so I'll have to call from there. Kathryn, you coming with me?"

"I'll stay for a while if Mimi can give me a ride home."

Immersed in guilt, Carrie Ann sat huddled in the corner of the couch while Kathryn and Mimi cleared the table. Before he left, Duke called El Paso House and then tried Fred's number once more. He hung up and sat next to her, taking her hand.

"We'll find her. Don't worry."

"It's all my fault. How could I have been so stupid? I never should have left her."

"But you've left her with Willie, and with us, and it's always been okay before. Willie's like your brother, he loves Rorie, and he would never have hurt her or let this happen if he could have prevented it. How were you supposed to know something weird like this could happen?"

Carrie Ann had no answer for that. But she had let this happen. She had lost her child.

It was a long night. Carrie Ann could not stand to be in the bedroom she and Rorie shared, with Rorie's drawings taped all over the walls and her little mattress in one corner, stripped of its sheets, empty. After Mimi went off to her room, Carrie Ann stretched out on the couch, close to the phone, and shut her eyes. It was hard to relax with her clothes on, but she thought she should stay dressed in case something happened and she had to leave in a hurry. The sofa's upholstery was rough against her skin; it seemed long ago and far away that she had sat on Glenn's soft leather couch and wished it were her own. This old couch smelled faintly of sour milk, a reminder of a toddler's many mishaps.

Maybe she should pray. She wasn't sure quite how; the only prayer she'd ever learned was the one that went, "if I should die before I wake," and that phrase brought up images she could not contemplate. She turned on her side, drew her knees toward her chest, and hugged her pillow.

Perhaps if she could sleep, the night would pass quickly, and in the morning, Rorie would be there. She imagined a knock on the door, and a friendly stranger holding Rorie's hand. If only she could make it so, will it into reality.

But she could not even make herself go to sleep, never mind bring Rorie home. Each time she began to doze, she would remember what had happened and her stomach would clench, her eyes well up, and the litany begin again. If only she had never let Rorie go. . .

Somehow, it was light, and the ringing phone was jolting her awake. It was Duke.

"I got hold of Fred. I'm afraid it's not real good news. He and Paula had a fight, and she took Rorie and said she was going down to L.A."

"To Los Angeles? Oh my God." The pain came back, to her stomach, her head, her mind. Her eyes, prickly with crying, filled again. "Now what do we do?"

"I think we have to go to the cops. Do you want me to come and get you?"

A hot shower helped, along with a reheated cup of Mimi's morning coffee. Carrie Ann ran a brush through her hair and put on a clean turtleneck with yesterday's jeans. The fog was in; she grabbed her denim jacket and went out to wait on the porch for Duke. Thank

God he was helping her. She didn't even know where the police station was.

Not that it seemed to do much good, once they got there. Maybe if she had dressed up, the police would have paid more attention, but instead, the man at the front desk seemed bored as he filled out the report form. Aurora Emerson a k a "Rorie," four years-two months, blonde hair (*pale and fine, Officer, put down "soft"*), blue eyes (*just like her father's—clear, pale crystal blue edged with dark lashes*). No distinguishing marks (*except for a little heart-shaped chin, Sir*).

Discouraged, they got back into Duke's van and headed for The Beadnik. In the kitchen behind the store, Kathryn poured coffee and urged Carrie Ann to eat some toast.

"I have a feeling it won't do much good to get cops involved," Duke said. "Just another lost little hippie kid. They don't give a shit. But at least he said they would notify the police between here and L.A. And I got half the roadies in California on the lookout. Fred said Paula took off hitchhiking, so somebody will probably see them somewhere. I'm thinking I might go down to San Luis Obispo, make some stops along the way, and see what Willie has to say."

"What about me? Can I go?" Carrie Ann asked.

"I think you should stay home, close to the phone, and keep calling El Paso House to see if anybody shows up," Duke said. "Maybe I'll take one of the guys from the band with me and we can pick up Willie's car and bring him home."

So it was decided. Carrie Ann tried to make the hours go faster by crocheting a sweater for Rorie to wear when she got home. She called everyone she could think of to ask them to keep an eye out for Rorie. In the early evening, after Mimi had gotten home and could stay near the phone, she walked up and down Haight Street, talking to shopkeepers and acquaintances, hoping for clues.

But by the time Duke drove up three days later with Willie in the passenger seat of his rescued VW Bug, there were still no clues to Rorie's whereabouts. No one had seen or heard a thing.

Carrie Ann knelt on the sidewalk outside her apartment, talking to Willie through the car window. He was still so weak that he had stayed in the car while Duke went to bring Carrie Ann out to see him. Now they were both crying, and Willie seemed to feel as bad as she did. His face was pale under his mop of curly hair, and his arm felt thin where Carrie Ann's hand rested on the sleeve of his old plaid flannel shirt.

"Shit, Carrie Ann, I am so sorry. I would do anything if I could find Rorie. I just couldn't help it. I hurt so bad I couldn't even stand up, I was doubled up with pain, and they sort of shoveled me into the back of Raven's van and took me to the hospital. There was nothing I could do. I had no idea something like this would happen—and by the time I was really thinking straight again, there was Duke on the phone telling me Rorie was lost."

"I know. It's not your fault. I should never have left her for a whole weekend, especially when you were planning to go someplace. I don't blame you, Willie. Now listen, you go home and go to bed and get better, okay? I'm going to need you to help me keep looking for her."

Still weeping, Willie leaned out to wave goodbye as the Bug headed up Haight. Carrie Ann watched them go, then dragged herself up the steps to her front door. Somehow, Willie's return made it all seem so final. Willie was back, but Rorie was not, and Carrie Ann was beginning to wonder if she would ever see her baby again.

Three weeks later, there was still no sign of the missing child. The police had taken a bit more interest after Duke and Carrie Ann made their third trip to the station but still offered no hope. As soon as Willie felt well enough to be out, Duke drove him and Carrie Ann all the way down to Los Angeles, with Willie stretched out on the bed platform in the back of Duke's van. They crashed on the floor with a friend of Duke's and made the rounds of hippie pads and shops. But Los Angeles was a big city, more spread out than San Francisco, and they were getting nowhere. Carrie Ann fought off despair as they drove around the endless, alien streets of this sprawling place, so different from the city she now thought of as home. Willie was still frail, their money was running low, and they were all depressed.

There seemed no point in hanging around this strange place, so they drove back up the coast. Carrie Ann settled near the phone and waited.

A week after their return, as she sat listlessly hemming a shirt she was making for one of the guys in Duke's band, Willie called.

"Carrie Ann, you better get over here right away. There's a guy here who might know where Rorie is."

"Oh God! What did he say? Where is she?" Carrie Ann dropped the shirt, needle and thread dangling, and knelt to reach under the couch for her shoes.

"He says she's in Hawaii, someplace called Maui. Somebody over there wants to adopt her. I think you're going to have to go and get her."

Chapter Two

The Maui air touched her cheek like velvet, soft and warm, as she stepped off the plane. Carrie Ann blinked against the bright sunlight. Her eyes burned from the airplane's dry air, and her nose felt parched. She clutched the railing and descended steep steps behind the other passengers. The couple ahead of her chuckled; big yellow footsteps were painted on the tarmac, as if a barefoot giant had led the way to the terminal. Carrie Ann stood for a moment beneath the plane's wing, refreshed by the moisture-laden breeze. A swath of green edged the runway, and beyond that, a great mountain loomed against a cloudless, brilliant blue sky.

Somewhere on this island was her little girl.

She hoisted the strap of her bag higher onto her shoulder, then nervously checked to see that it still held the little notebook with the phone number and address for the Maui Legal Aid office. The lawyer in the San Francisco office had arranged everything—she had an appointment with the Maui lawyer tomorrow, and Friday they would go to court. With any luck, she'd be back at this airport within a week and on the way home with Rorie. She took a deep breath of sea-scented air and followed the other passengers along the yellow footprint path.

Inside the terminal, a living tree spread its branches wide and reached up through a hole in the roof. Beyond the tree, the terminal was open to the air. Carrie Ann hadn't seen many airports, but somehow she didn't think trees were among the usual furnishings. She retrieved her suitcase and went outside to look for a taxi. She didn't want to start right out hitchhiking here, though she'd done it often enough in California. At least until she knew her way around, she was willing to spend a little of her precious money. Besides, she had no idea where she would stay tonight.

"Yes ma'am, you need taxi?" A dark-skinned man with a big smile and a flowered shirt greeted her. Carrie Ann thought he looked vaguely Mexican, but his accent was unfamiliar.

"I need a taxi, and I need a good cheap hotel. You know someplace where I can get a room? It needs to be near, uh . . ." She fumbled in her shoulder bag for the Legal Aid address. "Wahluckoo?"

The man smiled, said, "Wye-loo-koo," and opened the cab's back door. "No more hotel in Wailuku," he said, "but get some in Kahului, not too far away. I take you there."

At the hotel, the front-desk clerk greeted her with a smile as big as the cab driver's and gave her a room in a detached cinder-block building. It was pretty basic, but then that's all she could afford anyway, a place to sleep and shower. The room was small but looked clean enough. Right outside the window was a plant with brilliantly colored leaves—green, red, yellow, orange—the colors mixed on each leaf as if someone had splattered different paints across the plant. Carrie Ann hung her one dress in the closet, splashed her face with cold water, and set out to explore. She spotted a little shopping center across a wide street lined with tall palms and crossed over to look for a grocery store. Tonight, she thought, she'd have yogurt for dinner and save the cost of eating out.

But there was no yogurt in the grocery store, and the clerk looked blank when she asked for it. She bought crackers, an apple, and cheese and took them back across the road. Instead of going to her room, she wandered around to the other side of the hotel and discovered it was set on a beach.

The beach was narrow, with an industrial-looking pier at one end. But it was a beach nonetheless, with silvery water lapping at the shore. Across the bay, mountains rose into the sky, sharp ridges blocking the late-day sun so that its rays shot up in spears behind them, piercing the clouds clustered around the peaks.

Carrie Ann sank onto the warm sand and sat simply staring at this incredible sight. She'd never seen anything like it in Texas or California, green mountains rising steeply above the shining water, golden light imparting a glow to misty clouds. Peace settled over her. Even though she had no idea when she'd see her child again or what the judge would say in court, at least she knew where Rorie was. And sitting on this beach, watching the sun go down, she thought Maui was a fine place to be.

Her peaceful mood lasted as she took a hot shower and crawled into bed. Clean sheets were luxurious after long hours of travel. She was surprised at how tired she was after the flight, her first time ever on an airplane. Images of clouds floated through her mind as they'd floated below the plane, white and fluffy like the bubbles in a fresh-filled sink of dishwater.

A strange chirping sound startled her out of a doze. She turned on the light and lay without moving. The chirp sounded again. It was coming from a little lizard high on the molding at the ceiling's edge. She contemplated the creature for a moment. She'd never heard of a lizard bothering anyone. Okay, buddy, she thought, turning off the light—you stay in your corner, and I'll stay in mine.

But now she was awake. For days she'd been buoyed by the logistics of getting to Hawaii and by the knowledge, after nearly a month of anxiety, that Rorie was alive.

Finally, Carrie Ann was here, on an island she'd never heard of until a week ago, and the anxiety was rising again in her chest. She knew no one in this place. Tomorrow she'd have to tell a stranger, the Legal Aid lawyer, how she'd lost her child, and win him to her side so he'd help her tell her story to a judge.

What if they didn't believe her? And should she tell them how she came to send her baby off with Willie and his space-cadet friends in the first place?

No, she decided, it was best not to mention her weekend with Glenn. She turned over to face the wall, trying to find comfort in this strange hotel bed that only a short time ago had seemed luxurious.

No one here needed to know she'd wanted to be free for a few days so she could spend time with Glenn. And so what, she thought—her motives were righteous weren't they? Yes, of course she needed a man, but not only for herself. If she found the right one, he would be a father to Rorie. She couldn't help it if they all ran as soon as they realized she came with a child attached. Glenn had seemed different, willingly including Rorie in their walks through Golden Gate Park, treating her to ice cream, waiting patiently while Carrie Ann put her to bed before he pulled out his hash pipe.

Carrie Ann turned onto her other side, sighing as she plumped the pillow. Outside a slow rain fell, heavy drops hitting the roof and pattering on the bushes near the window. The sound of rain relaxed her once again, and she finally slipped into sleep.

Birdsong woke her in the morning. There must have been hundreds of them outside her window, headquartered in a big spreading tree like the one in the airport terminal. She sat up and put her face to the screen. Was it her imagination, or did the air smell sweet?

She crossed the street again to find somewhere to eat breakfast. The little shopping center was already busy. Old men sat playing cards at tables scattered under shady trees, and people pushed carts into the grocery store. Carrie Ann stopped, looking around for a restaurant. At one of the open-air tables, a man sat reading a newspaper. He spotted Carrie Ann and scowled, looked down at the newspaper and then at her again, still frowning. Puzzled, she glanced around. She was the only white person in sight—was that why he frowned? She had no idea how the races got along here. Everyone had been friendly so far. Could it be the way she was dressed? She wore bell bottoms and a tie-dyed T-shirt, along with the earrings and necklace she'd made with beads from her friend Kathryn's store. Maybe she should have worn a bra.

Well, whatever it was, she had to get going. She peered into the window of a drugstore and saw that it had an old-fashioned counter and stools like the one she remembered from her elementary school days. Inside, she chose a stool, ordered a ham-and-egg sandwich, and looked around. Only a few customers were at the counter. An elderly Asian man sat a few seats away, eating some sort of soup full of noodles, and another man sipped coffee, reading the paper. By the time she had finished her sandwich, he was gone, leaving the newspaper folded on the counter. Carrie Ann picked it up. When she saw the front page, she realized why that man outside had frowned at her.

A photo depicted long-haired dancers somewhere outdoors, with palm trees in the background. *"Love-in Desecrates Hawaiiana, Says Maui Councilman,"* the headline read.

> *Councilman Joe Rodrigues called last Sunday's rock concert at Baldwin Park a desecration of Hawaiian values. Speaking at a Chamber of Commerce meeting Friday, Rodrigues said the event was typical of those sponsored by the "hippie newcomers who have washed ashore" in recent years.*

> *"Half-naked women, dirty little children with no diapers on, men who need a shave and a haircut—all gyrating to loud rock-and-roll. We need to do something about this invasion," the councilman told a group of about 30 Chamber members.*

THE ISLAND DECIDES

Rodrigues said the recent quarantine of Guava Gulch was one example of the problems these newcomers are bringing to the island. "Besides the health hazard of them exposing our people to filthy diseases, it cost a lot of money to keep the police on patrol and bring food to those people.

"Even worse, they found one child down there that didn't belong to anybody, had to put her up for adoption by a good local family. These people can't even keep track of their own kids!"

Carrie Ann stopped reading. Her face burned. No wonder that man outside had given her such a terrible look, and he had not even known that she was probably the parent of that child, the very person who could not keep track of her own kid. She folded the paper so the story and its accompanying picture were hidden and hesitated for a moment. No, she did not want to keep that story. She carried the paper with her out of the drugstore and dropped it into a trash can. The man who had frowned at her was no longer at his table, but she was self-conscious now of her San Francisco hippie looks, and she avoided eye contact with the solid citizens of Maui as she left the shopping center and crossed the road to the hotel.

Carrie Ann changed into the conservative navy-blue dress she had bought especially for this trip, then contemplated her image in the mirror. Why had she seen that damn newspaper, today of all days? She was already nervous enough, without reading about her own irresponsibility on the front page of a local newspaper. She wondered if the lawyer had seen it. Everyone on Maui must be talking about her.

Once in a taxicab, her thoughts switched to another topic of anxiety. If she kept staying in hotels and paying for cabs, she would be broke in no time. At least the ride to Wailuku was a short trip. If she had known where she was going, she probably could have walked, though the hill between the two towns was steep. Wailuku was more village than town, a quiet cluster of buildings set in the foothills of the mountains she'd admired from the beach the night before.

The cabbie dropped her off outside a small green cottage with a Legal Aid sign above the front door. Carrie Ann stood nervously combing her hair with her fingers, gathering courage to enter. She hoped she looked okay. She'd gone secondhand-store shopping with Kathryn when she learned she had to go to court, and they'd picked out this little navy-blue number with its neat white collar. She'd put on her bra for this meeting, and there were stockings in her suitcase for the actual day in court, along with real shoes instead of the Indian leather sandals she usually wore. Kathryn had trimmed inches off her hair so it swung straight and thick just to her shoulders and had counseled her to wear a little lipstick to court.

She was early. The Legal Aid secretary said the attorney, Rick Stinson, wouldn't be able to see her for a while. Carrie Ann sat down and stared out a window at a tree with pink blossoms that reminded her of the simple cartoonish flowers Rorie liked to draw.

"Carrie Ann Emerson?"

The man standing in the doorway was young and bearded, with wire-rimmed glasses, rolled-up shirtsleeves, and long hair pulled back into a braid. Carrie Ann let herself relax. This guy looked like someone she might have met back in San Francisco, not the stuffy, judgmental old man she'd expected. Kind of handsome, she thought, automatically checking his left hand for a ring. Not that a bare finger really meant anything.

"Have you seen Rorie?" Carrie Ann asked as they settled into chairs on each side of a scarred wooden desk. "Is she okay? Will I get to see her pretty soon?"

"I haven't seen her myself," the lawyer replied. "But I talked to her social worker, and he says she's doing fine, staying with a nice family with another kid. You'll probably see her Friday when we go to court."

Carrie Ann bit her lip. "Well, at least she's okay. At least I know where she is."

Rick leaned back in his chair and tugged on his beard. "So tell me. What's happening here?"

"You mean how Rorie got lost?"

"Yeah. You gotta admit this is a pretty unusual situation."

Carrie Ann clasped her hands tightly in her lap and plunged in. "Last month, I let her go on a camping trip with Willie Sampson, an old friend of mine—we grew up in the same neighborhood, and he's known Rorie since—well, since before she was born. He babysits her sometimes, and I had some other stuff happening that weekend. He was going camping, so we thought it would be cool for her to go on her first camping trip, you know?

"Anyway, while they were camping Willie got this terrible stomachache, and someone took him to the hospital. Turned out he had appendicitis and they had to operate, like right away."

Carrie Ann paused. Tears stung her eyes. "So somebody named Paula ended up taking care of Rorie, and then she had a fight with her old man and split for Los Angeles. My friends and I searched for weeks, but we couldn't find her."

Rick reached back and took a box of tissues off the shelf behind him. He pushed it across the desk to Carrie Ann, who blew her nose and tried to get control of herself.

"Is Rorie's dad still in the picture? Did he help search?"

Carrie Ann looked down at her hands, twisting the damp tissue.

"No. His name is Jack. That's how I got to San Francisco. I quit school to follow him out there when he went to join this rock band. I caught a ride with Willie; he was transferring to San Francisco State. Anyway, Jack got a draft notice and split to Canada, and right afterward I found out I was pregnant. I wrote to him about it, but I don't even know if he ever got my letters."

"So, it's just been you two?"

"Yeah, except I have some really good friends who've helped a lot—my girlfriend Kathryn and her husband, Duke—he manages the band Jack played in—and my roommate, Mimi, and of course Willie." Carrie Ann shook her head. "Poor Willie, he freaked when he found out what happened. As soon as he could get out of the hospital, he helped me look for her. And Duke called his rock-and-roll connections—he knows a lot of people all over California. Then Duke and Willie and I drove down to L.A., since that's where Paula headed after the fight with her old man, but we couldn't find any sign of them. Plus of course we told the police, but they weren't much help. I guess they figured I was some hippie who couldn't take care of her kid."

Carrie Ann dabbed her eyes with a fresh tissue. "And my social worker—she was really pissed, not helpful at all. She said maybe I shouldn't get to keep Rorie even if I found her. And she was going to cut off my welfare right away, but I begged her to keep it going, so I wouldn't have to find a job, and I could keep looking for Rorie."

"Did she go for that?"

"Yeah, she let me stay on welfare until the end of this month. I called her when I heard where Rorie was, and then she was helpful—told me to call Legal Aid in San Francisco and get them to set up an appointment with you. And here I am."

Carrie Ann wiped her cheeks dry again.

"How did you find out where Rorie was?"

"About a week ago, somebody Willie knew from San Francisco State showed up. He had been here on Maui, living in some commune, and I guess they had an epidemic?"

Rick nodded. "Hepatitis. It's pretty much over, but they were under quarantine for a while. That's where Rorie showed up."

"Well, this guy said the cops found Rorie and turned her over to foster parents and she was really happy . . ." Carrie Ann began to sob and almost couldn't finish her sentence, "and they wanted to adopt her and keep her." She pulled another tissue from the box.

For a moment, Rick sat, letting her cry, then asked, "Any idea how she got from California to Maui?"

Carrie Ann shook her head. "No idea. I don't know if Paula brought her or someone else—we never did manage to track down Paula. I don't know how anyone could take a child that wasn't theirs and bring her all this way across the ocean. It's unbelievable."

"Yeah, pretty weird," Rick said. "You want to hear what I know?"

She nodded, trying to compose herself.

"I got involved in the Guava Gulch situation representing a couple of the people there who were not sick and didn't want to be quarantined. I knew about Rorie—they found her with a woman named Sundance, kind of a freaky lady who was one of the last ones to get sick. Anyway, she didn't really know who Rorie belonged to, and Rorie seemed to have forgotten her last name and where she lived, so they put her into foster care. And you know about the legal ad that ran in the *Maui News,* we sent that to you after the San Francisco attorney contacted us."

"Yeah, that freaked me out." The ad, creased from much rereading and refolding, was tucked into her wallet. She could almost quote it verbatim. "To the parents of Rorie, a 4-year-old female child, greetings: you are hereby notified that the Department of Social Services and Housing has petitioned the Second Circuit Court, County of Maui, for legal custody of the above-named infant." Be in court on Maui on September 17, 1971, the ad said, or lose your child.

"And this family that has her. They really want to adopt her?"

"I guess so. But that's not the immediate problem. No one can adopt a child until parental custody has been terminated, and that's what we face in court the day after tomorrow. You have to prove to the judge that you are a fit mother."

Carrie Ann chewed her thumbnail. How could she prove a thing like that to a judge in court, especially after ending up in this freaky situation? She looked at Rick, so handsome, so competent; a lawyer who knew about court and judges and how these things worked. He would know what to do. She had to trust him to guide her. She had no choice. "I can see her Friday?"

"Yeah, not in the courtroom, but probably with the social worker in a private room before the court session. The social worker says Rorie's doing okay now, but she was pretty scrawny when they found her, with head lice and pinworms." Carrie Ann closed her eyes and groaned. "But she's doing a lot better," Rick repeated hastily.

"Poor baby," Carrie Ann whispered, shaking her head. She blew her nose. "How did something like this ever happen? It's unreal."

"Yeah, it sure is. Well, listen—we need to spend some time together tomorrow. I have to be in court today, unfortunately, and we see the judge Friday. How can I get hold of you?"

"I was going to ask you. I stayed in this little hotel, down the road in, uh . . ."

"Kahului?"

"Yeah, Kahului. But if I stay there even a few more nights, I'll be flat broke. And if I have to stay longer . . . Oh, God, what am I going to do?" Her voice broke again, and her eyes filled.

"Hmmm, yeah, I see your point. I guess you need someplace right now, and as cheap as possible."

"I could go back down to the hotel tonight, but I'd really rather not. Is there like a YWCA or something?"

"No, nothing like that. But tell you what, why don't you go hang out in the reception room, and I'll make some phone calls. I might be able to find you a place."

THE ISLAND DECIDES

Five minutes later Rick stuck his head out of his office door. Carrie Ann looked up from the magazine she'd been staring at.

"I found you a place. I can take you there after I get out of court this afternoon. You can handle rock-and-roll, can't you? And all that goes with it?"

Carrie Ann managed to smile. "Oh, yeah. I'm used to rock-and-roll. And all that goes with it."

Chapter Three

"This is sugarcane," Rick said as they drove through green fields toward the great round mountain Carrie Ann had seen when she landed yesterday. Rick said its name was Haleakala, a word she could barely pronounce.

"You'll see lots of sugarcane here." Rick pointed off to the right. "See those smokestacks? That's a mill where they process the cane."

Carrie Ann's hair flew in the warm wind blowing through the open sides of Rick's Jeep. Sugarcane swayed in the fields like giant blades of grass. A few peaceful-looking clouds drifted in the wide blue sky.

A town appeared ahead, along with another smokestack.

"This is Paia," Rick said. "The beginning of country and also the beginning of where the freaks live—the West Coast transplants, hippies, surfers, and other assorted strange haoles."

"Strange what?"

"Haoles. That's us. It means foreigner, but mostly it means Caucasian. Paia, Haiku, all this area we're heading into—it's filling up with haoles, mainland dropouts. First new people to come here in many, many years. This place was practically dead, the old plantation villages closing down, until the longhairs started moving in a few years ago."

Paia had an old-fashioned western look, with rickety buildings that needed a coat of paint. The tiny town disappeared after a couple of blocks, and the road continued through more cane fields and past a few well-landscaped houses.

"And coming right up," Rick said as his Jeep rounded a curve, "is Hookipa." Suddenly, they were driving along the coast, with waves pounding at the land's edge yards from the Jeep. Rick pointed out to sea. "See the surfers?"

A cluster of tiny figures floated near the wave line a few hundred yards out. A wave swelled, and several of them paddled madly. A few stood and rode the wave nearly to shore before diving into the water.

"Wow," Carrie Ann said, craning her neck to watch the surfers as the Jeep moved past. "I wonder if I could do that."

"Are you a good swimmer?"

"Not very."

"Well, that's the first requirement. The ocean is powerful. You have to be able to handle yourself out there."

Carrie Ann settled back to watch the scenery, which became more beautiful by the minute. The cane had disappeared, replaced by orderly rows of spiky gray-green plants Rick identified as pineapple. This was the country all right, with few houses and little traffic. She saw someone riding a horse down a road heading toward the ocean, and farther along a man in a cowboy hat loading cattle into a shiny red truck.

Rick turned off the highway and headed uphill. Slowing, he pointed to a dirt track into the jungle, a road so poorly marked she'd never have recognized it on her own.

"That's the road to Guava Gulch," he said. "That's where they found your little girl. It belongs to this old guy with real old-time liberal views—has a big picture of FDR on his wall. He started letting people stay there a few years ago. They built shacks and planted gardens, and he let them have all the bananas they wanted, as long as they kept the banana trees weeded. First thing you know he had a little colony going."

A couple of miles up the road, Rick shifted into a lower gear, turned onto a dirt driveway, and slowed to ease the Jeep over ruts and rocks on a rust-colored muddy track winding down into green jungle. In the golden light of late afternoon, Carrie Ann saw heavy vines climbing up the trunks of enormous trees and red waxy-looking flowers growing from clusters of foliage that must be as tall as she was. Giant stems lifted enormous heart-shaped green leaves. The air was humid, with a rich, fruity scent. They drove over a tiny stream trickling across the road and then started uphill again, passing a forest of thin green bamboo.

One final turn and they were back in the sunlight, in a carefully tended yard where a tall, gray-painted house stood at one end.

"This is the O'Connor place," Rick announced, turning off the Jeep. "Come on in and meet Jerilyn."

The strains of "Honky Tonk Women" greeted them from the open windows of the living room as they climbed the steps. Rick took off his shoes and walked right in. Carrie Ann hesitated briefly, fighting back a sudden surge of anxiety. Her life seemed to be one new challenge after another lately; now she'd meet the people who'd offered to put her up while she went through the process of getting Rorie back. She hoped they would like her, but she also hoped they wouldn't be too weird. What kind of people let someone move in, sight unseen? Well, she had no choice at this point. She took a deep breath, decided she'd better follow Rick's example and go barefoot, then slipped out of her sandals and followed him.

Inside, a woman in cut-off jeans and a tank top was vigorously polishing a windowpane with newspaper, singing along with the Stones as she rubbed. Her sun-streaked brown hair was pulled up into a knot on the back of her head, anchored by an orange chopstick. The room smelled of vinegar.

"Jerilyn!" Rick shouted over the music.

The woman turned, grinned, and stepped over to the record player to lower the sound. Carrie Ann felt better, seeing the tanned, smiling face of her hostess. She looked friendly and wholesome. Maybe this wouldn't be so scary after all.

"That's my window-washing music," Jerilyn said. "Hey, how you doin', Rick?" She gave him a kiss on the cheek; Rick patted her plump shoulder.

"And this must be Carrie Ann?"

Carrie Ann took her outstretched hand and smiled nervously. "Hi, Jerilyn."

"That's me—and this is the O'Connor Manor." She gestured at high ceilings painted sky blue. Each of the walls was painted a different color—lavender, chartreuse, coral, turquoise. The room was sparsely furnished with a wood-framed couch, a few rattan chairs, and piles of cushions. "It's an old plantation house. Used to belong to a sugar mill manager, years ago, before everybody moved to town. Then we came along and found it empty, got it for a song. It's roomy, but boy does it have a lot of windows! I'm forever cleaning windows—that and sweeping up termite shit. Well, listen—you guys want some coffee? Johnny will be home soon. Carrie Ann, where's your stuff? I'll show you where you'll be staying."

"I left it in the car."

"I'll get it," Rick said. "You go take a look at your room. I'd love a cup of coffee, Jerilyn."

Jerilyn led Carrie Ann through the kitchen, lit by slanting rays of sun that shone through wide windows over the kitchen sink. Jerilyn paused for a moment. "This is where I spend a lot of time—I cook for my husband and son and our foster daughter, but also for the band. One of the guys lives down the road, one lives downstairs, and one lives in the cottage up behind our house. They all show up for dinner most nights, and the bass player's girlfriend is usually around too. She's not much help, I have to say. Anyway, nice kitchen, huh?" She gestured to the warm peach-colored walls, gleaming wooden cabinets, and big windows, with their view of sky and tall waving bamboo. "This is the one room we really fixed up when we got this place. Johnny built the cabinets out of koa. It's a native wood, really pretty."

"It's beautiful," Carrie Ann agreed, running her hand along the edge of a cabinet whose wood seemed to glow. How Kathryn would love this kitchen; hers was small and dim, with a stained sink and out-of-date appliances. Carrie Ann had spent many an afternoon there with Kathryn, making dinner for Duke's band and whoever else happened to show up.

She followed Jerilyn through a short hallway to a room where dark-purple walls were decorated with psychedelic rock posters. Two single mattresses covered with pink Indian bedspreads lay on the floor, and a wooden chest of drawers stood in one corner. More Indian bedspreads shaded the windows, darkening the room.

"It's not much, and you have to share with Allison, but you've got your own bathroom." Jerilyn gestured to a closed door. "And dig the view." She pulled back a curtain to show another of those enormous trees, this one sprouting giant ferns here and there on a gnarled trunk. Flowers in shades of pink clustered around the tree's base.

"I can't get over the plants here," Carrie Ann said, moving closer to the window to get a better look.

"They're pretty amazing, huh?" Rick said as he set her suitcase next to the door.

Jerilyn pulled open a drawer of the dresser and sighed at the crumpled wads of clothing it held. "That girl—no wonder she never has anything decent to wear to school." She shoved the drawer shut. "Looks like you'll have to live out of your suitcase for a while, Carrie Ann. Allison's got this thing crammed full."

"That's okay," Carrie Ann said. "I'm hoping I'll be on my way home soon anyway."

"Well, come on into the kitchen and sit down and tell me all about it," Jerilyn said.

Carrie Ann was finishing her story when she heard the sound of an engine rumbling up the driveway. It stopped, and a door slammed. Jerilyn got up from her seat at the kitchen table and peered out the windows over the sink.

"Hi, baby!" she called out the window. "Come on in and meet our new roommate."

"Does he know Carrie Ann is here?" Rick asked as Jerilyn refilled his coffee cup.

"Oh sure, he called an hour or so after you did, and it's fine. You know Johnny. He's always cool with another face at the table. Of course, then he disappears with everybody else to play music after dinner, when the sink's full of dirty dishes."

"I'll help with the dishes," Carrie Ann said. "I know what it's like. My friend Kathryn has the same problem. Her old man manages a band, too, and Kathryn's always stuck with the dirty work."

"Dirty work? What dirty work is that?" A large man with fluffy brown hair and beard appeared at the kitchen's back door. He plopped a six-pack of beer onto the table and leaned over to give Jerilyn a quick kiss before lowering himself into a chair.

"I'm getting too old for house building," he said, pulling a cigarette from his shirt pocket. "Those damn musicians better get rich and famous, and they better do it damn quick."

"Johnny, you left your boots on again," Jerilyn said.

"Shit. Oh well, if I do it you got no excuse to yell at anybody else." He leaned back and looked around the table. "Hi Rick, howzit. And is this our lost mommy?"

Rick grinned. "Well, that's one way to look at it. Carrie Ann Emerson—Johnny O'Connor. Jerilyn said you guys would put her up until she goes to court and we see what the judge has to say. Then we'll have to figure out what to do next."

"So what's the prognosis? You gonna get her little girl back?"

"We'll have to see. Depends on the judge, I guess. It's Yoshioka, and he tends to be pretty conservative."

"Is that bad?" Carrie Ann asked anxiously.

"Well, it could make things tougher. But on the other hand, he's basically a nice guy, and there's the traditional belief that kids belong with their moms unless there's a real good reason for other arrangements, so keep your hopes up."

Johnny frowned. "Speaking of kids, where's Allison?"

"She went motorcycle riding with Michael," Jerilyn said.

"Oh, great. That asshole is practically old enough to be her father, and all he's interested in is getting in her pants, if he hasn't already."

"Oh, baby, he's not that old, and Allison's not exactly an untouched virgin, you know."

"As long as she stays on the pill. Hey, forget that shit, how about a beer, Rick? Carrie Ann? And let's roll one up, it's been a long, hard day."

Jerilyn glanced at Carrie Ann, then at Rick. "I hope Carrie Ann is used to being around people smoking dope."

"Hell, she's from San Francisco, of course she is," Johnny stated, stretching one long arm to reach a flower-painted metal box on top of the refrigerator.

"Oh, I don't mind. I kind of like a little smoke," Carrie Ann said, a blush heating her cheeks. "But, Rick, I didn't know lawyers smoked it—not that I know any other lawyers."

Rick laughed, a bit uneasily. "Sure, lawyers smoke it, especially if they're lawyers who spent their school years in Berkeley and then moved right to Maui. Just don't tell the judge, okay?"

"I won't, don't worry." Carrie Ann accepted the roach Jerilyn passed her, took a deep toke, and handed it to Rick. She held her breath a moment, savoring the sense of having her head fill with something that made her very, very peaceful.

"What's the latest on Guava Gulch?" Johnny asked, his voice choked as he held in the first toke from the new joint he'd rolled.

"Everybody's free to come and go, they're all well, and now there's the building permit hassle. But the best part of the story—have you heard this one? You know where it turns out the hepatitis came from?"

Johnny stopped in the process of rolling another joint and looked up. "Where?"

"The Lono Poi Factory."

"You're shittin' me."

Carrie Ann sat mystified as Johnny, Jerilyn, and Rick grinned and shook their heads.

"I don't get it. What's the Lono Poi Factory?"

"It's a place where they make poi—the traditional staple food of the Hawaiian people. The native equivalent of bread or rice, really basic," Rick explained. "And the irony is that the local politicos have been using this hepatitis epidemic as an excuse to come down hard on haoles in general and hippies in particular. Anybody who looks weird or has long hair has been getting hassled, and the chief weapon has been the claim that 'da heepies' are bringing disease to our fair isle and contaminating paradise."

"So when they find the source of the nasty old germs, and it's a poi factory, it shoots that theory to shit," Johnny said, still grinning.

"Man, that's too much. I can't believe it," Jerilyn said.

"It's pretty far out, all right," Rick agreed.

"How did hepatitis get to the Gulch? And why didn't anyone else get sick, if the germs were in poi?" Jerilyn asked.

Rick shrugged. "I guess some of the people in the Gulch are into eating poi pretty regularly. And then once someone was infected—they have such poor hygiene down there; you gotta wonder about those outhouses above the stream, and they all bathe in that water—anyway, it got passed along. Then I guess somebody carried it to Makena and infected some people down there.

"And here's the really political part. There were locals with hepatitis. One whole family ended up in the hospital, but it was hushed up somehow. Nobody told the reporters there was anybody else sick, so it got no press. All the health officials and politicians just carried on about the dirty hippies." Rick wasn't smiling anymore. "It pisses me off. I'm trying to figure out if there's any way I can use this when I go to court with the building permit cases."

"Yeah, that's pretty disgusting," Johnny said. "Maybe you need the ACLU or somebody, or at least a friendly reporter."

"This one guy from the Honolulu paper was showing some interest, and one young guy at the *Maui News,* but they have to get whatever they write past the editors, so who knows."

The roar of a motorcycle interrupted the conversation. Johnny rolled his eyes and put the pot back into the metal box, closed it firmly, and set it on top of the refrigerator. "I'll be damned if I'll get that asshole high," he said, shoving the remaining beer into the refrigerator.

Footsteps clomped up the back stairs, and a girl appeared in the doorway, a stunning redhead wearing jeans, a black leather jacket, and heavy boots. She stepped inside and bent to remove her boots. "Hey, smells good in here. Got any more?"

Behind her, a tall man appeared. A zing went through Carrie Ann's body, as if seeing the man in the doorway had somehow given her an electrical charge. His eyes met hers, and for a moment they simply looked at each other. Johnny broke the spell by belching loudly.

"Sorry," he drawled. "We done used up our quota for the afternoon." He took another gulp of beer.

"Allison, this is Carrie Ann Emerson," Jerilyn announced, ignoring Johnny. "She's gonna be your roommate for a little while."

"Oh?" Allison straightened up slowly, one boot in hand. "How come?"

"Because she needs a place to stay, and your room's the only immediate possibility. Carrie Ann, this is Allison, and that's Michael Wharton, our neighbor from down the road."

Michael stared at Carrie Ann without smiling, a distracted sort of stare as if his mind were halfway somewhere else. But he kept his eyes on hers, and she couldn't take hers away. They were beautiful eyes, she thought; so blue.

"Hi," he said, looking down from a height that must be inches over six feet. Long, pale-blond hair framed a chiseled face. Carrie Ann had never seen anyone that handsome. She was glad he didn't cover that face with a beard. He looked like a Viking.

"Hi," she said in a small voice

"You got any homework, Allison?" Johnny asked, keeping his eyes focused on the beer bottle he was sliding in a slow circle on the tabletop.

"Yeah, some."

"Well, you better get with it."

"Fine." Allison dropped her boots with a clunk on the floor, turned, and stood on tiptoe to give Michael a kiss. "Thanks for the ride, Michael. See you later."

"Later," the Viking replied, as Allison stomped off to her room. "I guess I better hit the road myself. Nice to see you folks, Rick—and Carrie Ann, is it?"

She nodded, speechless.

"Hope to see you again sometime," he said and was gone, rapid footsteps down the back stairs and the sudden roar of a motorcycle engine. Carrie Ann let out a long breath and took a sip of her beer, listening to the engine as it disappeared into the distance. She very much hoped to see him again, too.

Chapter Four

Carrie Ann knocked timidly on the door to Allison's room, heard a muffled "Come in," and opened the door. Allison was balanced upside down in a shoulder stand.

"You're doing yoga?"

"Mmmm." Allison opened her eyes briefly, then touched her toes to the floor in front of her and rolled slowly down to lie on her back.

"I gotta do something to stay loose," she said, "since I have to go to that dumb school all day, and Johnny is so stingy about sharing his dope."

Carrie Ann pulled her T-shirt and jeans out of her suitcase.

"Thanks for letting me stay in your room. I really needed a place."

"Mmmm," Allison replied, rolling over onto her stomach and grabbing her ankles to pull herself into an arch. Carrie Ann went into the bathroom and closed the door. She changed, then washed out her dress in the sink with a bar of Ivory, so it would be clean for court on Friday. There must be somewhere outside she could hang it.

Allison was sitting in a lotus position, facing the wall, and said nothing as Carrie Ann left with her wet dress wrapped in a towel.

Sure enough, there was a clothesline outside. Carrie Ann hung her dress and the towel, then wandered around, admiring the plants. Butterflies fluttered over a vegetable garden, and beyond that, chickens clucked in a wire-enclosed yard. Carrie Ann watched the chickens for a moment—she hadn't seen live chickens up close since she was a kid—then headed back to the kitchen. She had promised to help cook dinner.

Jerilyn was there, pulling a big pot out of a cabinet.

"Hey, now you look more like you belong around here."

"That's my court dress. I got it just for this trip."

"Well, I'm sure the judge will be impressed. You look very straight and responsible in it. Around here, we're pretty responsible, but we're not straight!"

Carrie Ann smiled. "I can tell. Do you want me to wash the carrots?"

"Hey, great. Then maybe you can chop them up. The knives are there, by the cutting board."

Carrie Ann fell into the familiar kitchen rhythm she'd often shared with Kathryn, who usually had a house full of mouths to feed. Rock-and-roll musicians always seemed to be hungry, no matter how many drugs they had taken the night before. She glanced at Jerilyn, who was swishing water through a pot full of brown rice.

"What kind of band does Johnny manage?"

Jerilyn carefully drained the wash water from the rice and refilled the pot.

"Oh, you know—good old noisy rock-and-roll. Their name is Blend. They're pretty good, got a lot of original songs. They've played in the club over in Lahaina and even went to the Crater Festival in Honolulu last year."

"What's the Crater Festival?"

"A big daytime concert in Diamond Head Crater. They hold it every summer, the past few years. There are bands, craft booths, all that stuff."

Carrie Ann sliced carrots in silence for a moment. Jerilyn set the rice on the stove and turned the burner flame to high. "What's Allison doing in there? I don't suppose it's homework, by any chance."

"She was doing yoga. Said she needed to get loose."

Jerilyn rolled her eyes. "Oh, right. That's her latest, ever since she's been hanging out with Michael. Allison's such a flexible young thing, she could do all the postures and stretch farther than anyone the minute she started. I don't think she's getting any spiritual value out of it, but I guess it's good for her body."

"So Michael is into yoga?" Carrie Ann tried to sound casual as she dumped a pile of sliced carrots into the bowl Jerilyn had given her.

"Yeah, he teaches classes in Paia. Actually, I think it's his way of meeting chicks. He wouldn't even be coming around here if not for Allison. You may have noticed he and Johnny don't get along."

"How come?"

Jerilyn shrugged and measured out a cup of whole-wheat flour. "Long story. You know how guys are."

Carrie Ann wasn't sure she did. She changed the subject. "You said Allison is a foster child?" It wasn't clear exactly how this teenager fit into a house full of rock-and-rollers.

"Yeah, kind of an informal foster child," Jerilyn replied. "She was on the verge of running away, showing up here at odd hours. Johnny and I took her home one night and met her parents. Then one day Allison asked if she could move in, so we went and talked to them, and they actually agreed, much to my surprise. They couldn't handle it—Allison smoking dope, screwing around, skipping school." Jerilyn sighed. "Sometimes I wish they'd said no. It was kind of fun, at first, having a girl around—I always wished I had a daughter. Lately, she's been pretty hard to deal with. But she's okay, just a teenager, and I guess she'll get over that if she doesn't O.D. or run someone's motorcycle off a cliff or something."

"That's awful nice of you all to do that."

Jerilyn laughed. "Part of our service here at O'Connor Manor—musicians fed, vegetables grown, and teenagers saved from a life of sin, or at least allowed to sin in a controlled environment. We make her go to school, be home for dinner every night, do her homework, take the pill, and smoke no more than one joint per day—after school, not before."

"And she goes for all that?"

"It's better than living at home."

"What do her parents think of it?"

"Well, they don't know about all of it—like the dope rule, for instance—but they know she's on the pill. Like I said, this kid is no vestal virgin and hasn't been for a long time."

"At least she's got the pill. I didn't, and I did it one time too many without my diaphragm, which I hated, and first thing I knew, I was a mom."

"And that's how Rorie got started?"

"Yep. I kind of thought about getting an abortion, because her dad had taken off to Canada, and I was on my own. But that's hard to set up, and I didn't have any money, and I thought it would be cool to have a little baby anyway." Carrie Ann shrugged. "So I had her, and she was adorable. I fell in love with her. But it's hard being a mom by myself." She took a deep breath. "Then I lost her."

Jerilyn patted her on the shoulder, then returned to her mixing bowl. "Don't you worry. Rick will get her back for you. He's a pretty good lawyer. And as he said, they usually don't like to take kids away from their moms unless they're really screwed up."

Carrie Ann shook her head. "I would think most people would consider a mom who lost her kid to be pretty screwed up."

"Listen, weird things can happen to anyone. It was one of those things. I think the judge will be cool."

Jerilyn's assessment was something to cling to. Carrie Ann hoped she was right.

Jerilyn had just put the casserole into the oven when the musicians began to show up.

The first one brought a strong barnyard smell with him. Carrie Ann looked up from the silverware drawer to find a husky young man with glossy dark hair and beard grinning at her as he removed rubber boots and peered around the door frame from the back porch.

"Hey there, foxy lady, where did you come from?"

"This is Carrie Ann, Allison's new roommate, and you can come inside and say hello after you wash off that stinky chicken shit," Jerilyn said.

The man's grin widened, and he disappeared, bare feet clumping down the wooden steps.

"That's Tom, the one who lives downstairs," Jerilyn said. "He works at the chicken farm and comes home real smelly every day. He does keep us supplied with eggs and with plenty of chicken shit for the vegetable garden and banana trees, but I refuse to let him in the house until he's had a shower."

"He goes outside to shower?"

"There's a furo house in the back. You know what a furo is? A Japanese bath—a big tub with a copper bottom. We fill it with water and light a fire underneath. We'll have to fire it up while you're here, it's incredible. Anyway, there's a shower out there, too. Tom's a real sweet guy when he's clean. He's our drummer."

Carrie Ann couldn't imagine how Eppie, the drummer for Duke's band, would react to Tom. Eppie probably wouldn't know a chicken if he saw one. He rarely left the house before sunset, spent his days reading science fiction and practicing his riffs, and was so thin and pale he looked a bit ill most of the time.

The next musician was no less a surprise. "This is Stevie," Jerilyn informed Carrie Ann when a rosy-cheeked boy trudged into the kitchen with an enormous stalk of bananas on his shoulder. "Stevie's our son and also Blend's rhythm guitarist!"

Stevie blushed even rosier red, mumbled in Carrie Ann's direction without looking at her, and turned to hang the bananas from a rope attached to a large hook in one of the kitchen rafters. Jerilyn winked at Carrie Ann.

"I had no idea bananas grew like that," Carrie Ann said, edging closer to the bunch. Stevie shot her a terrified look and backed up to the door, turned, and disappeared.

Jerilyn chuckled. "That boy. He isn't quite ready to deal with chicks yet. Allison scares the shit out of him, and now you're here. Poor baby."

"He's awful young," Carrie Ann said, peering up into the hanging stalk to see how the fruit, familiar in the singular, formed a bunch with dozens of bananas.

"Yeah, but he sure can play." Jerilyn reached for the tin canister on the refrigerator, sat down, and put her feet up on a chair. "Ever since he was a little squirt he's been watching his dad's musicians, sitting in on rehearsals with his eyes practically glued to their fingers, learning those licks." She lit one of the leftover roaches, took a toke, and offered the roach to Carrie Ann. Carrie Ann hesitated for a moment, then took a tiny hit and handed the roach back to Jerilyn. This Maui dope was strong stuff.

Jerilyn took another deep toke and, when Carrie Ann declined a second hit, licked her fingers and snuffed the roach. She stood up.

"I'm going to go see if Johnny's out of the shower and get cleaned up myself," Jerilyn said. "You make yourself at home—do whatever you want. The casserole will be ready in about half an hour, and I'll come back to make a salad after my shower."

After Jerilyn left, Carrie Ann sat for a moment. Might as well clean up some of the kitchen mess, she thought. That took a few minutes. Now what? She hesitated to invade Allison's space. Finally, she headed outdoors.

The birds were in chorus again, as they had been this morning when she woke. Chirping seemed to come from all around. Giant old trees were everywhere. The sun was out of sight, but pink and gold light reflected from fluffy clouds overhead and cast a warm glow that deepened the colors of everything in the O'Connors' yard. Big trees, bamboo forest, and clumps of flowers that Carrie Ann could not identify surrounded the lawn. It was as if she were in a magic place, a safe, beautiful space on an island far from the realities of the busy and plastic world. Carrie Ann breathed the sweet scent of some nearby flower and lay down on a cool carpet of soft grass.

Staring up into the sunset sky, she thought about Michael. He certainly was gorgeous. And what was that she had felt when their eyes met, that electric shock thing? She had never experienced anything like that before. Just her luck that he lived on Maui. Plus, he was going out with Allison, and from what Jerilyn said, there were other ladies in his life. Oh well, what did it matter? She would be going home to San Francisco as soon as she got Rorie back. Restless, she stood up and wandered around the yard, waiting for dinnertime.

Meals at the O'Connors' were served around a table in the space that once must have been a formal dining room. Ornate molding edged a high ceiling painted the same sky blue as in the living room. None of the dishes on the table matched, but there was a bouquet of fresh flowers and plenty of food, with the casserole, a giant salad, a couple of loaves of homemade bread, and a jug of tangy yellow juice made, Jerilyn told her, from lilikoi.

"Also known as passion fruit, Carrie Ann," Tom said, grinning and wiggling his eyebrows at her. "Better watch out—you may be overcome with a burning passion. Let me know, maybe I can help you out."

"Tom, leave her be!" Jerilyn scolded, as Carrie Ann blushed, Allison rolled her eyes, and a couple of the musicians laughed with their mouths full. "Don't mind him, Carrie Ann, you know how these rock stars are—or at least they wish they were rock stars! And hey, you guys, you know Carrie Ann's fresh out of San Francisco, and she probably does know some real rock stars. Right, Carrie Ann? You hang out with a band over there, don't you?"

"Yeah. With Red Dog."

Everyone except Allison stopped eating and stared at Carrie Ann, who felt her face heating up again.

"Red Dog? You hang out with Red Dog?" Johnny asked.

"Wow," said Tom.

"Cool," Stevie said, actually looking her in the face for the first time.

"Well, I really hang out with Red Dog's manager, Duke, and his old lady Kathryn. Kathryn is one of my best friends."

"Duke?" Johnny hadn't moved since she said "Red Dog." "THE Duke?"

"Like, big deal," Allison interjected. "What's so great about Red Dog and Duke?"

This set off a chorus of male voices as Johnny, Stevie, Tom, and the two other musicians Carrie Ann hadn't quite sorted out yet explained to Allison that Red Dog was only the hottest band in the city at the moment. Duke was legendary both as their manager and as a leader in the late lamented hip community of Haight Ashbury.

Carrie Ann herself was surprised to hear such adulation of Duke. To her, he was just Duke, Kathryn's old man, a nice guy who managed a band and liked to play horsey with Rorie.

But the revelation seemed to secure her place in this small society. Even Stevie seemed more comfortable with her, actually speaking to her as he delivered dishes to the sink where Carrie Ann had begun to wash. She was uneasy about being pegged as an expert on an era in which she herself had been a confused newcomer surviving on the fringe. She'd barely had time to sample the cultural explosion that culminated in the media creation known as the Summer of Love. The Haight was in full bloom when she arrived, a naive college dropout, chasing after Jack when he left El Paso to join Red Dog. Before she'd even begun to feel at home in San Francisco, Jack was gone to Canada, and she realized she was pregnant.

She'd had this beautiful baby, with Jack's crystal-blue eyes. Then she'd managed to misplace that baby. And now here she was in a strange place, where the people she counted as friends were somehow seen as legends.

She sighed and rinsed a handful of clean silverware.

"What's the big sigh about?" Jerilyn asked as she wiped down the kitchen table. "Miss your baby?"

"Yeah, I do. Even though it's been hard to be a mom without Rorie's father to help. Thank God for welfare and food stamps. At least now I have a place to live, with a nice roommate who likes kids." Carrie Ann shook her head. "I had to move four times after Rorie was born. Babies don't fit in too well with the scene in San Francisco."

"Yeah, I can imagine. I was lucky to have Johnny and to lead a pretty peaceful life when Stevie was little. He was born when we still lived in Arkansas, before we moved to L.A. and Johnny got into rock-and-roll." Jerilyn began to wipe down counters. In some distant part of the house, Carrie Ann heard the familiar screeches and thumps of a rock band tuning up.

"Rehearsal time," Jerilyn said, grinning. "I hope you're not too tired, because they won't quiet down for a couple of hours at least. Want to go down to listen after we're pau?"

"After we're what?"

"Pau. It's a Hawaiian word. It means finished, all done. You'll hear it a lot; everybody says it."

"Pau." Carrie Ann tried it. She was learning a lot of Hawaiian words, if she could only remember them. "Pau. Like that?"

Jerilyn laughed. "Yep. Well, I'm about pau, as a matter of fact, and it looks like you are too. Why don't you leave that pan to soak, and let's go listen to some music. They're not bad, actually."

Blend practiced in the basement. Funny, Carrie Ann thought, how bands seemed to have an affinity for basements. But while Red

Dog's rehearsal room was a dark little space with red-brick walls and a few dangling bare light bulbs, this room took up about half the area beneath the house and had white-painted walls. Rather than a musty space dug into the ground, this basement existed because the house was set up on posts. Lots of Island houses were built this way, Jerilyn explained, but this one had more room under it than most, with space for storage and Tom's room as well as this rehearsal area. And though the ceiling was low, it was tall enough for even the lanky bass player to stand up straight.

Jerilyn and Carrie Ann joined Johnny on an assortment of cushions that lined one wall. Rock posters in psychedelic colors were tacked up here and there. Carrie Ann recognized some of them from concerts and dances in San Francisco. White paper lanterns covered the light bulbs, giving the room a diffuse brightness.

Carrie Ann could understand why Blend's members were impressed by Red Dog. They played the same loud, pounding hard rock, with intricate guitar solos laced through the steady thump of bass. The lead guitarist shouted lyrics, tossing his hair out of his face. Stevie kept his eyes down, stroking a steady rhythm, and Tom's sun-tanned arms and long dark hair flew above the drums.

Carrie Ann was no connoisseur of rock music, despite her association with Kathryn and Duke. She'd fallen in love with Rorie's dad, Jack, more for the excitement of watching him perform than for any appreciation of his guitar licks, and because she was with Jack, she had grown to know his band and their manager. But she liked to dance, and Blend played music that made her want to dance, so she decided they must be good. Still, her ears were ringing after a few songs. She waited until a break and then told Jerilyn she was off to bed.

Upstairs, she found Allison hunched over a textbook on one of the mattresses in her bedroom. The girl looked up with glazed eyes as Carrie Ann entered. "Had enough band?"

"Yeah. I think I'll take a shower and crash."

"Me too. This history is boring as hell."

The room was dark within a quarter-hour, and soon Carrie Ann could hear Allison's breathing deepen even over the sound of the band, still pounding away downstairs. Carrie Ann stuffed her ears with tissue and turned on her side, putting a pillow over her head. She tried to imagine how much Rorie had grown in the nearly six weeks since she'd seen her. Only a couple more days, and she'd find out.

Chapter Five

Carrie Ann shifted her weight on the hard wooden courthouse bench and tugged at the tight sleeve of her go-to-court dress. It rubbed against skin burned tender by the sun over Jerilyn's backyard. She wished once again that she had a watch. Rick was off on some errand in the courthouse basement, and it seemed like ages she'd been sitting here, waiting to see her child, waiting to see what the judge would say.

Yesterday had passed in weeding the garden with Jerilyn, a surprisingly satisfying activity, followed by a trip to town in Johnny's old red truck and an afternoon of going over and over her story with Rick. After dinner, there was rock-and-roll again, but she'd stayed downstairs only briefly. The sooner she slept, the sooner the morning would come.

And now here she was, biting nervously on a fingernail still stained, despite her scrubbing, with Haiku red dirt.

A door opened down the hall, and a woman peered around its edge. "Mrs. Emerson?"

Carrie Ann decided not to correct the Mrs. "Yes, I'm Carrie Ann Emerson."

"Come this way, please. The social worker is here with your little girl."

Carrie Ann gulped air and stood quickly, feeling dizzy. The woman opened the door wide, then left, and Carrie Ann stepped into a small, sparsely furnished office. And there was Rorie, in a pink dress with ruffles, clutching a teddy bear. She sat on the lap of a young Asian man. Rorie didn't move, just stared at her mother with a slight frown. Carrie Ann had expected her daughter to run to her, begging to be picked up, but Rorie simply sat and looked at her.

"Honey? Don't you remember me?" she asked. "It's Mommy. I came to get you and take you home."

Still Rorie didn't speak. She looked down at the floor, then up at the young man who held her.

"Rorie, aren't you going to say hello to your mommy?" the man asked.

Rorie pulled at a button on her teddy bear. "Hi," she said, and then was silent.

Carrie Ann didn't know what to do next. After a moment, the young man broke the silence.

"Miss Emerson, my name is David Hara. I'm the social worker who's been helping with Rorie. I found her down at Guava Gulch during the quarantine, and we kind of hit it off, so they put me in charge of her case." He bent his head to speak to the child, who was still twisting the teddy bear's button. "Rorie, your mom came all the way from California to see you. I think it would be good if you talk to her a little bit, don't you? Come, I'll set you down and you folks can talk story."

He stood, placed Rorie on the chair where he'd been sitting, and waved Carrie Ann toward the seat next to it. She sat and leaned over to stroke Rorie's head. She'd have liked to grab her child, hold her, nuzzle her, and inhale her familiar scent, but Rorie's peculiar reaction warned her off. She'd better take it slow. All the nights when she'd lain awake, wondering if Rorie was okay, her child had been lying somewhere alone and afraid. Who knew how many times she'd cried out for her mother? Who knew what she'd been through in the weeks she'd been lost? Carrie Ann had not foreseen that this reunion would be so difficult. Now she realized it might not be easy to regain her child's trust.

At least Rorie did not draw away when Carrie Ann stroked her hair, though her face remained set and she said nothing.

"Is that your new bear? What's his name?" Carrie Ann asked

"Kimo."

"Kimo?"

"That's the name of her foster father," David interjected. Carrie Ann flinched.

"And what's the name of your . . . foster mother?" she asked Rorie. Might as well get it out in the open. Rorie looked confused, until David said gently, "Linda."

"Oh yeah," Rorie said, nodding. "Auntie Linda."

"And have they been taking good care of you? Are they nice?"

Suddenly, Rorie was all words, animated and focused on her mother for the first time since she'd walked into the room. "Yeah, they're really nice, and they have a dog and a kitty cat, and Charlene lives with them, she's a big girl, she goes to school, and she lets me help her with her homework, I draw the pictures for her. And we went to the beach, and I can almost swim, Mommy."

Somewhat taken aback by the sudden change, Carrie Ann could only be grateful that, at least, Rorie had called her "Mommy." Still, it hurt to hear Rorie's enthusiasm about this family with whom she'd lived for less than a month. She gazed at her child, whose pale-blonde hair was trimmed shorter than usual, the heart-shaped face with its dark-lashed crystal-blue eyes—her tiny, exquisite, irreplaceable daughter. Surely nothing that had happened in the short time they'd been apart could truly destroy the bonds of birth and nursing, of all the days they'd been together. Carrie Ann knew she'd been a less-than-perfect mother—when had she ever been a perfect anything? But she was this child's mother, and she would not give up her child to anyone.

"Well, maybe when we get home to San Francisco we can get a kitty cat—not a dog, but a kitty cat—and we can find a pool where you can go swimming."

Rorie resumed her stubborn look.

"Don't you want to go home?" Carrie Ann had to ask, then wondered if that was the right question, especially with David standing off to one side, leaning against the wall with his arms folded, watching and listening.

Rorie stuck out her lower lip and tugged at the bear's ear but said nothing.

"You know everyone misses you, especially Mommy." Carrie Ann tried to keep her voice steady. "I've been looking everywhere for you. You know I didn't want you to get lost, don't you? And every day since you've been gone I've worried and wondered where you were and how you were doing and when I would find you. And Willie—he feels terrible because you got lost when he was sick. Remember the camping trip? And how he had to go to the hospital?"

Rorie was silent, but she had stopped pouting. Carrie Ann decided she must be on the right track. "And Kathryn and Duke and Mimi miss you, too." Rorie perked up, looked at her mother's face. Yes, this was working. "Duke took me and Willie all over the place in his bus, looking everywhere, and we couldn't find you. And Kathryn was crying almost as much as Mommy, worried that you were lost and were sad and missing us. And Mimi called her friends in Los Angeles to see if they knew where you were, but no one knew. No one ever thought you would come to Maui. When we found out where you were, Mommy got on an airplane and came to get you. Today we're going to see the judge—did you know that?" She glanced at David, who nodded. Rorie frowned at the teddy bear.

"Is Rorie going to see the judge too?"

"He'll talk with her separately. She won't be in the courtroom with us."

Oh boy. What would this moody and confused child tell the judge? Carrie Ann continued her campaign.

"Well, when you see the judge, I hope you tell him about your friends in San Francisco who miss you, and about the nice apartment we have with Mimi, right across the street from the park, with the swings, and all the toys you have. Remember your trike? The one Duke gave you for Christmas?"

Rorie nodded, but she still wasn't meeting her mother's eyes. Despair rose in Carrie Ann's chest. Surely Rorie would want to go home with her mother, back to her familiar life and the people who'd helped care for her since she was born. Surely there was nothing here worth trading for her real home. No one knew better than Carrie Ann how hard the first months of Rorie's life had been, but since they'd moved in with Mimi, things had settled down a lot, and Rorie wouldn't remember those difficult early days.

David broke the silence. "Miss Emerson, Rorie and I are supposed to be in the judge's chambers in about ten minutes. I think we better start winding this up."

The time pressed in on her, so little time to make up for such a great loss, for the hours and days and nights when they'd been apart. So little time to make Rorie love her again, and to make David the social worker know that they were a good pair, a real family, just the two of them, a mother and child who should never be parted again.

"Honey, is there anything you want to tell Mommy? Is everything okay?"

"I hafta go shishi," Rorie replied. Mystified, Carrie Ann looked at David. Shishi? He laughed, smile lines crinkling beneath straight dark brows.

"That means she needs to go to the restroom. Looks like your daughter is getting used to Hawaii, starting to talk like a local. Come on, I'll show you where it is, and you can take her in."

David was leaning against the wall next to the door when Carrie Ann came out of the restroom, clutching Rorie's hand. She was encouraged by the chatter that had started up again as she helped her daughter rearrange her frilly dress over an equally frilly slip. The familiar care-taking tasks of helping a four-year-old use the bathroom seemed to ease the strain of meeting for both of them, and Rorie even appeared to be reluctant when David took her down the hall to the judge's office, promising that she'd see her mother again later.

Drained, afraid to feel hopeful, Carrie Ann went in search of her lawyer.

Rick treated her to a quick sandwich before their court appearance, at the Kress store cafeteria a few blocks away. She had trouble swallowing, wondering what Rorie and the judge were discussing at this very moment. Rick led her back up to the old courthouse in the noonday heat. It was a relief to step into the shade of the front porch, its roof supported by classical-looking pillars. Carrie Ann splashed her face cool in the women's room, then joined Rick. She couldn't remember ever being this tense. Finally, they entered a room down the hall from where she'd met with Rorie and David. Rorie was not there, but the social worker sat next to another man at a table facing the front of the room; Rick briefly introduced the stranger as the state's attorney, and he and Carrie Ann exchanged nods. She and Rick sat at another table next to theirs, facing a desk and an empty chair. Carrie Ann guessed it was the judge's. She chewed her fingernail as they sat waiting, jumped to her feet when the judge entered the room, then sank into her chair again, twisting her fingers together.

Judge Yoshioka was a stern-looking middle-aged man, with heavy dark eyebrows drawn together in a frown. Carrie Ann wasn't sure whether to smile when he looked at her; she didn't feel like smiling, so she decided not to try.

Yoshioka first had David describe the circumstances in which Rorie had been found, a rendition that sent Carrie Ann searching in her purse for a Kleenex. She was relieved when he said the doctor had found Rorie's physical problems recent and temporary. There was no sign of abuse, and the child had been well-nourished most of her life, the doctor had reported.

Next, David told of the search for Rorie's family: the visits around the island's hippie community (Jerilyn had told Carrie Ann the social service people had even stopped by her house), the calls to other islands, and finally to the Social Services offices in California. Why on earth, Carrie Ann wondered, had no one in California recognized that this was the missing child she had reported? She thought bitterly of her social worker's condemnation when she heard about Rorie's disappearance.

It wasn't until the San Francisco Legal Aid lawyer put Carrie Ann in touch with the local office that they were able to identify the mystery child who called herself "Rorie" as Aurora Emerson, David said, and then they had called the San Francisco welfare office and asked about Rorie and her mom. Carrie Ann's social worker had verified that her child was missing, that Carrie Ann had been searching for her, and that there had never been a sign of abuse or neglect in the four years Carrie Ann had collected aid money and taken Rorie to well-baby clinics. Well, at least she was honest, Carrie Ann thought grudgingly.

"Very well," the judge said as David sat down. "Mr. Stinson, do you wish to say anything, or to have your client speak?"

"Yes, Your Honor, we'd like to put my client on the stand," Rick replied. Carrie Ann took a deep breath, shrugged her shoulders to release the growing tension, and walked to the chair next to Judge Yoshioka's desk.

They'd rehearsed the story well yesterday, and anyway, it was the truth, so Carrie Anne found it wasn't hard to get the facts straight.

What was hard was to get her voice to work, with the judge, David, and the state's attorney all staring at her intently. She answered Rick's questions and finally, when the story was told, sat waiting for someone to make the next move.

At last, the judge spoke. "Miss Emerson, do you want your child back?"

Carrie Ann tried to speak, had to clear her throat, finally managed to croak out a "Yes, Your Honor."

"What will you do when you get her?"

"I'll take her home to San Francisco and try to get back to a normal life."

The judge was silent again. Finally, he seemed to make up his mind. He picked up a stack of papers and briskly straightened them, banging the pile against his desktop.

"Miss Emerson, the court sympathizes with the difficulty you've been through in the past few weeks and hesitates to add to your burdens. However, I can't in good conscience let you get on a plane and take off with that child." Carrie Ann's throat went dry; her heart pounded.

"I realized it's unlikely a similar situation will arise in the future, especially now you've been through all this," the judge continued. "But in light of the circumstances, I am not going to give you legal custody of your child just yet. I want to keep you close at hand, let Mr. Hara here keep an eye on you until we see how things work out between you and Rorie. There seems to be some hesitation on her part to go back to you." Carrie Ann bowed her head and bit her lip. "That may be a result of the trauma she's been through," the judge said. "But I have to be sure things will work out well for the child's benefit.

"Therefore," Yoshioka said, "I've decided to award you physical custody of Aurora. You can take her with you today." Carrie Ann's head jerked up to face the judge. "And you may keep her with you, subject to Social Services finding any reason why that should not continue. But you may not leave the island until the court returns Aurora to your legal custody. In other words, you stay on Maui. You do not go back to San Francisco until I say so. I want you back in this courtroom in six months to review the situation. If I find in the meantime that you've left the island, you'll face legal action and possible loss of parental rights. Is that clear, Miss Emerson?"

Carrie Ann's eyes had been fastened on the judge's. She swallowed, moistened her dry lips, and nodded. "Yes, sir," she said in a faint voice, though in truth she was not entirely sure she understood what the judge wanted her to do.

The main thing was that she could take Rorie with her today. Everything else would work itself out in time.

It wasn't until they were back out in the corridor, waiting for David so they could walk down to his office to pick up Rorie, that the judge's words really began to sink in.

"Rick, he's saying we can't leave Maui? We have to stay here?"

"That's right. Physical custody but not legal. You have to stay here."

"But how on earth am I going to do that? I have nowhere to live, no clothes except what's in my suitcase, no money . . ." Carrie Ann was beginning to experience a profound sense of shock. The future yawned before her, an unknown place where, if she stepped forward, she would find no solid ground on which to place her feet.

Rick grimaced. "Yeah, it's tough. I must admit I'm not entirely surprised—this is too unusual a situation for the judge to casually hand over the kid—but you never know what a judge will do until he rules. I guess we'll have to have a powwow when I get you back to the O'Connors'; they might have some ideas. And I'm sure you can get welfare to help you financially. It's not that expensive to live here, especially if you're willing to share rent with someone. Don't worry, we'll figure it out."

They walked across the street to David's office, where a secretary had been keeping an eye on Rorie as she played with toys from a box in the corner. Rorie glanced up briefly, said "Hi, Mommy," and went back to dressing a half-bald Barbie doll.

"Have a seat, folks. I need to ask a few questions before I turn you loose," David said. He took a pen from his pocket and opened a notebook. "First things first. We'll fill out the paperwork for food stamps and financial aid before you leave; might as well get that process started. Miss Emerson, do you have enough cash to keep you going for a while? Where are you staying, anyway?"

"Call me Carrie Ann, please," she replied; this "Miss Emerson" stuff was far too formal for comfort. "I'm staying with Jerilyn and Johnny O'Conner, out in Haiku. Rick set it up for me, and they're letting me stay for free, but none of us thought I'd be here for long. I don't know how they'll react when they hear I have to stay on Maui. And I'm sleeping in a room with their teenage foster daughter, which is already crowded, so I don't know how that's going to work out now that I have Rorie back."

"The O'Connors? The ones who bought the old Aiken place?"

"Yeah, that's them," Rick replied. Carrie Ann wondered how on earth David knew these people and where they lived, far out in the country. This really must be a small community, a place where eyes were always on you, and everyone knew everyone else's business.

"I'm familiar with them and with this teenager they've taken in. I give them credit for trying to help out. Well, it is a big old house. Maybe they can find a spare room for you somewhere. If not, we'll have to see what else we can come up with. Maybe we can find you a good roommate. The judge wants to see you in six months, so you need something for at least that long."

David smiled sympathetically. "You've been through a lot, Carrie Ann. And so has Rorie. The more we can stabilize your situation, the better. I hope you can work something out with the O'Connors, because they are pretty steady folks, from what I can tell. Why don't you talk it over with them and give me a call. If this doesn't work out, we'll have to see what we can do to find something else that will make Judge Yoshioka happy. It's important for you to keep that in mind, because if he's not satisfied with your progress, he does have the power to terminate your parental rights." He glanced at Rorie, whose attention still was focused on Barbie. "The foster family has grown very attached to your daughter, and Mrs. De Silva let me know they would be happy to adopt her, so you have a lot at stake here."

Carrie Ann bit her lip and nodded. Rorie seemed oblivious to the fact that her fate was under discussion, but her mother knew better. Just finding her daughter had not been sufficient. Now she had to prove that she was worthy of keeping her own child, here on this island where her resources and her courage were shaky.

David helped Carrie Ann fill out the paperwork to qualify for food stamps and a welfare check and promised to expedite the processing so she'd have some money soon. Her last check from California was almost gone.

When the final paper had been signed, and David had set up an appointment to see Carrie Ann and Rorie again in two weeks, she stood to go. Rick got up from the corner, where he had been sitting on the floor encouraging Rorie while she put together a jigsaw puzzle.

"I guess we're ready to go, honey," Carrie Ann said as David handed her a pink cardboard suitcase. Rorie did not look up from her task of carefully placing a bright green jigsaw piece amid the branches of what looked like part of a tree. "Rorie. Let's go."

The adults exchanged glances. "Come on, Rorie, we're going in my Jeep," Rick said.

"Time to go with Mommy," David chimed in. Carrie Ann blushed. Two strangers had to urge her child to acknowledge her.

Rorie sighed, a loud exhalation that indicated she had been interrupted in an important task, dropped a handful of puzzle pieces to the floor and stood. "Okay," she said, sounding exasperated. "Where are we going? Uncle Kimo and Auntie Linda's house?"

"No, honey, we're going to Johnny and Jerilyn's house. You'll like them. They have a big boy named Stevie and lots of chickens and stuff."

Rorie looked distressed. "I want to see Uncle Kimo and Auntie Linda and Charlene."

Carrie Ann waited for David to answer; she'd wondered herself about the future of Rorie's relationship with the foster family.

David squatted to look Rorie in the eyes and held both her hands. "Rorie, you're going with your Mommy," he said in his gentle voice. "She's your real mom, and the judge said it's okay for you to go with her. She came all the way from California to find you, and you're her little girl. You're supposed to be with your mom, who loves you. Uncle Kimo and Auntie Linda and Charlene love you too, and they'll miss you, but they knew you could stay with them only for a little while until your real mom came to get you. See?" He gestured to the pink suitcase Carrie Ann clutched to her chest. "Auntie Linda packed your stuff and sent it along so you could go straight home with your mom if the judge said it was okay. I'll call her after you leave and tell her you went with your real mom, and you're not coming back to her house. Okay?"

Rorie's lower lip had been creeping out during this speech, and a tear spilled over her lashes and down her cheeks. "I want to see Charlene."

"I'm afraid not, Rorie. Time to go with Mommy," David said, wiping away the tear. He stood up, still holding one of Rorie's hands. "Come on, I'll walk you folks to the door," he said.

It seemed a long hike up Main Street to the Legal Aid office where Rick's Jeep was parked. Carrie Ann held one of Rorie's hands while Rick held the other and carried the pink suitcase. Carrie Ann could think of nothing to say that would ease her child's pain or her own anguish, so they trudged wordlessly in the afternoon heat, Rorie with her head hanging and her feet dragging. Rick kept a diplomatic silence, and Carrie Ann wondered, sneaking a glance at him, if he too felt the irritation that edged her worry with guilt: Couldn't this child pick up her feet and get with it? What the hell, she was only going with her own mother, and surely their life together hadn't been that bad.

Bleakly, she faced the reality that had been submerged in the recent weeks of frantic searching and fear. Motherhood was not easy. Especially alone, especially in the hippie world of San Francisco, where babies and their needs, toddlers and their tantrums did not fit a lifestyle of late nights, easy dope, freedom to come and go, to crash wherever and whenever. How often she had lain at night with a fussy, crying baby pulling at her breast while others partied, or tried to hush her child when the house was silent and others slept. And then next morning, the sour looks from those others, whose lives had neither room nor desire for an infant's company.

No wonder Rorie had settled happily into a middle-class life of comfort and security, with two parents and a big sister, a dog, and trips to the beach. Especially after going through whatever she had in the weeks before they found her in Guava Gulch. Carrie Ann wondered if she'd ever find out what really had happened to Rorie in all that time; who had had her, what they'd done, what she'd eaten, where she'd slept. A rush of concern overcame her irritation—her poor baby, alone with strangers, and now dragged away from the comfort she'd found in her foster home. Carrie Ann sniffed and lifted her head. Somehow, she'd have to make this up to her child. She hoped Maui would cooperate. She had no idea how she'd make it here, even with welfare and food stamps to ease her way.

"Rick, wait up," she said and stooped to pick up her daughter. The walk back to Rick's office was a tough trek for such a small person; she needed a lift, even though her weight was heavy on her mother's hip.

Once at the Jeep, Rorie refused to sit in her mother's lap for the ride to Haiku. She sat sulking on the back seat as they drove out of town, and within minutes sprawled across it, asleep, thumb in her mouth.

"Needed a nap," Rick commented, glancing over his shoulder.

"I'm sorry she's being such a drag," Carrie Ann apologized. The anxiety she'd lived with for four years, the need to apologize and cover up for her daughter's misbehavior and shortcomings, rose in her chest.

"Don't sweat it. She's had a hard time for such a little girl. She'll be okay once she gets used to being with you and the two of you get settled down someplace."

"Got any ideas about where that might be?"

Rick shrugged. "We'll think of something. Between us, Johnny and Jerilyn and I know a lot of people. We'll come up with something."

Johnny's truck was already home when they pulled up the driveway. Rick lifted the groggy Rorie out of the back seat. Carrie Ann bent to brush wisps of hair out of her face and straightened out her frills. Then she led her child into the kitchen, where Jerilyn was up to her elbows in a brown mound of bread dough that gave the kitchen a sweet, yeasty smell. Jerilyn stopped her kneading and looked delighted at the sight of Rorie, who was trailing at arm's length behind her mother, eyes on the ground and lower lip at full pout.

"Hi," Jerilyn said, drawing the word out and smiling broadly. She dusted flour off her hands and bent to get a better look at Rorie.

"Look who's here." She grinned up at Carrie Ann. "What's the deal? You get to keep this little angel?"

"I get to keep her, but we can't leave the island."

"Wow. No kidding." Jerilyn stood up. "Like forever?"

"For six months," Rick said. "The judge gave her physical custody but not legal. He wants to see how they get along."

"Wow," Jerilyn said again. "That's a trip. Never thought he'd pull a number like that, huh?"

"No way," Carrie Ann agreed. "Rorie, this is Jerilyn, the nice lady who's been letting me stay here. Can you say hi?"

Rorie, who'd been sneaking peeks around the kitchen, put the sulk back on her face and stubbed the toe of her black patent-leather Mary Janes against the kitchen floor.

"Well, better take her on into your room and get her stuff stashed. I hope there's something more suitable for country life in that suitcase there. Rick, Johnny's out in the front, clearing weeds from banana trees. Why don't you take a couple of cold beers out there, and when I get done kneading this bread, we'll join you guys on the porch."

Rorie's suitcase did contain several pairs of shorts and T-shirts, Carrie Ann found, along with another dress, pajamas, the teddy bear she'd held earlier, a pair of rubber thongs, a small long-haired doll, a toothbrush, and assorted hair clips in bright colors. Knowing how fine her daughter's hair was, Carrie Ann wondered how Linda ever had managed to get a hair clip to stay in. She slipped the pink dress over Rorie's head and helped her into shorts and a shirt. She looked around for a place to put the dress; this room was getting crowded. Where would Rorie sleep? Probably on the single mattress with her. It would be a tight squeeze, a temporary solution at best. She wondered how Allison was going to handle this development.

She gave Rorie a hug, then, on an impulse, lifted her. "My, you're big. I think you've grown since I saw you last. Have you been eating lots?"

"Mm-hmm," Rorie answered, pulling on a hangnail. The child's nails were chewed; it looked like she'd inherited her mother's bad habits. Carrie Ann lowered herself to the mattress, settling Rorie on her lap.

"So, tell me some things you like to eat over here in Hawaii."

Rorie examined the ceiling. "Ummm. I like pineapple. And bananas."

"And what kinds of things do you like to do?"

"I like to go to the beach. And play with Charlene."

"Does Charlene ever tickle you? Like this?" Carrie Ann blew on her daughter's neck, usually a move guaranteed to get a giggle. It worked.

"Mommy, that's too tickly!" Rorie said, squirming and smiling.

"How about this? It's the eensy-weensy spider. . . " She walked her fingertips over Rorie's forehead, down her cheek to her neck, then jumped to her bare arms and finally her legs. Rorie laughed and wriggled in her mother's lap, and Carrie Ann stopped tickling and held her daughter tight.

"Oh, baby girl, I missed you so much. I'm so glad I found you. I love you, Miss Rorie Emerson! Don't you ever get lost again!"

"Okay, Mommy, and don't you ever get lost again too."

Chastened, Carrie Ann kissed Rorie's head and gave her another squeeze. "Okay, let's hold onto each other tight."

Rorie stretched her arms to hug her mother. Carrie Ann blinked away tears and stroked her daughter's soft, shining hair, rocking her gently. They sat like that for a few minutes, holding each other. Then Rorie looked up. "Mommy, I'm thirsty," she said.

"Okay, let's go get some juice." She set her daughter gently onto her feet and stood, holding out her hand for Rorie to grasp, grateful that their familiar tickle game had passed through some invisible barrier to reach her child's heart.

"How's it going?" Jerilyn looked up with a smile as they entered the kitchen. "I see you found some shorts. You look a lot more comfortable, Rorie."

"Mm-hmm," Rorie said, nodding without looking up. Carrie Ann opened the fridge and pulled out a jug of bright yellow juice, the lilikoi-orange they had drunk at dinner last night, sweet and tangy and full of a unique flavor. It would be too strong for a child, so she diluted it for Rorie, then poured a cup of straight juice for herself.

Jerilyn had finished her kneading. She tossed a clean dish towel over the mound of bread, and they joined the men outside. Johnny had quit weeding and settled on the shady front porch steps next to Rick. He put down his beer and held out a big, grubby hand for Rorie to shake. To Carrie Ann's surprise, she shook the hand and even looked at Johnny, smiling shyly. Within minutes, she had begun to climb up and down the steps, then onto the wide concrete half walls that edged the stairs.

"What's your next move?" Johnny asked as Carrie Ann sat, close to where Rorie played so she could grab her if she seemed about to fall into the bushes alongside the steps.

Carrie Ann shrugged. "I don't know. I thought I was going to get on the plane and go home as soon as I got Rorie back, but I guess that's out. Do you guys have any ideas about where I could live? Shit—I had such a good scene going. I'll have to write Mimi and ask her to send my stuff and tell her she has to find a new roommate."

"I thought you lived with Duke and Kathryn," Jerilyn said.

"No, their place is too small, only a couple of rooms above Kathryn's store. I did crash on the couch there a few times when I really needed a place to sleep, but Rorie was little, and they had the band practicing downstairs all night—they don't eat dinner and go play like your guys do, they don't even start 'til ten or eleven—it was hard, with a baby trying to sleep." Jerilyn nodded sympathetically.

"When Rorie was born, I lived with a bunch of friends from El Paso," Carrie Ann said. "But the guy with the lease didn't like kids, and he said we had to leave. I was lucky to find Mimi. We have this great old apartment on Haight, not up in the business district but a little way down, where you don't have to see the junkies and stuff all the time." Carrie Ann shook her head. "The Haight has really changed since I first got there. It was nice then, real exciting. Now it's awful." She sighed. "Anyway, that doesn't matter much right now, does it? What I need is a place on Maui."

"Well, something will happen. Maui's a pretty magical place," Johnny said. "My theory is, if Maui wants you to stay, you get to stay. Whatever you need to make it here sort of shows up at the right moment. If Maui doesn't want you to stay, things don't work out for you. The island decides whether you stay or not."

"I don't know about Maui, but Judge Yoshioka sure wants me to stay," Carrie Ann replied, and finished off the dregs of her juice, swirling the last tart mouthful on her tongue.

"I tell you what," Jerilyn said, looking thoughtful. "I don't know if you could handle listening to another band every night, but we have a tiny little space out in the furo building. Maybe we could fix that up for you, at least until you find something else. Then you wouldn't have to share with Allison the teen queen, and you and Rorie could have a little place of your own."

"I don't know about that place," Johnny said. "What about the centipedes?"

"What's a centipede?" Carrie Ann asked.

"You don't want to know," Rick said, grimacing.

"Don't worry about that. We can clean it out good and cover up the pukas in the screens and maybe you could build a platform to put a mattress on, Johnny. I think we can do it, Carrie Ann, and make it work for a while. There's even the shower and a toilet out there—of course, you'd have to put up with the scent of chicken shit when Tom comes home from work every afternoon, but that's minor. I tell you what, I've got to go put a casserole into the oven and get that bread made into loaves, and then we'll go out there and look it over, okay?"

"Okay, sure." Carrie Ann's eyes stung with tears, a far-too-frequent occurrence lately. "I sure appreciate the help you all are giving me."

"Don't worry about it. You're cool, and we like you." Jerilyn stood and reached over to give Rorie a pat as she paused in her climb from one slab topping the half wall edging the steps to the next. "And you're cool too, Rorie-child," she said, then turned and ran up the steps.

"I guess I ought to go do that last tree in the row," Johnny said, stepping on his cigarette butt as he lumbered to his feet.

"And I ought to hit the road. I gotta get up early to go into the office," Rick said. "I'm running behind on a couple of things."

"I'm sorry I've taken up so much of your time," Carrie Ann said. "I'm sorry to be such a nuisance."

"Don't sweat it," Rick replied. "I'm glad things are working out. They don't all have such happy endings, you know."

Rorie was on the top level of the wall, arms spread. "I can fly! I can fly!" she announced, jumping down to the next level. Carrie Ann flinched, but before she could move to stop her, Rorie was already jumping to the next level, and the next, and finally into the waiting arms of Rick as he stood on the grass below.

Rick carried her up the steps, her cheeks flushed, wisps of hair stuck to her sweaty forehead. "You're quite a girl, Rorie," he told the child as he handed her to Carrie Ann. "What are you going to be when you grow up?" he asked as Rorie settled down comfortably into Carrie Ann's lap. Rorie seemed not to notice that her mother's eyes were streaming tears as she clutched her child, inhaling the scent of her hair, still sweet with the baby shampoo Linda must have washed it with that morning. Rorie turned to face Rick and Johnny, who stood watching the reunion on the porch steps.

"When I grow up," she said calmly, "I'm going to be strong and smart."

Chapter Six

Carrie Ann had to get up and call her mother. She knew that. She'd do it, soon, she promised herself. Last night, she'd made the same promise to Kathryn, whom she'd called as soon as Rick left. The two of them had ended up blubbering at each other over the long-distance line, crying with relief at having Rorie back and with sadness over the judge's order that Carrie Ann stay on Maui.

"I can't believe I'm not gonna be seeing you guys for six months," Kathryn said, sniffing.

"Maybe you can come visit when I get a place," Carrie Ann offered. "Airfare's not that much, right? Could you get someone to watch The Beadnik for a while? Maybe you and Duke can come, and we can have a Hawaii vacation together."

Kathryn sighed. "Maybe. We'll have to see. The bead business barely keeps our bills paid. I don't know how I could afford somebody to watch the store. And Duke says he thinks things are really starting to move for the band. You know how they are—if Duke leaves, they're likely to smoke dope all night, sleep all day, and never practice. But we'll see—something will come up. Have you called your mother?"

Instead, Carrie Ann had called Willie, and then she'd called Mimi. She hated to think how much she already owed the O'Connors for long-distance bills, and anyway, she told herself, it was too late to call Texas. So she had put off calling her mother until this morning, and she really had to. Any minute now, she'd get up. It was still early. Carrie Ann turned on her side and looked at Rorie, curled into a ball on the big cushion they'd dragged in from the living room. Carefully, she reached out to touch her daughter's soft cheek; no point in waking her up. She looked perfect asleep. She'd grown so much. Carrie Ann wondered if any of the clothes back in the apartment would still fit the child. Kathryn said she would help Mimi pack up Carrie Ann's and Rorie's stuff and send what she thought they'd need here, stashing the rest in the loft at The Beadnik until they could get back home.

Home. Carrie Ann drew in a deep breath. How could this ever have happened; how could they have ended up on Maui, of all places; how would they manage until they could get back home? Mimi would have to rent out her room. Would she be able to find someone to rent it for only six months, so they could move back in when they got home? Shit, it had seemed so perfect. And Mimi said Glenn had called. Damn. What were the chances he'd still be interested when she got back, whenever that might be? Maybe she'd write him a letter, try to keep it going.

Carrie Ann sat up slowly, looking around the eggplant-purple room filled with the deep breathing of Allison and Rorie and the pink glow of morning sun filtered through Indian bedspread curtains. It was pretty crowded in here with three people. Today they'd start work on the tiny space in the furo building, Johnny had promised, and he'd build them a bed up off the floor.

That would have to do, for now, Carrie Ann thought, though she was doubtful about the furo building, which had been too dark to inspect by the time they'd gotten out there last night. Johnny said he had to fool with the wiring to get the overhead light to work. She sighed, thinking of the high ceilings, bay windows, and old-fashioned footed bathtub in the apartment she shared with Mimi. And now to start over again, in this strange place. Beautiful, but not home, not San Francisco.

Well, nothing she could do about it. She'd better get with it and call her mother. Pulling on her jeans and a shirt, she wondered if anyone else was up. Saturday morning, so no work for Johnny, she guessed, and the band had played late last night. Probably everyone was still crashed.

Sure enough, the kitchen was silent and empty. Carrie Ann poured herself the last of the lilikoi-orange juice, rinsed the jug, and went to sit on the cushion next to the phone in the living room. What time would it be, in Texas? She knew it was later than California, which was at least a couple of hours. Probably sometime around midday. Good. Her dad would be out in the garage tinkering with his clock collection, and her mom would still be fairly sober. She didn't want to talk to her mother drunk, or to her father at all.

Not that he'd say anything mean; in fact, he probably wouldn't say much of anything. That was kind of the problem. It was hard to keep up a conversation with someone who had so little to say, even about something as big as his granddaughter being lost and then found.

Her mother answered on the second ring.

"Hi, Mom, it's Carrie Ann. I went to court yesterday, and I got Rorie back."

"Oh, sweetheart, I'm so glad." Her mom's voice broke with emotion. "How is she? Is she okay? Is she glad to see you?"

"She's fine. Bigger than ever. I haven't had much time to talk to her about it—it's kind of weird, you know, getting back together again after this long—but so far she seems to be fine, and the social worker said she didn't seem to have been mistreated or anything. Kind of neglected, you know, without any one person taking care of her." Carrie Ann didn't want to go into detail about the pinworms and so on. Her mother would freak out if she heard that stuff.

"Well, what on earth happened? How did she get to Maui?"

Carrie Ann recounted the little that she knew, then told her mother about the court date yesterday and the judge's order.

"Oh my gosh, you mean he can make you stay there? With no friends or family or anything? I wish your father was here—he went grocery shopping—I'd get him right to work on this. They don't understand who they're dealing with here. Maybe he knows someone, and he can pull some strings or something. They have no right to do this to you!"

"Mom, I don't think there's anything anyone back there can do about this. I have a lawyer, and he's real nice. He seems to think it's okay; this is just the way it is. I'm sure if there were any way to change the judge's mind he would have tried. And if I make a fuss, they're likely to take Rorie back. They were ready to take away my rights and adopt her out, you know, if I hadn't shown up to get her. I don't think I have much choice."

"But if that judge knows you come from a good family, and you've always been taken care of, and—well, what if you and Rorie came back here to stay with your father and me? Would that make a difference?"

Carrie Ann cringed. "No, I don't think so, Mom. Maybe if he sees I'm doing my best to get it together he'll change the order and let us leave in a few months."

"Mommy?" A thin cry came from the bedroom where she'd left Rorie sleeping. "Hold on, Mom," she said, and bolted for the bedroom to grab Rorie before she woke up Allison. The teenager cast a grumpy glance in Carrie Ann's direction, then turned over and closed her eyes.

With Rorie in her arms, Carrie Ann settled back onto her cushion in the living room. She picked up the phone. "Rorie just woke up, Mom. I'll put her on, but I don't know if she'll have much to say. Want to talk to Grandma, sweetie?"

Rorie frowned, leaning back against her mother. "Grandma?"

"Yeah, honey, you know, Mommy's mother," she whispered, covering the phone's mouthpiece as she passed it to Rorie. "Talk to Grandma," she repeated in a normal voice as Rorie clutched the receiver with both hands, still frowning.

Carrie Ann wrapped her arms around Rorie and bent her head to inhale her child's fragrance. She could hear her mom's gravelly voice, seeping past Rorie's little ear. Why did her mother always sound as if she needed to clear her throat? Probably it was from all the years of vodka and cigarettes, she guessed. Carrie Ann swore to herself she'd stay away from that crap; nothing but good old pot for her, none of that junk that had ruined her mother's life.

Rorie was nodding and saying "Uh-huh," but not much else. It was a one-sided conversation. Finally, the child said, "Bye, Grandma," and handed the phone back to Carrie Ann.

"Well, she sounds normal enough," her mother said.

"Yeah, she looks fine," Carrie Ann said, brushing the hair out of Rorie's eyes.

"I'm going to talk to your father. I'm sure he can do something," her mother said.

"Well, I don't know, Mom. Listen, I've got to get off the phone. These people are being real nice to let me stay here, but I'm going to owe them a big phone bill if I don't keep it short. It's a long way to Texas."

"Oh, I know. You're so far away, my two babies." Her mom's voice sounded weepy again. Carrie Ann closed her eyes and tried to be patient; little as she believed in her mother's histrionics, usually alcohol-induced, she had to admit this was a dramatic situation, and it seemed to make everyone involved cry.

"Have you heard from Jack?" her mother asked. The usual question, the one she asked every time they spoke.

"No, Mom, I haven't," she answered, as always. She doubted she'd ever hear from Rorie's father. He was long gone into the wilds of Canada. Maybe he'd turn up again someday if the war in Vietnam ever ended, but she knew she couldn't count on it.

"I wish you could find a good man," her mother said. "A woman needs a man; it's the nature of things."

"I know, Mom, me too," Carrie Ann replied. "Listen, I've got to go. I'll give you the O'Connors' number, so you can keep in touch, and I'll get someone to take a picture of Rorie and me under a palm tree or something and send it to you, okay?"

"Honey, do you need any money? Shall I tell your father to send a check?"

"No, Mom, I'm fine. Thanks again for the plane ticket, but we can manage, as long as I'm careful." She hated taking money from her parents, had hated having to ask for help with the airfare, and was glad when she finally could say goodbye and return to her own world. Unfamiliar as it might be at this moment, at least it wasn't suburban El Paso.

"Mommy," Rorie asked as she hung up, "are we going to live with Grandma?"

"No, honey, we're not, but she wishes we were. The judge said we had to stay right here, remember? And then we'll go back to San Francisco. Did you like talking to everybody on the phone last night?"

Rorie smiled and nodded. "They miss us, huh."

"They sure do, and I miss them too. But we have to stay here, and this is a pretty nice place. I guess we'll have to make some new friends, won't we?"

Rorie nodded again, looking uncertain.

"Tell you what, why don't we get you some clothes, and let's sneak a piece of Jerilyn's homemade bread and go for a walk. Want to?" This time, Rorie smiled and nodded vigorously.

A quarter of an hour later, the two of them trudged down the driveway into the gulch with its muddy ruts and incredible flowers. Carrie Ann stopped to sniff at one of the giant red flowers and found it had no scent. But a delicate crown of yellow blossoms growing on a nearby stalk gave up a deliciously sweet fragrance. She pulled two of the flowers off the crown and stuck one behind her ear and one behind Rorie's. "Now we're island maidens, out for an early morning stroll," she said, setting off again with Rorie's hand in hers.

The air was cool and fresh, and birds sang in the tall trees and bamboo that lined the driveway. For a while, Carrie Ann and Rorie walked in silence. This morning was the longest she'd been alone with her child since she'd gotten her back, Carrie Ann realized. She wondered if it was too soon to begin asking about what had happened while they were separated.

They climbed up the sloping driveway and into an open area with a well-mown lawn off to one side and a view of blue-hued mountains straight ahead. Across the paved two-lane road at the end of the driveway, Carrie Ann recognized the orderly rows of pineapple plants. A red-dirt road ran into the field.

"Let's cross the road and walk in the pineapples, okay?"

"Okay," Rorie agreed.

The road through the field, marked with thick ridges where heavy tires had traveled, led them up a gentle slope. At its crest, they found the island spread out before them, pineapple plants gleaming down the hillside, the bright-green carpet of sugar cane spreading onto the flat isthmus of Central Maui at sea level, and the peaks and ridges of the mountains on the horizon, surrounded by a glittering silver-blue ocean.

"Wow." Carrie Ann stopped, and Rorie, still holding her hand, leaned against her hip. "It's really a pretty island, isn't it," she said. The little girl nodded.

"Do you like it here? Do you like Maui?"

Rorie cocked her head and pursed her lips. "Umm, yeah. I kind of like it. Sometimes."

"What parts do you like?" Carrie Ann settled on the hardened dirt at the side of the road. "Come on, let's sit down here for a while and talk. We haven't talked for a long time." Rorie plopped down next to her mother.

"Okay, tell me more about the stuff you like. I know you like going to the beach, and bananas and pineapple. What else?"

"It's pretty. I like flowers."

"And what else?"

"And I like Uncle Kimo and Auntie Linda and Charlene and I like their house and I like the toys they have there."

Carrie Ann tried not to grimace. "Do you like Johnny and Jerilyn and Stevie and Allison?"

Rorie wrinkled her nose. "Allison's not very nice."

"Did she do something mean?"

"She isn't very nice." Not an illuminating response, Carrie Ann thought, though she could understand the sentiment. But she didn't want to get into a discussion about Allison. She decided this was as good a time as any to plunge into a conversation about the missing weeks when Rorie had been away from her.

"I've been wondering," she began, not sure how to carry on. "Can you tell Mommy what happened when Willie got sick, and someone brought you to Maui? Do you remember that?"

Rorie picked up a chunk of hardened mud and tossed it across the road. "I don't know," she said, and reached for another clod.

"Did you come on the airplane?"

"Um-hmm."

"Who brought you?"

"Rosemarie."

Who on earth was Rosemarie? Carrie Ann searched her memory. It was Paula, not Rosemarie, who'd taken Rorie when Willie got sick. She could not remember anyone among her acquaintances or among the people they'd talked to in the search named Rosemarie.

"Who were you with before Rosemarie?"

Rorie twisted the hem of her shorts. "Carolyn."

Carolyn. Another unknown name. How many people had this child been handed off to? Carrie Ann tried to stay calm, to fight the hysteria that had often taken over her mind in the past weeks.

"Do you remember Paula? She was camping with you, and she took you to Los Angeles."

"Um-hmm."

"And then you were with Carolyn, and then Rosemarie brought you to Maui."

"Um-hmm."

"And who did you stay with on Maui?"

Rorie frowned and set the dirt clod she'd been picking at on the ground. She lifted one foot and smashed it into bits. "Some people."

"More than one? Did you go to different houses?"

"Yeah. I didn't like it. It was cold at night. And Sundance was mean."

Carrie Ann was afraid to ask, but she had to. "What did Sundance do?"

"I don't know." Rorie stood and tugged her mother's hand. "Let's go."

Carrie Ann hesitated, watching her scowling child. "You can't remember what Sundance did? Is Sundance a boy or a girl?"

"She's a girl," Rorie said. "I don't like her. Come on, let's go."

Carrie Ann stood. At least it was a woman, not a man, whom Rorie called "mean." David the social worker had said there were no overt signs of abuse, only neglect, when they found Rorie, but who knew what some man might have done to her, alone and vulnerable. Carrie Ann took a deep breath, stood, and chose her words carefully.

"I'm glad David found you and took you away, and I've got you back, and Sundance can't be mean to you again." Rorie said nothing; no telling what was going on inside the child's head. "Tell you what, let's not talk about this anymore right now, okay? Because it's making Mommy feel too sad, and maybe it's making you feel sad too. Let's go back to the house and see what's for breakfast. But let's talk about it some more later; I want to hear all the things you can remember, okay? And if you think of something you want to tell me, you tell me anytime, okay?"

Rorie nodded, apparently glad to get off this tense subject. She put out one dirt-stained hand for her mother to hold and headed back toward the house. They were both silent as they walked, Carrie Ann still trying to imagine what it had been like for her baby to be alone in a world of strangers. It was all her fault. She'd been a bad and selfish mother, wanting to be alone with Glenn. But then, she reminded herself, she'd sent Rorie off with Willie, who was completely trustworthy. How could anyone know he'd get sick like that? And she'd hoped that Glenn might want to take on the two of them, to become the man they needed in their lives. Still, she could not shake off her guilt.

"Yoo-hoo!" A chirpy little voice came from behind a hedge dotted with large red flowers. "Good morning!"

Carrie Ann stopped. The hedge bordered one end of the wide lawn at the top of the O'Connors' road. Now that she looked, she could see a rusty tin roof behind it. Must be a house back there; probably the dirt track at the other edge of the lawn was its driveway. The hedge parted, and a smiling brown face peered through.

"Good morning, how you?" The face was old, its wrinkles formed in the shape of a perpetual smile, as if its owner had been cheerful all her life. Her gray hair was tucked up under a wide-brimmed straw hat. The old lady stepped back and then appeared at the end of the hedge and came toward them.

"Good morning," Carrie Ann replied. Rorie stood staring, with her mouth hanging open. "We're fine, how are you?"

"Oh, fine, fine. It's a lovely morning," the old lady said, except, Carrie Ann thought, the "morning" sounded more like "mawning," in the peculiar local accent she'd heard from some of the people here. The old lady bent down with her hands on her knees to look at Rorie more closely. "Oh, what a pretty girl! Did you go for a nice walk with your mommy?" She grinned up at Carrie Ann. "I saw you folks leave before, I was out watering my anthuriums, they like water in the morning so they stay cool all day. You folks staying with Johnny-dem?"

Johnny-dem? It took Carrie Ann a moment to realize it was "Johnny-them," presumably meaning Johnny and them. She'd have to get used to this way of talking if she stayed here.

"Yes, we are. They're letting us stay while we look for a place to live."

"Your husband here too?"

"Um, I don't have a husband . . . . "

"No worry, maybe you find one on Maui, one nice Hawaiian boy, take good care of you and this little one." The old lady reached down to pat Rorie's head. The child still stood staring at the old lady, a birdlike being so tiny she seemed almost closer in size to Rorie than to Carrie Ann. The old lady looked back up at Carrie Ann and grinned. "Local boys, they like pretty blonde haole girls. My grandson, he wen' marry one haole girl, move back to her home in Michigan. But they be here pretty soon, for the baby luau. You folks coming to the luau with Johnny-dem?"

Carrie Ann was vaguely familiar with the word luau; she thought it meant some sort of feast, or maybe a form of entertainment. Uncertain, she nodded and smiled.

"You tell them bring you. You tell them Auntie Nani said bring you." She turned her attention again to Rorie. "What's your name, little one?"

"Rorie."

"Oh, one nice name, Rowree." She grinned back up at Carrie Ann, who hastily introduced herself.

"You came here from California?"

"Yes, San Francisco." Carrie Ann didn't want to get into a big explanation of why she'd come. Too complicated to share with a stranger, even one so benevolent. "I think we'd better get back; no one was up when we left, and they might be wondering where we are. It was nice to meet you."

"Okay," the old lady replied cheerfully. "Nice to meet you and little Rowree. See you at the luau, yeah?" She stood waving and smiling as they headed back down the dirt road into the O'Connors' gulch. Rorie turned and waved back. A nice old lady, Carrie Ann thought, wondering again exactly what a luau might be.

It was indeed a feast, Jerilyn informed her as they cleaned up the kitchen after an oatmeal breakfast. "They serve some Hawaiian food, plus the other kinds of stuff the different immigrants have brought to the Islands: maybe some sushi, that's a rice roll from Japan, and chow fun or some other Chinese-type stuff, plus of course good old macaroni salad, and usually white cake with coconut frosting."

Jerilyn wiped crumbs off the counter. "It's good fun, you'll like it. Give you a chance to see what local life is like. Auntie Nani has this big family, she's pretty much pure Hawaiian, I think, but between her and the two husbands she's outlived, they've added a little of everything to the mix. She's got grandkids that are almost blond. They call it chop suey—all mixed up."

"She said her grandson lives in Michigan?"

"Yeah, he's the reason for the luau—or at least his baby is. They're bringing him home for a baby luau. People give a luau to celebrate the baby's first birthday, I guess because in the old days, if you could keep babies alive until they were one, they'd probably survive."

Jerilyn surveyed the kitchen and wiped her hands on the damp dishtowel. "Well, looks like that will do until we have to mess it up again. Want to go look over the furo shed and see what we're in for? Come on, Rorie, let's go see your new house."

Johnny was already in the little wooden building out behind the house, in the shade of the enormous tree across the driveway from Allison's window. Carrie Ann followed Jerilyn through the front door, which opened into a concrete-floored room with dark wooden walls. Most of the tiny room was filled with a square tub made of concrete, covered with a rough wooden lid. Jerilyn pried up one end of the lid, exposing an edge of blue tile around a dark pool of water.

"This is the furo," Jerilyn said. "Ever seen one before? It's a Japanese bath, here when we got the place. It's great. You make a fire underneath the building in a special fireplace, and it heats up the water in this tub. It has a copper bottom, but we put wooden pallets over it, because it would burn your butt if you sat on the copper. Anyway, it's really great when you've been working hard. You sit in there for a while, get relaxed, then get out and take a cold shower over there." Carrie Ann lifted an eyebrow. "No, really," Jerilyn reassured, "it feels wonderful. We'll probably fire it up tonight."

She turned to look around. "Over there behind that door's the toilet, and there's the laundry sink. You can use that for tooth brushing and stuff. Now here," she turned toward a closed wooden door and pushed it open to peer inside, "here is where you'll be staying. Oh boy. This is gonna be fun."

Jerilyn opened the door wide to reveal a tiny room with a low ceiling and small windows. Dusty cardboard boxes were piled in one corner, and a light bulb hung from a wire in the middle of the ceiling. Johnny was measuring one wall while Stevie stood by, jotting down the measurements as his father called them out.

"Looks like there's just about enough room to squeeze in that old double mattress and still get in and out," Johnny said as the women peered into the cramped little room. "You can put your stuff under the platform, and we can put a shelf over here, to hold a lamp and shit. What do you think, Carrie Ann?"

Carrie Ann swallowed. It was hard to see how this filthy little room, its windows clouded with a film of dirt, light peeking in through cracks in the wall, would ever be livable. But what choice did they have? "Looks fine," she replied. "Rorie, honey, don't pull the paint off the wall, okay?"

Rorie started back, looking guilty, but Jerilyn laughed. "We'll probably peel off a lot more than that when we start cleaning. This is going to be dirty work. Got any grubby clothes, or do you want to borrow some of mine?"

For the rest of the morning, with Johnny and Stevie outside patching holes in the walls and sawing up old boards, Jerilyn and Carrie Ann swept and scraped and wiped to get off the first layer of what appeared to be an endless supply of dirt. Carrie Ann had begun sneezing shortly after they began; her eyes were itchy and her nose running. Rorie, fortunately, seemed happy to explore the edges of the jungle that surrounded the lawn, stopping from time to time to watch the carpenters work.

After lunch, the guys put together the new-sawn boards to make a bed platform, while the women cleaned windows from the outside and stitched pieces of new screen over tears in the old ones. By mid-afternoon, they had dragged in the old mattress left sunning on the grass since morning, covered it with faded but clean sheets, and set a kerosene lamp on the new shelf.

"I'll look at the electric in here tomorrow," Johnny promised, taking a slug from a cold beer. He wiped sweat from his forehead. "Stevie and I want to go down to Hookipa, catch a few waves."

"Me too, I'm ready for a swim." Jerilyn bent to pick up a paper bag full of dust and paint chips. "Carrie Ann, wanna go? You haven't been in the ocean yet, have you?"

"Yeah, I'd like to—but I don't have a swimsuit."

"I think we can borrow one of Allison's, she's got several. And she's off somewhere, probably won't be home 'til dinnertime. Come on, let's go. Does Rorie have a suit? She can always swim in her underpants, or naked for that matter."

Rorie did have a bathing suit, a couple of bright-flowered scraps of fabric tucked into a corner of her suitcase. She was excited about going to the beach and headed straight for the water's edge after Stevie lifted her out of the back of the truck. She stood watching on the wet sand as Stevie and Johnny headed down the beach with boards tucked under their arms.

"This area right here is cool for little kids," Jerilyn said, dropping a towel-stuffed bag onto the sand. She skinned off her T-shirt. "Rorie can play in the little tide pools, see, by the coral ledge." She pointed off to the left, where the waves lapped directly onto the sand, breaking into foamy scallops. "I'm going out over there. The surfers either hang out at that end, where the guys went, or right off here, and I usually try to swim where they aren't. I like to really get out there, and I keep thinking how much it would hurt to get hit by a surfboard, so I avoid them!"

Carrie Ann eyed the waves, deep blue and restless, and decided that, even if she hadn't had Rorie to watch out for, she'd prefer the shallow tide pools. She'd been in the ocean a few times, quick dips in the cold gray water off Bolinas. This was nothing like that ocean. And it was lifetimes away from the neighborhood pool where she'd learned to stay afloat back in elementary school.

Rorie was already happily knee deep in one of the tide pools, bending down to splash, then leaning over to inspect something on the coral. Carrie Ann stepped gingerly into the water. The coolness sliding up her calves felt good after the sweaty day of dirty work. She started to sit on the coral ledge, then thought better of it—who knew what sort of creatures might be on there? Instead, she sank slowly, cross-legged, to the sandy bottom of the pool. Clear water lapped around her shoulders. Carrie Ann wiped her dusty face with wet hands, then on impulse dipped her face in, eyes squeezed tight.

She held her breath for a moment, came up for air, bent her neck so the water cooled the back of her head. She uncrossed her legs, let her body slowly relax, and rested on the soft sand, arms floating loosely in the water.

It was the most restful thing, she discovered, to sit like this, ears full of water, eyes closed to the sun, limbs washed by the little surge when a wave splashed over the coral barrier and into the pool. The next wave splashed water in her face; she sat up quickly. Rorie was fine, humming as she waded around, arms outspread, bobbing on wave ripples. Sun slanted over the water from the mountains where Carrie Ann had watched it set only a few nights ago, her first night on Maui. The ridges were hazy, topped with a mass of clouds that masked the setting sun.

Carrie Ann glanced off to her left; yes, there was Jerilyn, a lone swimmer splashing steadily parallel with the beach. Out on the water, people sat on barely visible boards, waiting for waves. She could not distinguish her friends from the others.

Rorie drifted close to her mother and put her hands on Carrie Ann's shoulders. "Mommy, I can kick," she said, straightening her body in the water. Her slippery hands gripped tighter as her small legs churned up foam. "Uncle Kimo showed me how."

"Wow, that's good. You probably swim better than your mom does."

"Yup, I'm pretty good," Rorie replied, kicking harder.

"Hey, good kicking!" Jerilyn came dripping up the beach, picked up a towel, and spread it to stretch out next to the tide pool.

"I was just telling her, I need some lessons," Carrie Ann confessed.

"Well, we can fix that. Next time we come, okay?" Jerilyn lay back and fell silent. Rorie kept kicking for a while, then said, "Whew! I'm tired now," and got out of the water to dig in the sand.

Carrie Ann was inspecting the water wrinkles on her fingers and thinking it might be time to get out of her pool when Johnny and Stevie returned. Soon they were back in the truck and heading toward Haiku, with Stevie and Rorie sitting in the truck bed. As Johnny took a left onto the highway, Jerilyn fished under the seat and came up with a plastic bag. She took out a joint, lit it, and passed it to Johnny. Carrie Ann glanced back through the truck window; Rorie was talking to Stevie, using her hands in animated gestures. Carrie Ann had never worried about smoking it in front of her daughter before. She took a hit and handed the joint back to Jerilyn. "Do you think I could get in trouble for smoking pot, and maybe lose Rorie again? To the law, I mean?"

"Umm." Johnny exhaled. "I wouldn't worry too much unless you do something really stupid. Nobody pays too much attention to us hippies out in the boonies here, unless you start some big growing operation or something."

Reassured, Carrie Ann took another hit. Soon they were climbing the hill that led to the now-familiar dirt driveway. Johnny pulled up under the giant tree that faced Allison's bedroom window. Hey, Carrie Ann thought, I have a room! Rorie and I have a room!

"Jerilyn, you said that shower out here works? Could Rorie and I take our showers out here?"

"Sure, why not? And later on, we'll have a furo. Johnny likes to light it up on Saturday nights."

It turned out Johnny had lit the fire under the tub before they left for the beach. Carrie Ann heard his voice outside the tiny concrete-floored room where she and Rorie shared a shower of lukewarm water.

"Carrie Ann," he called, "how 'bout hoisting up that wooden cover on the furo and checking to see if it's getting hot yet?"

She wedged her fingers under the edge of the rough wooden cover, lifted it, and checked the water. "Yeah, it's hot, or at least pretty warm," she yelled toward the window in the back wall.

"Okay, I just added wood. It oughta be nice by the time we're pau dinner." Carrie Ann heard a door slam behind the shack and then the rustle of Johnny's feet through the litter of leaves. The water pressure dropped; probably someone else was showering. They'd better go next door to their new room and get ready for dinner.

Her skin smooth and glowing, her body tired but relaxed, Carrie Ann dug into the bags she'd hauled down from Allison's room. Rorie was sitting naked on the edge of the bed brushing her doll's hair with her own brush. The little room was dim, its flaws hidden. Tonight, she and Rorie would sleep in peace and privacy, and who knew what tomorrow would bring? So far, things seemed to be getting better. A surge of well-being filled her body as she pulled Rorie's T-shirt over her head and sniffed the scents of clean baby, woodsmoke, and some flower whose name she did not yet know.

Dinner was less chaotic than usual. The band was going to Lahaina tonight to jam with another group who had a gig at the town's only nightclub. All but Stevie and his dad had left earlier in the day. No one had much to say as they ate; everyone was tired from the day's work. Johnny's plan, he told them, was to take a quick furo, lie down for a nap, and then drink black coffee to keep himself awake the rest of the evening. After dinner, Jerilyn told Carrie Ann they weren't going to bother with washing the dishes tonight, just pile them in the sink and put everything off until morning. Carrie Ann lifted the half-asleep Rorie from her chair and carried her out to bed.

Carrie Ann lay down with her child until Rorie's breathing was deep and even, then slipped off the bed and into the next room, closing the door. Johnny was lifting the lid off the tub; steam rose from the water in the dim light of a kerosene lantern set on a windowsill.

Jerilyn dropped her shorts in the corner and stood naked beside the furo, testing the water with one hand. "Whew! That's hot!" she exclaimed, and then swung one foot over and lowered it slowly into the tub. Johnny shucked his jeans and eased into the steaming water. "Come on in, Carrie Ann, the water's fine," Jerilyn said, then relaxed with a sigh.

Carrie Ann hesitated; she'd run around a Big Sur beach naked one weekend but wasn't used to this casual disrobing. Oh well, there was no other way to try this tub, and Johnny was leaning back with eyes closed, neck-deep in water. She slipped out of her own clothes and tested the water in the space next to Jerilyn.

"God, that's hot! I don't know if I can stand to put my whole body in there."

"You can. See, your hand is still in there, and if your hand can stand it, the rest of you can," Jerilyn said.

Cautiously, Carrie Ann sat on the side of the furo and lowered first one foot and then the other into the water. Her feet rested on a slatted wooden surface; beneath them rose waves of heat. Yes, it was hot, but yes, she could keep her feet and legs inside. Carefully she lowered her body. The hot water stung slightly when it first passed over her skin, but once she was all the way in, it was simply the hottest bath she'd ever had. Only her head topped the water. Everyone was silent.

They sat like that for a while, talking little, until Johnny announced that he was ready for a shower. His exit from the tub set off waves of heat. Then he was under the shower, and Carrie Ann felt a cool mist touch her face. "Man, that's good!" Johnny moaned as he turned under the stream of cold water. A moment later, Jerilyn crawled out and took Johnny's place under the shower. He wandered outside. Carrie Ann was beginning to feel groggy. She pulled her body out of the water and stepped carefully over to the shower as Jerilyn followed Johnny out the door.

At first, Carrie Ann was as hesitant as she'd been entering the tub. She stuck one overheated hand under the shower and turned it on, just a trickle. Then she braced herself, turned on the shower full blast, and stepped beneath it.

The cold was a wonderful shock, sending tingles of energy throughout her body. She stood under the shower for a moment, alive with an almost psychedelic surge, then stepped, still warm, into the night air. Johnny and Jerilyn sprawled on a beach mat, apparently unconcerned about lying around naked in their backyard. A few minutes ago, Carrie Ann had been shy about undressing for the furo, but now she was as relaxed as the O'Connors looked. One more new experience among many in recent days. She took a toke from the joint Jerilyn passed, then lay flat on a towel, breathed out smoke, stared up at more stars than she'd ever seen, and listened to the solitary notes of Stevie's bass drifting from the basement.

Chapter Seven

For a moment Carrie Ann was confused, uncertain where she was, disoriented by the dark and by the child's crying next to her ear, pulling her from a deep sleep. It was a different cry from the usual midnight calls for a drink of water or even for comfort after a nightmare. This was a piercing, insistent shriek.

Carrie Ann sat up and gathered Rorie's rigid little body to her own.

"Hush, baby, it's okay. Mama's here." She murmured the soothing phrases automatically, rocking her daughter and patting her back. Still Rorie screamed, and Carrie Ann wondered if people in the house could hear her.

It was several minutes before she could quiet the child. When at last her cries subsided into sobs, and then into deep sniffling breaths, Carrie Ann reached up to the shelf over the bed, glad she'd thought to bring a jar of water when she was organizing their little room yesterday. She wished she had a clock as well.

Rorie sipped water but refused to answer her mother's questions. Had she had a bad dream? Did her tummy hurt? A dreadful thought struck Carrie Ann as she remembered Johnny's comments about centipedes—had something bitten Rorie? The girl simply shook her head and clung to Carrie Ann. Gradually her body relaxed, and after a while, she slept. When her breathing deepened and her grip loosened, Carrie Ann carefully laid her daughter onto the mattress, pulled the sheet up over her, and settled back into her own place.

What on earth was that about? Rorie had been a good sleeper all her life, except for the infant months when she woke for feeding and diaper changes. She'd had an occasional nightmare, but never anything like this. Once again, Carrie Ann wished there were some way to find out what had happened during the weeks when Rorie was lost. Surely this night terror was a result of that time. She'd try again to talk to her about it, and maybe Rick or the O'Connors could help her find out more. What about those people down at Guava Gulch? Would any of them be able to tell her anything? She resolved to get down there, somehow, and ask.

Rorie seemed fine the next morning. When Carrie Ann asked what had bothered her in the middle of the night, Rorie looked at her blankly. She got the same reaction later, over a bowl of oatmeal, when she tried again with questions about the missing weeks. She'd thought that if she introduced the subject casually, with Jerilyn sitting nearby sipping a cup of coffee, she might get some answers.

But no. Rorie scowled and concentrated on her oatmeal, then managed to spill her milk. Jerilyn, grabbing for a rag to clean up the table, quirked an eyebrow at Carrie Ann, who shrugged, perplexed.

They cleared the sink of last night's dishes while Rorie crawled into the next room, dragging a length of string to tease the cat. In a low voice, Carrie Ann told Jerilyn about Rorie's outburst the night before. "Do you think we could go down to Guava Gulch and ask some people about it?"

"We could try," Jerilyn said. "A lot of people have left since the quarantine let up, but we might find someone. Maybe next time we go grocery shopping, we could take a trip down there. We could get Stevie or Allison to watch Rorie. I don't think we should take her along."

The day proceeded peacefully. Rorie seemed to be fine. Carrie Ann spent some time fixing up the little room with pictures clipped from an old calendar and curtains made from fabric Jerilyn gave her. Rorie played with the scraps, cutting up the leftover calendar pages and gluing together a messy collage of paper and fabric. She appeared to be absorbed and happy, though Carrie Ann noticed she had reverted to sucking her thumb, something she hadn't done for the past year. Carrie Ann decided to ignore the thumb-sucking; she'd outgrow it again.

Rorie slept soundly that night, and the next, and Carrie Ann hoped that the night terror had been an aberration. Perhaps she needn't bother to go ask questions at Guava Gulch. Perhaps Rorie would be okay if they simply got on with life. Living at the O'Connors' was certainly peaceful enough. Jerilyn seemed happy to have her and Rorie around, as much for company as for help with the chores, with Johnny at work and both Allison and Stevie off at school. Sweeping the big house took half an hour, and then there was weeding the garden, feeding the chickens, and the endless round of cooking and cleaning up in the kitchen.

She had about given up on the idea of going down to Guava Gulch when Jerilyn paused one day, broom in hand, and peered around the corner into the living room. Rorie was playing there with some of Stevie's wooden toy cars, climbing onto furniture to run first one, then another, along the seat backs and down to the floor again.

"Hey, Carrie Ann . . . ." Jerilyn's voice dropped to a whisper. "I'm planning to go into Paia later, since Johnny left the truck today, and I was thinking you might want to go down to Guava Gulch. We could leave Rorie with Stevie when he gets home from school. Want to go?"

"Yeah, sure. Maybe we should wait until she takes her nap. She's not going to like it if we go somewhere and don't take her along."

Jerilyn snorted. "Right, but who knows what she'll do when she wakes up! We'd better make it a quick trip."

A few hours later, the two women were in Paia. They hit the Mercantile and Horiuchi Market for groceries, then headed back to the country.

The turnoff to Guava Gulch was a familiar landmark by now, but Carrie Ann was tense as Jerilyn maneuvered the truck down a narrow dirt road. Stop that, she told herself, clutching her hands as she stared at the branches slapping the truck's windows. There was no reason to feel weird about this. Jerilyn had a friend down here she planned to visit; no one need know who Carrie Ann was, and she wasn't sure she wanted anyone to know. She clutched the dashboard, steadying herself as the truck rattled over a bump. Jerilyn pulled off the road onto a grassy area and rolled up the window.

"I hardly ever lock the truck, but we just bought all this food, and some of the people down here are pretty skuzzy, so maybe we better."

Carrie Ann climbed out, locked her door, then followed Jerilyn down the road into the valley. Trees arched over ruts too deep even for Johnny's truck.

"That place where we parked is where the cops set up the quarantine checkpoint," Jerilyn told her. "They wouldn't let anyone out past that checkpoint for more than a week. Of course, they brought in food, so nobody starved. Some people did leave—they climbed up the side of the gulch and cut across the pineapple field to the highway and hitchhiked to town."

They rounded a bend in the road, and Jerilyn pushed aside guava branches to reveal a trail. Once past its beginning, the path was well maintained, the bushes along the edges neatly trimmed. The trail ended at a small lawn, obviously one kept neat with a real lawn mower. At one end stood a building that could only be called a shack. It appeared to have been made from scrap materials. Windows that did not match formed one patchwork wall, boards of different sizes made another, and peeling paint in various colors marked much of the wood. Still, Carrie Ann saw a grace to the building that somehow took it beyond the "shack" category. Its peaked roof, formed of corrugated iron, was shaded by drooping tree branches; colored plastic in some of the window spaces gave a stained-glass effect; wind chimes tinkled on the little screened-in front porch.

Jerilyn's friend was a thin young woman with long braids who sat on the porch nursing her baby. Jerilyn introduced her as Sandy and the baby as Lily. For a while, the three women sat, smoking a joint, sipping tea from a jug Sandy had brewing in the sun. Then Sandy bundled the baby into a shawl tied over one shoulder and led them farther into the valley.

The jungle was thick here, vines curling and crawling over guava bushes and banana trees, and the path was narrow. They walked single file. Somewhere to the left, Carrie Ann heard water running—the stream, Sandy told her, where they all got their washing water. Drinking water, at least at Sandy's house, came from rain caught on the roof and stored in 55-gallon barrels.

"But some of the people were drinking out of the stream," Sandy told them. "I think that might be how they got sick. The outhouses are uphill, you know, and the stream is probably polluted. My old man's too smart to set up anything like that, and we never got sick."

Sandy pointed at the side of the gulch. "Here's where Big Al the Biker lived before the quarantine. He got bummed and split, and no one's moved in. Your little girl was there for a while, Carrie Ann. Big Al and his old lady, Betty, took care of her, but they weren't really into kids." Carrie Ann peered through the bushes and saw, high on the valley walls, a shack more deserving of the name than Sandy's colorful little house. This one seemed haphazardly put together, with windows of plastic sheeting that had begun to tear loose and flap in the breeze.

There were more shacks perched on the valley walls, similarly constructed of scrap wood and used windows, with rusty metal roofs. Some had water barrels alongside. Here and there, a long-haired inhabitant peered out to wave at Sandy. Somewhere, a flute played. Woodsmoke scented the air.

At last, the winding path came to an end at the steps of the sturdiest building Carrie Ann had seen down here. Sandy turned and spoke in a low voice.

"This is where the cops found Rorie. It's Sundance's place. She's probably not here, or she'd have heard us coming. She's kind of weird. I was glad when they took Rorie away. If I hadn't been so close to giving birth, I might have taken her when Al and Betty gave her up, but it just wasn't happening."

Finally, someone who knew something about the time when Rorie was lost. "Do you know who else she was with?" Carrie Ann asked. "Or who brought her here?"

Sandy shrugged. "Some chick came in from California, stayed at Big Beach at Makena for a while, I think, and then came down here. She moved into an empty house, but she didn't stay long—couldn't make it without an old man, I guess." Sandy shifted the shawl, lifting the baby higher on her breast.

"What was the chick's name?"

"I never really talked to her—Rosemarie, maybe?"

Carrie Ann's shoulders relaxed, as if a piece of a difficult puzzle had clicked into place, a puzzle she'd worked long and hard to solve. Paula had given Rorie to Carolyn, who gave her to Rosemarie, who for some unaccountable reason had brought her to Maui, then turned her over to Big Al and Betty.

"What's going on here?" The voice came, harsh and unexpected, from the path they had just traversed. Carrie Ann turned to see a tall, thin, deeply tanned woman, her shaven head incongruous with her great silver hoop earrings, silky blouse, and long skirt. From a strap around her waist hung a long, sharp-looking knife, the kind Johnny used to clear weeds around his banana plants.

"Oh—hi, Sundance." Sandy did not seem intimidated by this strange woman, whose fierce glare and sharp knife made Carrie Ann want to retreat behind the nearest tree.

"This is Carrie Ann," Sandy said. "She's the mom of Rorie, the little kid who was living with you."

"Oh yeah? And what does Rorie's mommy want? Come to see how well I took care of her little angel?"

This woman was heavy, Carrie Ann thought, biting her lip. She tried not to imagine what kind of foster mother Sundance would have made, if indeed that was the way to describe her relationship with Rorie.

"It's cool, Sundance," Sandy soothed. "She just wanted to see where Rorie stayed."

Sundance snorted. "Only the best house in the Gulch, the one Antone Cravalho himself built and gave me to live in." She frowned directly at Carrie Ann, causing her to take an involuntary half-step back. "I'm the original resident here, you know—the founder of Guava Gulch. And the way things are going, I may be the last one to stay." She turned to Sandy. "I hear you folks are splitting."

"Yeah, we got a piece of land up in Kanaio. Gonna build up there. Too much shit going down around here—too many people, the quarantine—we're heading for the hills."

"Those asshole cops and state flunkeys. They're dragging Antone into court, you know. Some shit about building permits."

"Yeah, well . . . it was fun while it lasted."

"Fun! Hell, this could have been Paradise, if not for a few fuckups. Antone, he's a great man. He's into freedom and peace, not like the fucking pigs. How do you think these people got sick, anyway? Somebody poisoned that poi, man, I'm telling you. They knew who'd be eating that stuff. They knew who'd be at that luau."

Sandy glanced at Jerilyn and Carrie Ann. "Yeah, well, I don't know about that, Sundance. How can somebody know who would be there, never mind which bag of poi to poison?"

"I'm telling you, they knew!" Sundance was vociferous. Her hand went to the knife at her waist. Carrie Ann eyed its silvery-sharp edge nervously. "I know what's happening, I'm not some airy-fairy space case like some of these idiots down here. They're after Antone, trying to clamp down on him before he gives away his land—no free land allowed here, no sir. Got to keep those peons tied to their jobs and paychecks. So they went after him through us, trying to make it look like living off the land is bad for your health. Shee-it!"

"Yeah, well, you may be right, Sundance. I just know we're getting out of here." Sandy shifted the weight of her sleeping baby. "This kid's getting heavy. We got to go now, Sundance. Nice talking to you."

Jerilyn and Carrie Ann followed Sandy as she turned to head back up the Gulch. Glancing back, Carrie Ann saw that Sundance had removed her machete and was whacking at some weeds next to her house, muttering to herself with a frown on her face. Carrie Ann walked faster, glad to be leaving.

"God, Jerilyn—what a trip," she said as they climbed into the truck to head home. "I can't believe Rorie lived with her. No wonder she had lice and stuff. That woman is freaky."

"Yeah, Sundance is kind of famous. They had her picture in the paper on the courthouse steps the day they went to court to get the quarantine lifted. The cops wouldn't let her into court with her cane knife, and she stood outside fuming for most of the morning."

Carrie Ann sat silent for a moment. "But you know, we still didn't find out exactly why Rosemarie brought Rorie to Maui. How could she afford to buy a plane ticket for a kid that didn't even belong to her? And then why abandon her?"

"Little kids can fly for free on their parent's lap. I think Rorie might be over the age limit, but she's petite—wrap her in a pink blanket, give her a baby bottle to suck on, and she'd probably look young enough. As for why anyone would do that? Honey, you might never know. Maybe it's always going to be a mystery. Maybe Rorie will come up with something someday, or somebody who knows what happened will show up, or maybe you'll have to get used to not knowing."

That night, with Rorie settled in bed, Carrie Ann tried again. Did Rorie remember Big Al and Betty? Did she remember camping at Makena, being at the beach every day?

But Rorie was having none of it. She pulled at a loose thread on the blanket, twisted the button eyes on her teddy bear, and said nothing but, "I don't know."

At last, sighing, Carrie Ann opened Stevie's old copy of *Charlotte's Web* and began to read. When Rorie's eyes closed, Carrie Ann put the book down. For a long time, she sat looking at her daughter. A mystery, Jerilyn had said. Perhaps part of the answer was locked inside Rorie's head, though she could have no idea of Rosemarie's motivations or of the others who had accepted her into their care only to pass her along to someone else. Carrie Ann was beginning to think this was a mystery that might never be solved.

Then, only two days later, Carrie Ann nearly bumped into Sundance in Paia. She'd been in the Mercantile, browsing through fabrics, and Rorie was right behind her as she stepped out the door onto the sidewalk. Carrie Ann stopped abruptly, drawing a startled breath as Sundance halted on her way into the store, a sneer on her face.

"Well, look who's here. The little mommy and her darling daughter. And doesn't she look nice in her pretty sundress! Remember me, sweetheart? Got a kiss for Auntie Sundance?"

Rorie shrank closer to her mother and clutched Carrie Ann's skirt. Laughing, Sundance reached as if to pat Rorie's head. Carrie Ann grabbed Rorie before the woman's hand could touch her. "We have to go," she said, lifting her child, and strode away. She went straight to the truck, set Rorie on the front seat, and climbed in, shaking. She locked her door and stretched to lock the driver's side. She knew it was irrational; surely Sundance would not follow them, but the locked doors made her feel secure. She pulled Rorie onto her lap and wiped off the tears running down her daughter's face.

"It's okay, baby, we're safe. Sundance is gone, and you don't have to see her anymore."

"I don't like her," Rorie said, clinging to her mother.

"I know, you said she was mean." Carrie Ann paused, then continued in as casual a tone as she could manage. "She sure looks mean, huh? Do you remember any mean stuff she did when you stayed with her?"

"Maybe."

"Can you tell Mommy?"

Rorie kept her eyes down, plucking at a button on the front of Carrie Ann's dress. "She spanked me. When I went shishi in the bed."

"Oh, honey! I'm sorry!" Carrie Ann stroked her scowling child's frail shoulders. "Did she spank you hard?"

"Sort of hard. I don't like her."

Carrie Ann drew a deep breath. "I don't like her either. But you're back with me, and you don't have to be scared. That mean Sundance shouldn't have spanked you. But she can't do it anymore, okay? Mommy has you now."

Jerilyn's face appeared in the driver's side window, and Carrie Ann reached over to unlock the door.

"What's happening?" Jerilyn asked as she settled behind the steering wheel.

"We ran into Sundance," Carrie Ann replied. "At the Mercantile."

"Ahh."

"Yeah. So we split and came back here, because neither one of us wanted to see her. And Rorie tells me Sundance spanked her kind of hard."

"Is that so!" Jerilyn turned the key and revved the engine. "Well, I tell you what, Rorie-child, if that old Sundance ever comes around our place, we'll give her a spanking, okay? Would that be good?"

Sniffing, Rorie nodded and smiled.

"Or maybe we could put her in the chicken coop, how about that?" Jerilyn continued, pulling out onto Baldwin Avenue and heading for home.

"Or make her weed banana trees," Carrie Ann suggested.

"Or clean up the kitty's poo-poo!" Rorie chimed in. Jerilyn and Carrie Ann laughed, trading glances over Rorie's head. At least they knew something about Rorie's time in Guava Gulch, Carrie Ann thought, pulling her daughter close, and maybe something about why she sometimes woke, screaming, in the night.

Carrie Ann went to bed half expecting to be wakened by those screams. But Rorie slept through that night, and the next. She was clingy for a few days after the encounter but soon reclaimed her usual independent self. Thinking about it as she braided Rorie's hair one morning, Carrie Ann came up with a theory. Perhaps her own instinctive reaction on that day, getting Rorie away from that weird woman and taking her straight to a safe place, had restored her daughter's trust. She fervently hoped so; it would mean she'd managed to do the right thing at least once in her life as a mother.

Chapter Eight

"I don't know what to get for a present for Auntie Nani's great-grandson," Jerilyn said as she and Carrie Ann sat at the kitchen table chopping vegetables for the night's stew. "The baby luau is this weekend. Got any ideas?"

Carrie Ann dumped a handful of chopped celery into a pot. "Oh, yeah, I almost forgot—Auntie Nani asked us to that party. He's how old? One?"

"Yeah, and they have to take any presents back to the mainland in their luggage, so that kind of rules out the wooden toys Johnny makes—too bulky and heavy."

"Well, I could make something. Like a little shirt, maybe. I make a lot of Rorie's clothes. You'll see some when Mimi sends my stuff. Do you have any good fabric? Like baby blue or something?"

The trunk where Jerilyn kept her fabric stash did contain baby-blue velvet, which at first seemed a bit much for a year-old boy. But Carrie Ann came up with an idea: a long-sleeved, hooded jacket with a gold crown embroidered on the chest, a perfect party jacket for the baby whose birthday occasioned a feast. She used one of Rorie's T-shirts to get the basic shape, stitched the shirt together on Jerilyn's old treadle machine, and picked up a skein of gold embroidery thread on a trip to Paia.

The day of the luau, Carrie Ann wrapped the little shirt and attached a homemade card decorated with Rorie's crayon scrawls and signed by everyone in the house and the band. It felt good to know they were contributing something to this household, and Carrie Ann was excited as she dressed for the luau in a long, flowered dress borrowed from Allison. This was her first social event on Maui, and the first time she'd see the band perform in public.

Music sounded faintly through the trees as the women set off down the dirt road to Auntie Nani's house. Johnny and the band had gone ahead, their speakers and instruments loaded on the back of Johnny's truck. Carrie Ann smiled as she picked her way along the rutted road, holding her skirt up off the red dirt. Rorie skipped along in her frilly dress and Mary Janes, and even Allison seemed in a good mood, chatting with Jerilyn as they walked in the fragrant late afternoon.

Rounding a bend, they found cars parked bumper-to-bumper along the side of the road and people clustered, drinking and laughing, on Auntie Nani's broad lawn. They cut through the crowd to the house, where an army-green canvas tarp was stretched from the porch to the limbs of a tree, sheltering rows of picnic tables where more people sat. The music they'd heard as they approached came from a trio perched on stools under yet another tarp. Three men, dressed in white pants and colorful shirts, plucked stringed instruments—an ukulele, a guitar, and a stand-up bass. They seemed oddly bored, as if the melody was one they'd played forever.

Behind them, Johnny and the band were busy with their collection of giant speakers, connecting wires and plugging in instruments. They would play later, after the meal, Jerilyn told Carrie Ann.

Rorie clung to Carrie Ann's hand as the two of them stood briefly alone. Jerilyn was over talking to Johnny, and Allison had disappeared somewhere—probably saw a friend, or maybe off to find a beer while Jerilyn's attention was elsewhere. All around were unfamiliar faces. Carrie Ann tried a tentative smile—it was a party, surely people would be friendly—but found few willing to meet her eye. She was beginning to feel uncomfortable when Jerilyn reappeared with Auntie Nani, who immediately bent to exclaim over Rorie, then stood to greet Carrie Ann.

"Come, come," she said. "You folks come meet my grandson and his wife and the baby." Auntie Nani grasped Rorie's hand and led them up the porch steps to find a handsome dark-skinned young man and his freckled, red-haired wife. Their chubby baby was a combination of the two, with golden skin, green eyes, and red highlights in his wispy dark hair. All three wore flower lei around their necks. The baby was shredding petals off his, but no one seemed to mind. With introductions complete, the old lady led them to an old-fashioned Coca-Cola cooler filled with ice, beer, and sodas, told them to help themselves, and flitted off into the crowd.

Jerilyn chose a bottle of beer, Carrie Ann found Cokes for herself and Rorie, and the two women stood sipping, watching the milling crowd. "Let's sit over there." Jerilyn pointed to one of the picnic tables under the tarp, where a young man sat alone. "Might as well stake out our territory, and Chuckie won't mind." She led the way across the lawn. "Hey, Chuckie-boy, this is our new roommate, Carrie Ann."

Carrie Ann had just settled herself when someone called to Jerilyn from across the lawn. "Oh, wow, it's Cathy—I gotta go talk to her, be right back," Jerilyn said, heading off to see her friend. Rorie watched Jerilyn weave her way through the crowd, then turned toward several children playing at the base of the tree supporting the tarp.

Carrie Ann sipped her Coke, tried to look as if she were having a good time, and sneaked a peek at the young man sitting farther down the table. He was kind of cute, with brown skin and big brown eyes. He seemed to be absorbed in his beer and in the performance by the Hawaiian musicians.

The table was covered with white paper, with a line of shiny green leaves and big red and yellow flowers running down its center.

Carrie Ann picked up one of the flowers, stroked its long velvety stamen, and sniffed the deep red of its center. She sniffed again. There was no smell. She frowned, then realized that Chuckie was grinning, watching her from the corner of his eye. She blushed at the sudden mental image of herself stroking the flower's stamen, and hastily laid it back on the table.

"It's one hibiscus," the man said. "That kind don't smell." He sipped his beer. "So, what . . . you staying with Johnny folks?"

"Yeah. Do you live here?"

"This my grandma's house. I never lived here, but I played here plenty growing up."

"Auntie Nani is your grandma? She's real sweet. She talked to Rorie and me one morning when we came back from our walk."

"Rorie. That's your little kid?"

"Yeah." Carrie Ann looked from the flower to her child, who was watching several others about her age play at the feet of a group of laughing adults.

"How long you been here?"

"Just a few weeks."

He grinned. "You like it? Where you came from?"

"Yeah, I like it, but I'm still planning to go back home to San Francisco."

"Oh yeah. I been there. When I was passing through on the way to Nam, after basic training."

"You went to Vietnam?"

"Yeah. Man, I never thought I'd see this place again. When I walked off the plane and saw that jungle, I thought, oh man, how am I ever gonna get out of here. I was so happy to come home." He took a swig of beer and stared off into the palm hedge lining one side of the lawn.

"When did you come back?"

"Last year. Almost eleven months." He sat up straighter, took a deep breath, and another drink of his beer. "Anyway, how come you like go back to San Francisco? Some cold, that place!"

"Well, it's where I've lived for the past four years, and it's where my friends are."

"Umm. Well, at least you get a nice look at Maui *no ka oi*."

"Maui what?"

"Maui *no ka oi*. It means Maui is the best. Some kinda motto or something." Chuckie had talked thus far without looking straight at her. Now he turned to face her. "So what's your name again?"

"Carrie Ann."

"Nice to meet you, Carrie Ann." He pointed with his beer bottle toward the porch, where Auntie Nani was holding the birthday baby while his parents embraced a family who had just arrived. "That's my cousin Joey up there. We used to have plenty fights when we were kids, but we're good friends now."

They were silent for a few moments. Carrie Ann felt she should say something. "It must have been nice growing up here. So different from where I grew up, and from San Francisco."

"Where did you grow up?"

"In El Paso, Texas, out in the middle of the desert. I don't think I ever saw a tree as big as that one over there until I moved to California. And California's pretty, but this place is something else."

"So what, you one hippie from Haight Ashbury?"

Carrie Ann laughed, a little embarrassed. "Well, kind of. I did actually live on Haight Street. And I got there the year before the Summer of Love, so I saw it when it was really cool, before it got weird." Talking about it brought back memories of her first summer in the city, of the 1940s fur coat she had found in a secondhand store, and the first boots she'd ever owned—right before the media showed up to chase the hippies, and the whole scene went sour. The summer Rorie got started. That summer.

"Hey, you want a beer or something?"

"Sure. I'm almost done with my Coke." She wasn't much of a beer drinker, but what the heck, it was a party.

As Chuckie swung one leg over the bench to stand up, a plump, dark-haired woman approached, said, "Chuckie-boy!" and gave him a kiss right on the lips, patting both cheeks.

"Hey, Claudia, howzit? Long time no see. Hey, I'm going get one beer for me and this lady over here. You like one too? Then we can sit and talk story. I never see you long time already."

"Okay." She settled herself on the bench across from Carrie Ann, smiled, then turned to call to Chuckie, "Try bring some peanuts, yeah?" She turned back to Carrie Ann. "Chuckie's my cousin. We used to play together at this very table. I hardly see him nowadays, I'm busy with my kids, plus I'm taking classes. So how do you know Chuckie?" She smiled again, dark eyes looking directly at Carrie Ann's in a way that made her know Claudia suspected something was going on here.

"Oh, we just met. He was sitting here, and I sat down, and we started talking. He told me he used to play here when he was a kid. My name is Carrie Ann. I came with the O'Connors and the band." She gestured to the band area, where Johnny was still fooling with speakers while the guys set up drums and fiddled with guitars. Soon rock would split the conversations of the night, fill the air with music, and perhaps, set the crowd to dancing.

"Will people dance, do you think?" she asked Claudia. "I've never been to a baby lua before."

Claudia laughed. "Luau, luau, not lua. That means a toilet! Lu-au. Like that. Anyway, sure, people gonna dance. I will! I heard these guys before and they're good, you know."

Chuckie arrived with hands full, distributed three beers, and set a bowl of unshelled peanuts on the table. Claudia grabbed a few and began peeling them immediately; Carrie Ann saw that the hulls were soft and soggy.

"Boiled peanuts," Chuckie explained. "Try 'em. They're good." He turned to Claudia. "So, Cuz, what's happening?"

The two began a conversation in the local accent that was almost unintelligible to Carrie Ann. She tried one of the soggy peanuts and found they were, indeed, tasty. She ate a few of the salty nuts, then turned to offer some to Rorie.

The child had edged closer to the group playing on the ground, and as Carrie Ann watched, Rorie stooped tentatively and picked up a toy truck no one else was using. Soon she was on her knees, pushing the truck in circles. The other children barely acknowledged her presence but made no move to take the truck away. Carrie Ann sighed, thinking about the red mud that was likely to be ground into Rorie's frilly dress, but decided it was a small price to pay as long as Rorie was having fun. Reassured, she turned her attention to the party, surveying the animated crowd that filled Auntie Nani's yard.

Oh my God. There was Michael Wharton, lounging against a tree at the edge of the yard. Carrie Ann hadn't seen him since that first day at the O'Connors'. He was as gorgeous as she had remembered. Carrie Ann sipped her beer, trying to look casual, as if her heart had not started to pound the moment she caught sight of him. Then, she spotted Allison cutting through the crowd, heading straight for Michael. The two stepped back into the shadows under the tree and talked for a moment. Allison looked over her shoulder, scanning the crowd, and then grabbed Michael's hand and walked away from the party.

Carrie Ann blinked. A wave of disappointment washed over her. Shit. What did he want with that little punk? Sure, she was gorgeous, but awfully young and not all that together. Why did the really cool men always seem to be attracted to someone else? Had Michael and Allison planned this meeting in advance? Down on the road, she heard the roar of a motorcycle. That must be Michael's bike. She wondered where they were going.

Across the lawn, she saw Jerilyn, still talking with her friend. Should she tell Jerilyn what she'd seen? Carrie Ann thought about it for a minute. They were probably only going for a ride, she decided. No big deal. After all, Allison had been hanging out with Michael for a while, so it must be okay. It's too bad it was Allison instead of me, she thought, reaching for another soggy peanut. Then she thought of Jerilyn's comment about Allison taking birth control pills and sighed. She might as well face it: Michael and Allison were probably heading off somewhere to get it on. Shit.

The Hawaiian musicians finished their song, and Auntie Nani's grandson, Joey, stepped up to the microphone Johnny had set up.

"Aloha, you folks. Can I have your attention, please!" A squawk of feedback screeched from the speaker, and Johnny hurriedly adjusted the mike. Joey spoke again. "It's time for kaukau, so first we pule. If everyone can settle down, please . . . ."

Carrie Ann looked around, wondering what Joey had said. The crowd was in fact becoming quiet, pausing in their conversations to turn and face the impromptu stage area where the musical equipment was set up. From behind the speakers came a wizened little man in a black suit, leaning on the arm of Joey's red-haired wife. Johnny adjusted the mike again, lowering it to the old man's face. Eyes closed, the old man spoke in a language Carrie Ann had never heard. Everyone else was bowing their heads, so this must be a prayer—grace before dinner? She bowed her head as well and waited for someone to say something she could understand.

"Okay, thank you, Papa Kalama." It was Joey back at the mike. "Time for eat! You folks line up for food!" There was scattered applause as the crowd resumed its conversations, and some people began moving toward a row of tables set up along one edge of the lawn. Smiling women removed the lids from stainless steel containers and stood poised with spoons, ready to serve the first in line.

"Carrie Ann, want to try some Hawaiian food?" Jerilyn reappeared. "Sorry to desert you—I haven't seen Cathy since she broke up with her old man. She had a lot to tell me. Men—I swear! They can sure put you through some changes, can't they? Hey, Chuckie—not you, of course. We know you're a good guy!"

Chuckie grinned and introduced his cousin, then kissed her goodbye as she headed off to find her family. "So, you folks ready to eat?" he asked. "Time for Carrie Ann to try some poi, huh? Maybe a couple opihi?"

Chuckie led her through the food line, explaining each dish, while Jerilyn made up a plate with things she said Rorie would probably like. Carrie Ann couldn't bring herself to try the opihi. Chuckie's description of a little shell-enclosed creature clinging to rocks by the shore made it sound too much like a snail. But the poi, she discovered once she had settled herself and Rorie at the table and begun to eat, was kind of tangy. It was not bad if you ate a mouthful at the same time you ate a bite of something salty like the kalua pig or the salmon mixed with chopped tomatoes. Rorie ate her poi straight, to her mother's surprise, gobbling that, white rice, and some kalua pig before scrambling back down to rejoin the kids' party under the tree.

Johnny and Stevie had just set their plates on the table when Jerilyn stopped with her fork in mid-air and looked around.

"Where's Allison?"

Carrie Ann swallowed a mouthful of macaroni salad.

"Uh . . . I think she went somewhere with Michael. At least, I saw them walk off, and I heard a motorcycle leave . . . "

Jerilyn rolled her eyes. Johnny, who had laid a hand on Chuckie's shoulder in greeting as he settled onto the picnic table bench, turned to look at Carrie Ann with a scowl.

"Oh, yeah? When was that?"

"Um, maybe half an hour ago? Not too long after we got here. Sorry—is that bad?"

Maybe Allison would get in trouble and not be able to see Michael anymore. But maybe Johnny would be mad at Carrie Ann for not alerting someone sooner to his ward's disappearance. She looked around the table; Chuckie was doing the same, probably trying to figure out what was going on.

But Johnny shook his head, still frowning, and dug into his food. "That kid. No wonder her parents couldn't handle her. She's outta control." He stopped to chew for a moment. "You gotta talk to her, Jerilyn. That Wart is an asshole, and the sooner she figures it out the better."

Wart?

Chuckie looked puzzled. "What you called him?"

Jerilyn shook her head, exasperated. "Oh, Johnny calls Michael 'Wart.' His last name is Wharton, and Johnny doesn't like him very much."

"And he deserves it," Johnny said. "That guy is a wart on the face of humanity."

Everyone laughed, including Jerilyn. "Come on, Johnny, this is a man thing between you two. Carrie Ann and I don't think he's so bad—kinda cute, huh, Carrie Ann?"

Carrie Ann ducked her head. "He's okay."

"Although I do wish Allison wouldn't take off with him without telling us," Jerilyn said.

"Damn right. He shouldn't be taking off with a seventeen-year-old girl without her elders' permission, and I'm her elder, and I'm going to have a talk with her if you don't want to. Thank God for birth control pills." Johnny took a swig of his beer and turned to Chuckie. "Let's change the subject. How's the fishing, Chuckie-boy?"

The three guys were soon deep into a discussion, recalling a trip Johnny and Stevie had taken in Chuckie's boat. Carrie Ann was left to think about the missing Michael and Allison. It was kind of amazing that Jerilyn and Johnny weren't more upset. If it had been Carrie Ann's folks, her mother would have been in hysterics and her father in the car combing the streets, looking for his daughter. Maybe it was because the O'Connors weren't Allison's real parents, or maybe because they were hippies and had different ideas about what was acceptable.

Anyway, at least they weren't mad at Carrie Ann for not saying anything when Allison left.

Stevie got up to go for seconds, though Carrie Ann couldn't imagine how anyone could eat more than one plate piled as high as his had been. Chuckie went to the dessert table and returned with small plates holding large slices of coconut cake.

Jerilyn was halfway through her slice when she looked up. "Hey, we didn't sing 'Happy Birthday' to the baby."

"Well, it's about time for Blend to go on. I'll tell Terry to sing it before they start their set." Johnny looked around. "I better go find those guys. They're probably out back smoking a jay before they play." He heaved his body out from between table and bench and headed back to the house.

Carrie Ann felt an anticipatory thrill when the band members finally began to tune up, and a bit of pride. She knew the band; she lived at the band manager's house; she'd heard their songs. They started off by leading the crowd in singing "Happy Birthday," and then the band swung into one of their original songs, one Carrie Ann had found herself humming as she went about her day, a catchy tune set to the pounding rhythm of Tom's drums. She wanted to dance to it. She'd spent several evenings standing in a corner of the basement, swaying and bobbing to the music and looking forward to this party. Now, on the wide lawn of Auntie Nani's house, she wanted to move—as long as someone else, someone from around here, broke the ice and made it okay for a stranger to join in.

That took only a moment. The music's surge of energy lifted people to their feet, and soon the empty space between band and tables was filled with moving bodies. Carrie Ann slipped her sandals off and walked over to where Rorie stood watching a circle of kids play marbles. "Honey, I'm going to go dance, okay? Do you want to come, or do you want to stay here and play?"

"Stay here," Rorie replied, and Carrie Ann gave her a pat and went barefoot on the soft grass to join the dance.

At first, she danced close to the table, where Jerilyn and Chuckie sat smiling, but the beat drew her nearer the speakers. Feet planted, arms and shoulders weaving sinuously, every part of her body responded to the guitar's wail, the pounding drums, and thumping bass. She closed her eyes, digging the music and her body's joy. Dance was a kind of meditation, a way into the center of her being and yet out of the shell of herself.

The band moved from the first number directly into the next, and the next. Afternoon turned to evening, and someone switched on lights strung under the sheltering tarps. A long time later, she wasn't sure how long, Carrie Ann finally ran out of fuel. She needed to sit down and catch her breath. Back at the table, she flopped onto the bench, panting. Jerilyn had joined the dancing crowd, and Chuckie sat alone, with a half-dozen empty beer bottles on the table before him. He smiled.

"You was dancing one psychedelic hula, eh?"

Carrie Ann laughed. "I never thought of it that way. I just get into the music and move."

"Yeah." He nodded. "I been watching you."

"Oh. Well. You should get up and dance sometime. It's fun." She looked over at the tree to see what Rorie was up to. She seemed to be somewhat engaged with the other kids, so that was good. As long as Baby was happy, Mama could play too. Carrie Ann took a sip of her half-finished beer. Yuk. Better go get a cold Coke. She didn't really want to sit here alone with Chuckie, anyway. He seemed kind of drunk, slurring his words.

The Coke revitalized her. She set it down half-empty and lost herself again in the dance. Psychedelic, Chuckie had said. Yes, this definitely felt psychedelic, letting her body be taken over by the rhythm and flow of sound.

"Carrie Ann!"

The voice interrupted her reverie, jerking her back to reality. Jerilyn stood with a sniffling Rorie in her arms.

"She's tired, I think." Jerilyn handed over the child, whose crying increased, the sound rising over the music, as she wrapped her body around Carrie Ann's.

"Mommy, where were you? I thought you were gone!"

"I'm sorry, honey, I was dancing—I thought you were playing with your new friends. I wouldn't leave you behind."

Carrie Ann looked around, embarrassed by her child's wailing in the midst of the party.

"Come on, let's find Auntie Nani," Jerilyn said. "There's probably a bunch of other kids already crashed somewhere."

Several toddlers, including the birthday baby, were sprawled across a wide bed on Auntie Nani's screened front porch. Carrie Ann tried to lay Rorie down next to them, but Rorie resisted, refusing to remove her arms from Carrie Ann's neck. She gave up and sat on the edge of the bed, hoping her rocking and Rorie's sobbing wouldn't wake the others.

Eventually, the sobbing subsided, but Rorie continued to cling. Every time Carrie Ann shifted, as if to set her down, her daughter would rouse and begin to whimper. Outside, the band was taking a break, and the sounds of conversation and laughter filled the night. A couple stumbled into the shadows outside the porch, giggling for a moment and then becoming silent except for heavy breathing and an occasional moan. A mosquito whined near Carrie Ann's ear.

The band was well into the second song of their next set before Rorie's arms loosened. Carrie Ann waited a few more minutes, to be safe, then gently laid her on the bed. She tiptoed to the door and waited a moment, watching the sleeping form to be sure there was no movement. It had worked; Rorie was finally asleep. Carrie Ann could party.

Several songs later, she stood sweaty and out of breath as the band stopped to replace a broken guitar string. The crowd was beginning to thin, mostly families with children taking advantage of the quiet moment to bid Joey and his wife goodbye. A few people were pretty drunk, talking and laughing raucously. She scanned the crowd for Jerilyn. She wasn't at the table, but Chuckie was still there, with a lopsided smile. He was looking at Carrie Ann. She waved, then resumed her search for Jerilyn.

There she was, over by Johnny's truck at the side of Auntie Nani's house. And she was talking to Allison, back at last from wherever she'd been. Jerilyn was doing all the talking; Allison looked bored. Carrie Ann scanned the crowd again and found herself making eye contact with Michael Wharton. He was standing under the tree where she'd seen him earlier with Allison, hands in his back pockets, staring at Carrie Ann. She straightened and reached up to push her hair off her forehead. She couldn't break the eye contact, but she didn't know what to do next. She tried a smile. He smiled back. Then he put his hand to his forehead in a mock salute, nodded, turned, and walked away. A moment later, the motorcycle roared, and she heard it move down the road.

Carrie Ann took a deep breath. The music began again, and she swayed in time with the beat. She didn't want to go sit with the drunken Chuckie, and she had to wait for the band to finish or else carry a thirty-pound child down a dirt driveway in the dark.

She might as well dance and wonder as she did whether Michael Wharton was thinking about her as he rode through the night.

Chapter Nine

Carrie Ann pushed hard on her needle, which finally poked through thick fabric and pierced her finger. Swearing, she dropped the shirt she was embroidering and stuck her finger in her mouth. Time for a break. She stood, stepped off the blanket spread in the shade of a tree, and stretched.

Rorie looked up from a pile of wooden blocks. Stevie had dragged them out of the back of his closet, a set of many-shaped pieces Johnny had made for him when he was small, Jerilyn said. Stevie was still shy of Carrie Ann, but he was clearly fond of Rorie, playing with her on the family's frequent trips to the beach and giving her piggy-back rides around the house. And she obviously adored him.

Watching them play sometimes made Jerilyn look wistful. "I always wanted to have another baby, especially a little girl, but I never got pregnant again," she told Carrie Ann one day. Carrie Ann silently hoped she'd have the same luck. One was plenty for a mother on her own.

Speaking of which. As soon as Rorie saw her mother stand, she dropped her toys and stood up herself. "Mommy, I want juice," she demanded, hands on hips. Her body was plump and brown in the morning sunlight.

"Can you say 'please'?" Carrie Ann could hear her own mother in that phrase.

"Okay, please."

"That's better."

Carrie Ann headed for the house, while Rorie dropped back to her knees in the lush grass of the O'Connors' front lawn. The house was quiet as she entered through the front door and crossed to the kitchen. She was trying to keep Rorie outside, knowing that everyone was sleeping late after the birthday luau last night. Everyone except Kevin, the bass player who lived in the cottage out back. He had left early in Johnny's truck to go to the airport. His girlfriend was coming back today from the Mainland.

Settled back under the tree, she sipped guava juice as Rorie glugged hers down without stopping to breathe. Rorie handed her mother the empty glass, wiped her mouth with the back of her hand, and turned to her blocks. Carrie Ann picked up the shirt, one of Johnny's favorites. When he'd seen the little crown she embroidered on the birthday baby's shirt, he had asked her to do a banana tree on the breast pocket of this one. Carrie Ann looked across the lawn at a row of real banana trees and considered whether to change to another shade of green when she finished this strand of thread.

A melody drifted through her mind, one she could not completely recall but hoped to hear again. It was a song she had heard late last night, when the party settled down to a small group sitting on folding chairs under the tarp. Blend had finished their last set, and almost everyone had gone home. But the O'Connors and Kevin had stayed, joining Auntie Nani and her family as several people strummed guitars and ukulele. Kevin joined in, with his electric bass turned low.

This music was unlike anything Carrie Ann had heard before, Hawaiian music, sung in the same language used in the prayer before dinner and by the musicians who played at the beginning of the party. Those musicians, she had learned, played regularly in one of the hotels. Maybe their look of boredom came from having performed the same songs night after night at work. The people playing after the party did not look bored. They poured their souls into this music, Carrie Ann thought, listening to a dozen voices harmonize on words she could not even pronounce. In between songs, there was a lot of laughter and joking. Carrie Ann had no idea what they were talking about most of the time—it was all in that local accent she found so hard to understand—but the good vibes in the little group were infectious.

Sometimes, someone would get up to dance a hula. Did everyone here perform? If they were not playing an instrument, they were at least singing, and the dancers included a plump young woman, a middle-aged man, the birthday baby's father, and Auntie Nani herself. The old lady was agile and quick on her feet, moving to a lively song with winks and gestures that brought laughter and applause from her audience. Carrie Ann wished she understood what that song was about, and she wished she could remember the entire tune, instead of only these fragments that kept repeating themselves in her head.

She stopped in mid-stitch at the sound of a vehicle coming up the driveway—Johnny's truck, she thought. Sure enough, Kevin pulled up to the house, hopped out, and lifted a couple of suitcases from the back. A woman climbed down from the passenger side.

"Hey, Carrie Ann," Kevin called, "this is Alexis, my old lady," then headed back toward the cottage with the suitcases. Alexis advanced across the grass, copper-colored ringlets bouncing and long skirts swaying. She looked like someone Carrie Ann might have met in the Haight, with gypsy strings of beads and dark-rimmed eyes in a pert freckled face. She tinkled as she walked, as if there were little bells hidden somewhere on her person.

"Hey, how's it going? Is this your famous little girl? Kevin told me how she got lost. Far out! How do you like Maui? Do you think you'll stay?" Alexis dropped to her knees at the edge of Carrie Ann's blanket and reached over to ruffle Rorie's shiny hair.

Carrie Ann didn't know quite which question to answer first, but it didn't matter. Alexis chattered on. "God, what a flight, all the way from Boston, my grandma's house, she's getting on and my mom insisted I spend a month there, but at least it was warm and I didn't have to freeze my butt off. Where are you from?"

At last, a pause and a question she could answer. "I grew up in Texas, but I lived in San Francisco for the past few years. I'm going back there as soon as they let me."

"So the old judge won't let you go, huh? I guess you'd be in big trouble if you got on the plane and split. Oh well, might as well have fun while you're here. Where have you been so far? Hana? Lahaina?"

"Actually, no—I've been into town a few times to see the lawyer and the judge, and to Paia, and to the beach with Johnny and Jerilyn. I don't even know where those other places are."

"Well shit, we'll have to get you out on the road when I get my car back. It's getting fixed up by this artist in Paia; he does this really cool artwork on people's cars. Mine's a VW, not very roomy, but old Kevin will be happy to stay home, he's about as much of a homebody as Johnny and Jerilyn. They never go anywhere except to the beach and the boys' gigs." She hopped to her feet and turned to look in the direction where Kevin had gone.

"I gotta spend some time with my honey, but we'll get together later, talk about going out and having some fun. Bye, kiddo." She stooped to muss Rorie's hair again. "We'll take you with us. See you later." Alexis reached down to remove her shoes and waved them in the air as she turned to leave. "No more Boston, no more shoes!"

Rorie, who had been sitting mesmerized by the whirlwind of Alexis's energy, watched her go, then turned to her mother. "Mommy, are we going someplace with her?"

"I guess. Do you want to go?"

"If you go too."

"Okay, we'll see."

The morning peace returned, and Carrie Ann went back to her embroidery. She'd finished the banana tree trunk and one whole leaf by the time anyone appeared from the house.

Jerilyn settled on the blanket next to Carrie Ann and sipped coffee from a mug. "Looks like you're making progress on Johnny's tree," she said.

"Yeah, it's going good. Hey, Kevin's lady is back."

"Well, that'll make Kevin happy." Jerilyn set her mug on the grass and stretched out on the blanket. "Man, I drank too much beer last night."

"It was a good party."

"Mmm." Jerilyn didn't seem to have much to say. Carrie Ann re-threaded her needle and started on the next leaf. She'd taken only a few stitches when a movement down the driveway caught her attention. A long-haired and bearded man, burdened by a large backpack, trudged up the drive. He saw the three of them under the tree and cut across the lawn.

"Good morning, sisters," he said, pushing his hair off his sweaty forehead.

"Hi," Carrie Ann said. "Are you looking for someone?"

Jerilyn stirred, opened her eyes, and frowned. She lifted herself onto one elbow and looked at the man.

He smiled, a creepy kind of smile, Carrie Ann thought, and nodded at Jerilyn. "Greetings, sister. I hear your home offers hospitality to wandering members of The Family of Love." He reached into the pocket of his cut-offs and pulled out a sheet of paper folded into a small square. Opening it, he showed Carrie Ann and Jerilyn a hand-drawn map. Carrie Ann couldn't quite figure out what it showed—just a bunch of lines and arrows—but Jerilyn groaned and sat up.

"Look, I don't know where you got this map, but we aren't a crash pad, we got all we can do to take care of our own family, and I'd appreciate it if you'd head back down the highway."

The man looked crestfallen. "Oh. Well, do you have any ideas about where I could find a place to crash? I just got off the plane."

"Try Guava Gulch, down the road. They probably have to move pretty soon, but a lot of people have left lately, and I think there are some empty houses." Jerilyn gave the man directions to the Guava Gulch turnoff, watched him trudge back down the driveway, then groaned again as she sank into a reclining position.

Rorie watched him leave. "Mommy, he smelled funny," she said.

"Where did he get that map?" Carrie Ann asked.

"Shit, I don't know. We get these people every so often; they just show up. Someone somewhere told them we'd let them crash. And we did, back when we first moved here, lots of people came and went. But that got really old—most of them didn't have any money, never did any work, and one gave us scabies. Have you ever had scabies? Awful! I thought we'd never get rid of them. So we decided to keep it to us, the band, and invited guests. But these flakes still keep showing up."

Carrie Ann's face grew warm. She looked over at Rorie, who'd stopped staring at the bearded stranger and gone back to playing with Stevie's wooden toys.

"I sure hope we're not imposing on you all too much. It was real nice of you to let Rorie and me stay here, and even fix us up with our own place."

"Oh, you're fine, you're invited. Don't worry about it. And besides, you actually help me out, which is more than I can say about a lot of people. Alexis, for one."

"Alexis doesn't help?"

"Well, she does keep up the cottage for her and Kevin—and she pays some rent, which is nice. But they usually eat dinner down here, and the princess never lifts a finger to help me with that. Before you came, I'd have to drag Stevie and Allison in to help with dishes."

"You call her the princess, huh."

"Yeah. You know, she's okay, it's not that I don't like her, she's funny and friendly. But she's a rich kid. Comes from this big-time

East Coast family, only child, never had to work. She's not used to this kind of family life, where everyone has to pitch in."

Carrie Ann thought of her own childhood, alone with a silent father and a boozy mother. Being an only child had been no advantage; it simply meant that there was no one else to do the things her mother never got around to. Carrie Ann had learned early to put together a simple meal and clean up afterward. And though she couldn't remember anyone ever really teaching her, somehow she'd gotten to the point where she was keeping the kitchen clean and the house in order, jotting things on the shopping list her father took to the store, putting away groceries he brought home. She often wondered how they were getting by without her. She'd not been home since she left with Willie five years ago, chasing after Jack when he moved to San Francisco to join Red Dog. They must have managed somehow.

Thinking of cooking made her realize she was getting hungry. Must be time to fix lunch. Jerilyn was snoring lightly. Carrie Ann gathered her embroidery supplies and tucked them into the paper bag she was using as a sewing basket. She'd have to find something nicer soon, maybe get into making shirts for the band as she'd done for Red Dog. Maybe she could even earn some money selling things.

But it was time for a break. She'd been up since dawn with Rorie and had eaten only a piece of toast. With Rorie trailing behind, she headed for the kitchen.

She'd just finished making peanut-butter-and-guava-jam sandwiches for the two of them when she heard an engine coming up the driveway. Peering out the window, she saw an old Army Jeep, painted shiny silver. It stopped, and Chuckie climbed out, reached into the back for a large white plastic bucket, and headed for the kitchen.

"Hui! Anybody home?" Chuckie called from the bottom of the back porch steps. Carrie Ann went to the door and stuck her head out. Rorie squeezed between her mother's body and the doorframe.

Chuckie's teeth gleamed white in his brown face. He wore a ragged T-shirt and red swim trunks. He seemed to have a pretty good body, Carrie Ann thought, even though he was kind of short.

"I'm here," she said, "and Jerilyn's out on the front lawn, but nobody else is awake yet."

"Ho, I better be more quiet, then," he said, dropping his voice. "Hey, I went fishing this morning, and I brought you folks some fish. How about I clean 'em outside and then cook 'em up, surprise everybody with fresh fish for breakfast."

"Well—sure, I guess so, why not? Rorie and I are eating peanut butter sandwiches, you want one?"

"No, no, I'll wait for fish. But if you got any rice, maybe you could start up a pot."

Rorie took her sandwich and headed out the back door after Chuckie. Carrie Ann waited for the pot of rice to boil, turned it down to a simmer, and put the lid on. Then she went outside to join Chuckie and Rorie.

She was glad she'd finished her sandwich before she came out. Chuckie was kneeling next to the chicken coop's water faucet, digging the guts out of a large fish. Rorie squatted next to him, clutching her half-eaten peanut butter sandwich, fascinated by the whole messy operation.

"Mommy, look, he scraped this stuff off the fish," she said, pointing to a silvery pile of fish scales.

Carrie Ann backed away a few steps. The stench was awful, drawing a small squadron of buzzing flies. Carrie Ann had never seen a fish being cleaned before. It didn't seem to bother Rorie, who chewed a bite of her sandwich without taking her gaze from

Chuckie's hands. He rinsed the first fish under the faucet, set it on the grass, and pulled another from his bucket.

"Good kind," he said, flashing a grin at Carrie Ann. "Parrot fish. It's ono. You got eggs and flour and oil? I'll fry 'em up. You'll love 'em."

"I think I'll go get the stuff out, so it's ready." Carrie Ann was happy to have a reason to leave.

Inside, Johnny was pouring himself a cup of coffee.

"Mornin'. Hey, what's happening? I see Chuckie's Jeep outside. He here?"

Carrie Ann explained, and Johnny left to join the fish watch. No sooner had he gone than Allison stumbled in, bleary-eyed, looking for coffee. Within minutes, the kitchen was filled with people, as Stevie arrived and plopped himself at the kitchen table, and Jerilyn came to re-fill her coffee cup.

"How the hell you have the energy to get up early and go fishing after a party like last night I'll never know," Johnny told Chuckie a few minutes later as they entered the kitchen carrying the cleaned fish.

"No problem, I never wen' sleep. Just go home, load up the fishing gear, and go down Hookipa. After this, I going crash."

Carrie Ann watched as Chuckie expertly dredged the fish in egg and flour, then tested the heat of the oil in Jerilyn's largest frying pan.

The fish, once covered in a reassuring golden crust, was in fact delicious, steaming on a plate next to brown rice and some sweet orange cherry tomatoes from Jerilyn's garden. Carrie Ann decided she'd have to learn to cook fish like that—once someone else had cleaned it. She supposed its being fresh from the sea might have something to do with how good it tasted.

She got up to make a fresh pot of coffee as Johnny reached to pull his pot box off the top of the fridge. Outside, she heard yet another car engine chugging up the drive. In the short time she'd been here, there never had been a day with this much activity—Alexis, the strange hippie guy, Chuckie, and now what?

This car turned out to be Allison's girlfriend from school. They had a beach trip planned, Allison informed Johnny and Jerilyn as she stuck her plate in the sink. They were going over to Makena to body surf.

"Don't break your neck, and I want you home by dark," Johnny called as he pulled out a rolling paper and began to cut tiny bits of pot off a glistening dark-green bud.

Carrie Ann woke from a nap a few hours later to the sound of another car pulling up. She sat up and peered out the window. Right behind the car came a motorcycle. It was Michael. Hastily, she ran her fingers through her hair. How did she look? Maybe she should change into that new sundress she'd made.

Outside, the car door opened, and Allison stepped slowly onto the driveway. Her left leg was wrapped in a white bandage. Michael took her arm and walked with her to the back steps, while the driver of the car backed cautiously around the motorcycle, onto the lawn, and then pulled swiftly out the driveway.

Carrie Ann glanced at the still-sleeping Rorie and then into the faded mirror propped against the wall. She gave her hair a few swipes of the hairbrush. What on earth had happened to Allison?

"I was riding along the beach, and I guess the sand was kind of soft in this one place, and the bike tipped over. I didn't get out of the way fast enough, and the muffler touched my leg. Burned it pretty bad," Allison was saying as Carrie Ann entered the kitchen. Jerilyn sat at the kitchen table, where Allison was seated with her leg stretched straight in front of her. Michael stood near the door, silent, and Johnny leaned against the kitchen counter, arms folded. He didn't look happy.

"Who put the bandage on?" Jerilyn asked.

"Old Doc Cummings," Allison replied. "He put aloe vera on it, and gave me some leaves to cut up later, and said once I got home and could keep it clean, I should take off the bandage and keep putting cactus on it." She grinned. "Plus, he gave me a shot of morphine, and some Demerol to take when that wears off. Cool, huh?"

"Jesus, you burned the shit out of your leg and all you can talk about are the drugs you got! Did you by any chance call your parents?" Johnny sounded pissed. Carrie Ann took a step back into the hall. Michael didn't move, except for the muscles in his jaw, which seemed to be clenching.

"Yes, as a matter of fact." Allison sounded defiant. "Doc Cummings called them before he gave me the shot. My mom wasn't home, but my dad came down and looked at my leg and said Doc could give me the morphine and stuff." Allison paused. "He didn't stick around for long," she added in a subdued voice.

"Well, I'm going to call him myself. I think we need to have a talk. You're too far outta line, young lady. And you!" He turned to Michael. "Haven't you got anything better to do than hang out with a kid who must be at least ten years younger than you? That was a dumb-ass stunt, letting her ride your bike on the beach. Jesus! I'm telling you, Wharton, I don't want to see you around here anymore. And I don't think Miss Nevels here is going to be available to play, anyway. In fact, you can go to your room right now, Allison. Take one of your damn Demerols, and I don't want to see you 'til dinnertime."

"Johnny, I'm sorry, I screwed up—" Michael began, but Johnny cut him off.

"I don't really want to hear it. I think I made myself plain. Pau. No more messing around. She's over jail-bait age, but not by much, and I've had enough, okay? So split."

Without a word, Michael turned, tight-jawed, and walked out the back door. Carrie Ann, stunned by the tension in the O'Connors' sunny kitchen, hesitated a moment, then followed him.

Outside, she caught up with Michael as he climbed onto his motorcycle.

Shy, she stopped a few feet away. Michael straddled his bike and looked at her, shaking his head.

"Well, this is really a fuck-up, isn't it? I tried to tell him I'm sorry, I never should have let her get on the bike, but he doesn't want to hear it."

"He's pretty upset. Allison is kind of a handful, I guess. Was her dad really mad?"

"Yeah, but he didn't say much, just looked at her leg and told the doctor to go ahead and treat her, then stormed out without saying a word to me. I'm surprised he hadn't already called here before we got back."

"Well. I'm sorry you guys had such a bad time. Lucky she didn't get hurt worse, huh?"

"Yeah." He shook his head again. "Man, that was stupid of me. I keep forgetting how young she is, she always acts so much older."

"Are you really more than ten years older than Allison?"

"I guess I am. She's seventeen, right? And I'm twenty-eight." He looked up and directly at Carrie Ann, frosty blue eyes intense in a sun-browned face. "How about you, Carrie Ann? How old are you?"

"Twenty-three," she replied, shy again.

"Well, I guess you're definitely over the age of consent, huh? Maybe you and I should go out sometime." He kicked the starter, and his motorcycle roared to life. "That's if the master of the house will allow you to be seen in my company." He smiled. Carrie Ann's heart thumped. "See you around," Michael said, turned his bike in a wide curve across the lawn, and was gone down the driveway in a cloud of exhaust.

Chapter Ten

Dear Mimi,

Well, you won't believe how interesting things have been lately. Allison, that teenager who lived with the O'Connors, isn't living with us anymore! She got a motorcycle burn on Michael's bike—he's that gorgeous guy I told you about—and Johnny flipped out! He called her dad, and her parents came and got her the very next day. I couldn't believe how mad Johnny was! He doesn't like Michael, which is weird, because Michael is really a honey, and he was really sorry Allison got hurt. The best part of all this is that Rorie and I inherited her old room. It's a cool room, but I kind of miss our little jungle shack.

Anyway, we're at the beach. It's beautiful! This whole place is beautiful! If I didn't have so many friends back in the city, I'd think about staying. But then Kathryn said Jason called! Remember him? It's the first time he's called since right after I moved to your place. He wanted to know if I'm coming home soon!!! I can't wait! I hope he's still interested when I get back. When that old judge lets me go, that is.

The social worker came to see us the other day. He was really nice, and Jerilyn fixed him a cup of coffee and sweet-talked him, so I think we're cool. At least they didn't take Rorie away. But I'm still stuck with the six-month thing before we can leave.

Oh, well, could be worse. It's pretty here, warm but with this breeze that keeps you cool, and lots of flowers and fruit, and the people are nice. Like I said, if I didn't miss you guys so much, I'd be tempted to stay, especially if I can get somewhere with that Michael! He actually kind of flirted with me the day Allison got burned, but I haven't seen him since. Sigh. And there's this other guy, a local Hawaiian guy named Chuckie. He's kind of cute, but really short (and you know how I like tall guys).

Anyway, I think he likes me. Jerilyn says he never came over as much as he has since I showed up. But he hasn't asked me out or anything, he just comes over and hangs out. We'll see. Maybe someday I'll find my man. I don't know about Chuckie, but I sure could dig being Michael's old lady!

I'm sorry to hear about your Aunt Bea's divorce. She was so nice, taking us out to dinner that time she came to visit. But I guess her old man is really a pig, huh? Pulling a gun on her is too much! I hope she'll . . .

"Mommy!"

Carrie Ann looked up. Rorie was standing knee-deep in the tide pool.

"What, honey?"

"Mommy, come and help me swim!"

Carrie Ann smiled at the sight of Rorie, skin glowing golden in the sunshine, no longer the pale baby of her San Francisco days but a sturdy child of nature. This letter to Mimi was way overdue, with so much news to share, but Carrie Ann couldn't resist. She set her writing pad on her towel and stood up, waded into the cool water, and slowly lowered her body to sit on the floor of the tide pool. "Okay, baby girl. Now what?"

"Now you hold me up, and I swim."

Rorie flopped fearlessly facedown into the water, fully expecting her mother's hands to be under her belly. Thus supported, she flailed away with arms and legs until she had to come up sputtering for air.

"How's that? Am I getting better?" she asked, eyes scrunched against the water running down her face.

"You gotta learn to breathe, baby," Jerilyn said, wading into the tide pool after her long swim along the shore. She knelt next to Rorie and Carrie Ann, put her face down in the water, and stroked as if she were swimming, turning her head to catch a breath on alternate strokes.

"Okay, you stand up, bend over a little bit, and try that; I'll hold on to you," she told Rorie.

Carrie Ann decided to try it herself. She never had gotten the hang of breathing between strokes. She could hear Jerilyn coaching Rorie as the two of them splashed away. Every so often Jerilyn would call out instructions to Carrie Ann, who was beginning to think that she might master this thing if she kept it up. That would be cool. She was dying to get out on a surfboard, but Johnny warned her that she shouldn't even consider it until her swimming was much improved.

"Hey, what's this, swimming class?" Alexis came splashing in to join them, and Carrie Ann stopped her stroking and wiped her eyes. "Where'd you come from?"

"Paia—the Laundromat. My little VW is full of clean jeans and T-shirts. Those boys are such slobs, they let their clothes pile up for weeks until I finally take pity on them and haul their stuff into Paia. I saw Johnny's truck in the parking lot here and decided I needed a swim to cool off after hanging out by those fucking dryers all afternoon. Hey, listen, Carrie Ann, you wanna go party tonight? My girlfriend Emily and I are going to Lahaina. You haven't even been there yet, right? You should come! Jerilyn, you'll babysit, won't you?"

"Well, sure," Jerilyn said.

Rorie, hearing a new voice, had stopped her swimming lesson and now frowned. "I want to go. Where are you going? Can I go?"

"Darling, this is nighttime stuff, for grown-ups, and little girls are already asleep when we go out at night. You can stay with Auntie Jerilyn and Uncle Johnny and Stevie, and before you know it, it'll be morning, and your mommy will be home. You won't even know she was gone. How about it, Carrie Ann?"

Pleased at the thought of an adventure, Carrie Ann nodded. Rorie pouted.

"I wanna go," she said, her voice beginning to tremble.

"Darling, you can go with me and your mom on another trip to—let's see, how about Hana? Does she get carsick, Carrie Ann? I hate to think of a carsick baby in my little Bug. We'll do something, Rorie, something fun for all of us, you wait. How about Lahaina in the daytime? Have you been to Lahaina?" Rorie shook her head.

"Cool, we'll go there in the daytime real soon." Alexis winked at Carrie Ann. "Lahaina at night is definitely a place for grown-ups."

The full moon's light glinted off waves far below and "All You Need Is Love" blasted from the radio as Alexis steered the VW along a winding road. On the right, Carrie Ann could see steep cliffs, towering over the highway—the Pali, Emily called it, where a road carved into the cliffs led to the town of Lahaina.

"My grandmother used to travel from Lahaina to our place in Maalaea by boat," she told Carrie Ann. "That was in the days before there was a good road here, and it was easier by sea. Then they'd ride horseback to Wailuku." Emily leaned around the edge of the front seat to pass Carrie Ann the joint. She took a toke and handed it back; Emily held it so Alexis could get a hit without removing her hands from the steering wheel.

They had picked up Emily at her family's beach house, near a little harbor where small boats bobbed. They would drop her off later at the Upcountry house, an estate where Alexis said Emily's plantation-manager father had created a veritable arboretum of exotic trees.

"Lucky it's such a bright moon tonight. You'll be able to see what the place looks like. It's far out!" Alexis had said as she pulled into the driveway of the beach house. "Of course, Emily hates the place, because she's a leftist, and she says when she inherits, she'll sell everything and send the money to Cuba. I can relate. My family is capitalist to the core, and I really don't dig it either. That's why I'm out here. But wait 'til you see the trees!"

Emily and Alexis had been schoolmates at an exclusive East Coast girls' college, and Emily's presence had first drawn Alexis to Maui. "She's really a trip," Alexis said. "We used to go out and get stoned, party 'til dawn, and then sneak back in before anyone was awake. Of course, then we slept through most of our classes, but who cares about that shit anyway? Life is where you really learn, not some dumb classroom full of girls in sweater sets and pearls."

The cliffside road descended to sea level, where waves splashed along the shore. Lahaina crept up on Carrie Ann before she even knew they were near a town. There wasn't much to it—a few blocks of silent houses and then a few blocks of old-fashioned storefronts. Alexis turned off the main street and parked at the curb across from the only lit-up building on the block.

"This is the place, all the action you'll see in this town tonight!" she announced, holding the door while Carrie Ann unfolded herself from the back seat. The Day-Glo greens and pinks of the VW's new paint job shone in the light from across the street, where loud rock-and-roll emanated from a Western-style saloon door. "Welcome to the Blue Lagoon," Alexis said, then led the way across the street.

The three paused inside the door, checking out the scene. People sat at little tables around the room, or on stools at a long bar, laughing and drinking in the only lively place in the sleepy dark town of Lahaina. On a small stage at the back of the room, two guys with guitars wailed away while a third flailed at a set of drums. Carrie Ann immediately decided they weren't as good as Blend.

Out of nowhere, arms surrounded her and scooped her up. It was Chuckie, laughing, eyes bright in a handsome face close to her own. Where had he come from? What was he doing, swooping her up and twirling her around like that, holding her like a bride being carried across the threshold? Where did he find the strength in that little body to lift her so easily? Chuckie set her down again, ducking his head sheepishly. Alexis and Emily were cracking up, slapping Chuckie on the back in greeting, and Carrie Ann noticed a number of smiling faces turned to observe their dramatic entry, courtesy of Chuckie Ah Fong.

"Hey, ladies, howzit? You folks like come sit with us?" He gestured toward a table near the stage, where three local guys sat smoking cigarettes and smiling in their direction.

Emily and Alexis exchanged glances.

"Oh, thank you, Chuckie, but you know, ah, we don't smoke tobacco, so maybe we'll try to find a place where there isn't too much smoke," Alexis said. Still amazed by Chuckie's uncharacteristic greeting, Carrie Ann was wordless. She smiled and tried to look friendly. She was along for the ride; let Alexis decide where they would sit, and with whom.

Chuckie looked disappointed but patted Carrie Ann's shoulder. "Maybe we go dance later, eh?"

"Okay, Chuckie, sounds good." She smiled again and turned to follow Alexis and Emily.

"I'm glad we found our own table," Emily said as they took their seats. "Cramps my style too much to sit with a bunch of guys—this is girls' night out! Who knows what might happen? So, Carrie, Ann, what's going on here? Looks like Chuckie kind of digs you, huh?"

"Yeah, he's been hanging out at the O'Connors' an awful lot lately. What's the scoop?" Alexis asked.

"I have no idea. He always seemed so shy. I never would have thought he'd do that." Carrie Ann sneaked a peek at Chuckie's table. He was still looking sheepish as his buddies laughed and threw glances over at the table where the three women sat. "Actually, no one's ever done anything like that to me before. It's kind of cool; I feel real dainty, like feminine, you know? I don't know how he managed to pick me up like that."

"Oh, Chuckie's little, but he's been surfing and working in the cane fields for years, so I'm not surprised he's strong," Emily said. "He's a sweetie. I've known him since we were kids, plus we partied together in high school. His dad worked on the plantation, and every Christmas the plantation families would come to our house for a party, candy from Santa and all that. And his grandpa was the gardener at our place, and sometimes he'd come over to play while his grandpa worked. In fact, Chuckie's grandpa built my playhouse."

A waitress wearing hot pants and a harried look interrupted their conversation, asking what they wanted to drink. By the time she was gone with their beer and wine orders, Emily had spotted someone in the crowd she knew a good story about, and she and Alexis switched to gossiping while Carrie Ann surveyed the scene.

A few people were dancing—only couples, she noticed, so maybe she'd want to take Chuckie up on his offer later. As usual, there was no one she knew. Weird, after making a home in a city neighborhood where faces became familiar, to be in a place where everyone was a stranger.

But Maui was a small place, and Emily and Alexis certainly seemed to know a lot of people. As the evening wore on, several stopped at their table to talk, and the two chicks did some table-hopping of their own. Carrie Ann sat tight, except for twice, when Chuckie came to take her hand and lead her onto the little dance floor. He wasn't much of a dancer, and the space was too confined to allow Carrie Ann to move as freely as she liked, but it was rather thrilling to have a man ask her to dance, and surprising to see Chuckie overcome his shyness enough to be that man.

Slightly out of breath, she settled back into her seat after the second dance and looked around the room. It was beginning to seem familiar: the glossy golden wood of the bar, the blue-and-green mural depicting a tropical lagoon along the back wall behind the band, fake palm trees in the corners, people laughing in the dim, smoky air. She sipped her wine. She was feeling good, not at all unhappy to be sitting alone while the other two table-hopped.

Oh, wow. Her breath stopped. There was Michael, lounging in the doorway, looking around the room. Their eyes met, and that thrill ran through her body again, like the first time she saw him in the O'Connors' kitchen. Michael worked his way through the crowded room, between tables, coming toward the corner where she sat alone. He pulled out a chair, turned it around, and sat straddling it, arms folded across the top of the chair back.

"Hi, Carrie Ann." He had such a deep voice. It matched his looks, tall and Viking handsome.

"Hi, Michael."

"You here by yourself?"

"No, with Alexis and Emily." She gestured toward the other two, talking and laughing at separate tables across the room.

"Ah." He lifted one eyebrow. "Girls' night out?"

She smiled. "Yeah, I guess."

"So what's up with you, little Carrie Ann? What are you doing with yourself these days?"

She hoped her face didn't show the heat she felt rising. "Oh, hanging out, taking care of Rorie, doing some sewing, helping Jerilyn. And I've been learning to swim."

"You can't swim?"

"Not very well. I never really swam in the ocean before I came here, only a little bit in swimming pools."

"Yeah, the ocean is something else again. You don't want to get too far into it without being a good swimmer."

"Are you a good swimmer?"

"Yeah, pretty good. I was on a team in college, put in a lot of time doing laps, and I've been out in the ocean a lot since I got here, surfing, snorkeling, even took up scuba for a while."

"Scuba is where you go down real deep?"

"Yeah, and wear an air tank. It's trippy. Maybe I'll take you out sometime, when you learn to swim better."

That was the second time he'd mentioned taking her out. Carrie Ann held her breath for a moment, trying to stay calm.

"Michael, where'd you come from?" Alexis dropped back into her chair. She picked up her beer and leaned back, taking a sip.

"I came from Haiku, honey, just like you did. Where's old Kevin tonight? He let you out alone?"

"Hah. Kevin wouldn't even think of trying to stop me from going out. He likes to stay home, anyway, and the band always has to practice."

"Johnny runs a pretty tight ship, huh?"

"Yeah, he likes to keep them busy. He's hoping to get rich as a rock-and-roll manager, you know." They both laughed. Emily appeared and sat. Damn, Carrie Ann thought; everybody had to show up just when she'd been getting somewhere with Michael.

"What have you got for us tonight, Michael?" Emily was asking. Michael flicked a look at Carrie Ann, then around the room.

"Not so loud, Emily. I'm not into advertising."

"Okay, okay. Nobody can hear anything anyway, with this noise. Just answer the question."

Michael spoke in a low voice. "Ever try THC? It's better than speed or acid, if you ask me. That grass glow, with a real clear vibe to it, keeps you high for hours. Shit, it's so mellow you could take it every day, no reason not to stay high forever."

"That sounds good."

"Come on outside."

Michael stood, and Emily followed him out the door. Carrie Ann watched them go. Alexis sipped her beer. After a couple of minutes, Michael and Emily came back in and made their way to the table.

"Who wants some?" Emily asked.

"Me," Alexis answered. Emily slipped her hand into the pocket of her jeans and reached under the table. Alexis smiled, took her own hand out from under the table, and casually popped something into her mouth.

"Carrie Ann?"

"Uh, no, thanks." She'd taken anonymous drugs from people she didn't know very well one time too many in San Francisco. The white powder she'd sniffed had turned out to be pig tranquilizer, and she'd spent the day immobilized on the couch, barely able to respond when Rorie, still an infant, cried for her bottle or shit in her diapers. This wine was pretty good; she'd stick to wine, she decided.

Michael looked around the room. "There's old Chuckie-boy and the gang. Guess I'll go see what they're up to. Talk to you ladies later." He winked at Carrie Ann, stood up and turned his chair back around to face the table, then ambled over to Chuckie's table.

"He's a babe, that one," Emily said, watching Michael walk across the room. Carrie Ann tensed. Oh great. Did Emily like him too?

"Yeah, but trouble, don't you think?" Alexis looked thoughtful as she sipped her beer.

"That's the most fun kind." Emily laughed, Alexis smiled, and they turned their attention to a couple who'd walked in the door. "There's Karen and Fred—and, hey, Liz is with them! I thought they broke up. I don't know how two chicks can stand to share one guy."

The other two were off onto another gossip fest, on a tantalizing subject—two chicks with one old man? But despite her curiosity about this unusual arrangement, Carrie Ann could not keep her mind off Michael. He was deep in conversation with the guys at Chuckie's table. She wondered if he was selling the dope he offered, or if he was just generous.

A few minutes later, Michael got up and looked around the room. He started to move toward the stage, and Carrie Ann discovered she had an urgent need to pee. The ladies' room was on the other side of the stage, so of course she almost bumped into Michael as she worked her way around the dance floor.

"Hello again, Miss Carrie Ann," he said, smiling that slow smile. "Hey, how about a ride sometime? On my bike?"

"Yeah, that would be great," she managed to answer.

"Like maybe tomorrow? What are you doing tomorrow?"

"Uh, the usual." But what would she do with Rorie? Little girls didn't fit well on motorcycles.

"Considering how pissed off Johnny is, I don't think I should come down to the house. How about if we meet at the end of the driveway. Ridiculous, huh? Like a couple of teenagers sneaking out on a date. But you saw what he's like. I'm not into starting up a bummer like the other day. What do you say?"

"I could do that. What time?"

"About 3 o'clock? We could cruise around, maybe watch the sunset someplace?"

"Okay."

"Wear your jeans, now—don't want to have to bring home another lady with a burned leg from the muffler." He winked again, making her part of his world. "That would really piss off old Johnny, wouldn't it." He leaned over, gave her a friendly peck on the cheek, and headed for the stage, where the musicians were taking a break between songs.

Her smile wouldn't stop, all the way to the ladies' room and back to the table again, where Alexis and Emily eyed her speculatively.

"What's happening?" Alexis asked. "You look way too happy for someone who isn't even stoned."

Carrie Ann tried to be casual about it. "Michael asked me out."

"Oooh, hot stuff!" Emily cooed, glancing toward the stage, where Michael stood deep in conversation with the lead guitar player.

"Watch out—I hear he's a heartbreaker," Alexis warned.

"I hear he's also a great fuck," Emily added.

Carrie Ann's face heated. Would she never get over this blushing trip? How could she be cool if she was always turning red?

"Only one problem," she said, changing the subject. "I don't know what I'm going to do with Rorie. You know how Johnny is about Michael. In fact, I'm going to meet Michael at the end of the driveway, you know, to avoid any hassles. I kind of hate to ask Jerilyn to watch her."

"Well, I might be able to keep her entertained for a couple of hours," Alexis said. "When are you going?"

Chuckie appeared at Carrie Ann's side before she could answer, took her hand, and pulled her toward the dance floor, where a few couples were swaying slowly to a recording of Elvis singing "Love Me Tender."

"Uh, I'll tell you after this song," she said over her shoulder as Chuckie drew her onto the floor. He pulled her close. At the table, Alexis and Emily were grinning and whispering.

Chuckie said nothing through most of the song, simply clutching her in an embrace that was almost too tight, but he hummed along with the record. He smelled good, some kind of musky aftershave, she guessed. Carrie Ann found she didn't mind his holding her so tight, but her thoughts were on Michael and on the logistics of childcare for tomorrow afternoon.

The song ended, but Chuckie kept her on the dance floor.

"Carrie Ann, how about I take you out sometime? Maybe we could go out to dinner tomorrow night?"

This was too much. Carrie Ann couldn't believe she was attracting two men at once. But Michael had asked first, fortunately. She wouldn't have wanted to tell him no if it had been Chuckie who asked first.

"Actually, Chuckie, I'm busy tomorrow night. Maybe some other time."

"How about tomorrow morning? I'm not working. We could go beach, or maybe hike to the mountain pools at my uncle's place."

"Well . . . can we take Rorie?"

"Sure, no problem, no problem."

"Well. Okay then."

Chuckie walked her back to her table, then crossed the floor to join his friends.

"You won't believe this," Carrie Ann told Alexis and Emily. "Chuckie asked me out, too."

"I think he noticed the competition when Michael showed up," Alexis said.

"Wow, count your blessings, girl. Two to choose from," Emily said. "On the other hand, who says you have to choose? Maybe you can have your cake and eat it too. Chuckie for sweet lovin' and Michael for hot sex!"

They sang as they drove back along the Pali, Beatles songs mostly, some Elvis and a folk song thrown in here and there. Emily led, with a clear soprano. By the time they reached Paia, Carrie Ann's voice was worn out, but Emily was still going strong, singing in Hawaiian now, songs she said she'd been singing since childhood. Alexis occasionally hummed along, but Emily knew all the words.

Somewhere up the hill above Paia, they turned off the road into a driveway lined by trees, tall and straight in the light of the full moon. Alexis switched off the headlights, and Emily stopped singing. They cruised slowly past a big house, its tile roof gleaming in the moonlight. There were several smaller outbuildings, and Alexis parked next to the smallest one.

Whispering, so as not to wake Emily's parents, they climbed out of the VW. The full moon lit up a landscape where giant trees loomed over a rolling lawn that must have totaled several acres. "I'll have to bring you back in the daytime, when you can really look around. The flowers are fantastic," Alexis whispered. They followed Emily into the little building.

Inside, she lit a kerosene lamp, illuminating a miniature house.

"Wow. What is this place?" Carrie Ann asked.

"My playhouse. The one Chuckie's grandpa built."

Amazed, Carrie Ann explored the little house. The ceilings were high enough for an adult to stand erect, and it had working windows and doors exactly like those in a larger house. Fancy molding marked the border between the pink-painted walls and white ceiling, and the floor was tiled in dark blue. In the front room, a small rug covered the floor, and several large pillows were scattered about. Peering through a doorway, Carrie Ann discovered a tiny kitchen, complete with miniature sink, refrigerator, and stove. Ceramic tile lined the wall behind the sink, and the rest of the kitchen walls were covered with flowered wallpaper.

"The sink has running water, but of course the stove and refrigerator are fake," Emily said. "They didn't put power in the place, so I have to use the kerosene lamp if I come out here at night. When I was a kid, I usually had to be in by sunset, so they never got around to putting in power lines." She snorted. "Of course, it took an awful long time for them to put in power lines to some of the real houses, where plantation workers lived, not to mention running water and toilets. But, what the hell, those people were too busy working to need that stuff, right?"

"Now, now, no politics," Alexis said, settling onto one of the cushions. "Got anything to eat out here? How about another joint? And your guitar? Are you into playing a few of those Hawaiian tunes?"

Emily opened the little fridge, which turned out to be simply a cupboard, and pulled out a crumpled bag of cookies. She took glasses and half a bottle of red wine from under the sink and got her guitar from a little closet next to the stove.

THE ISLAND DECIDES

"This is it, nothing but the best Chez Emily," she said, plucking a guitar string to check the tuning.

"Nothing but the best," Alexis agreed, and pulling a fat joint from her purse, she leaned over the kerosene lamp to light it.

Chapter Eleven

Rorie was not in her bed. Cold fear flooded Carrie Ann's body, though her mind said her baby must be somewhere in this house. Calm down, she told herself—you know that Jerilyn is taking care of her. Look around.

She crept through the silent, dark house toward the room where Jerilyn and Johnny slept. The door was ajar. Inside, Johnny, snoring gently, was sprawled on one side of the bed. On the other edge, Jerilyn lay curled around a small figure whose blonde hair gleamed in a patch of moonlight.

Carrie Ann stood still for a moment, wondering if she should try to retrieve Rorie, but decided that would wake up everyone in the bed. Instead, she turned and made her way back to the room they had inherited from Allison. She left the door open in case her early-rising child wanted to come in, then pulled on a T-shirt and burrowed under the covers.

Rorie did arrive bright and early, entirely too bright and too early. In fact, everything seemed way too bright, even with the closed Indian bedspread curtains and dark walls of this room. Carrie Ann groaned as Rorie piled on top of her, chattering away.

In the kitchen, Jerilyn was measuring flour into the big bowl she used for making bread. Carrie Ann stood with her back to the windows, squinting.

"How did it go?" she mumbled, reaching into the cabinet for the granola.

"Well, not that great, actually," Jerilyn replied.

"What happened?"

Jerilyn paused in her work and looked down at the child, who stood waiting for her cereal. "Rorie, would you do me a favor? Would you run outside and look under the lilikoi vine and see if you can find me three yellow lilikoi?"

On a mission, Rorie headed out the back door.

Jerilyn looked down at her bowl, stirring in flour. "Rorie freaked out last night. It took me a long time to get her to sleep."

"Oh, I'm really sorry." Carrie Ann sank onto a kitchen chair. Shit, her head was beginning to hurt. "So what happened?"

"Well, she did okay until after dinner. She played with Stevie for a while, and then of course she got tired, and I tried to put her down in your room. But she would not go to sleep, and then she started really crying, and I couldn't make her stop." Jerilyn shook her head. "I finally got her to sleep by sitting with her in the rocking chair for a while, but every time I tried to put her back down, she would cry. The only thing to do was take her to bed with us and hope she would eventually pass out."

"I'm glad that worked, at least. I am really sorry, Jerilyn—I had no idea it would be like that. Nothing like a screaming kid to really wreck your evening."

Jerilyn shrugged. "It happens sometimes. I've done a lot of babysitting, and of course, I had a small kid myself a while back. I think it upset Johnny more than me."

"Shit. That's the last thing I want to do, make Johnny mad. And I certainly don't want to bum you out, either. You guys have helped me so much. I guess I'd better not leave her again."

"She seemed to be okay until she got too tired, but yeah, it might be better if you didn't go out at night, at least. For a while—until she gets adjusted."

And what about this afternoon, Carrie Ann wondered. What would happen if she went on the motorcycle ride? Should she even mention it to Jerilyn? Johnny hated Michael, but Jerilyn did not seem to share his feelings. Would she tell her husband if she knew that Carrie Ann was seeing Michael?

"Auntie Jerilyn, look what I found!" Rorie's arrival, with half a dozen lilikoi cradled in her T-shirt, temporarily distracted Carrie Ann. But the question remained, as she served Rorie granola and sliced open the fruit to make lilikoi-mint tea—what was she going to do about her date this afternoon? Rorie seemed to be fine this morning. She carried on as usual and asked for seconds. Maybe Carrie Ann could, like, sort of sneak away. She shook her head, irritated with herself. Of course that wouldn't work. She would have to talk to Alexis.

To her relief, Alexis encouraged her to go. "No problem at all, darling. Little munchkin and I will be fine. What about your other date? Is that still on?"

"Yeah, and I better go get ready. Chuckie called this morning and said to wear bathing suits. We're going to some pool."

The pool turned out to be like nothing she'd ever seen. She had visualized a turquoise concrete tank filled with chlorinated water and populated by screaming, splashing kids. Instead, Chuckie drove far into the countryside, turned up a dirt road, and parked near the edge of a valley filled with trees. Chuckie climbed out of the Jeep, lifted Rorie from the back seat, and threw a couple of towels over his shoulder.

Carrie Ann still sat in the passenger seat, looking across the grassy slopes on each side of the great gulch and up the hill to forest that stretched into the clouds circling the summit of Haleakala. "Where on earth are we? And where's the pool?"

Chuckie pointed to a path, barely discernible in the tall grass surrounding the Jeep. It led deeper into the valley. "Down there. This is my uncle's pasture, and there are pools in the stream down there. You're gonna love it. Come, Rorie, we go." He held out a hand, Rorie grasped it, and the two of them headed down the path into the trees.

Following, Carrie Ann found herself on a narrow, muddy track that wound between short, windblown guava bushes, dotted with the yellow fruit Jerilyn used to make juice and jam. The track led down the side of the gulch into the trees. Though light glinted above, through layers of dark green, the shade was welcome after the Jeep ride under dazzling sun. The air was warm and humid, scented with the now-familiar fruity smell of ripe guavas. Ahead of her, she could hear the deep tones of Chuckie's voice in conversation with Rorie. Off in the forest, birds sang.

Near the bottom of the trail, Carrie Ann heard the sound of running water, and soon they were climbing over rocks at the edge of a stream. Chuckie helped Rorie, for which Carrie Ann was grateful. She needed both hands to keep herself balanced.

The stream widened into a series of small pools, and then into a large one, surrounded by giant rocks. On the uphill edge, a mini waterfall poured into the large pool. Bright green ferns fringed crevices in the black stone around the waterfall. Chuckie stopped and stripped off his shirt.

"This is it. The pool where I spent some of my best summer days, small-kid time. Look, Rorie, this pool here is just your size." He helped the child skim her sundress over her head, then squatted in the small pool and stretched out his hand to help her in. Rorie dipped a toe, then giggled as Chuckie splashed her feet and legs.

"It's cold!"

"That's right." Chuckie grinned up at Carrie Ann. "And the rule is, if you don't get right in, somebody gotta throw you in." He turned his attention back to Rorie. "These rocks are slippery—see how they get the green stuff? It's real slippery. So you be careful not to fall. Don't try to walk around too much, just get in the water and kind of float, okay?"

"Okay." With eyes closed tight, Rorie sank into the pool and stretched out, as she had learned in her swimming lessons at the ocean. She came up onto her knees in the shallow pool, looking surprised. "It doesn't taste the same."

"You mean, not salty?"

"Yeah."

"That's because this is from the rain that falls on the mountain and comes down the stream. When it gets to the bottom it goes into the ocean, and then it gets salty, because the ocean's salty."

Carrie Ann decided she'd better make a move before Chuckie decided she needed help getting into the water. She slipped out of the T-shirt and shorts that covered her new homemade bikini and sat gingerly on one of the big rocks, dangling her feet into the larger pool. The water chilled her toes.

Chuckie stood and climbed to a nearby rock. "This is the diving rock," he instructed. "Don't dive from anyplace else, okay? In case you bump your head on the rocks underwater, and I have to carry you out."

Carrie Ann had no intention of diving. Chuckie, however, turned to face the water and went in headfirst, creating a giant splash. Drenched with cold water, Carrie Ann decided she might as well finish the job. She slipped awkwardly off the rock and into the water, finding it chilly but refreshing after sitting under the sun in the open Jeep.

"Good girl!" Chuckie surfaced grinning, his teeth white against his brown skin. "You gotta move around, now. Tread water at least, to keep warm." His expression changed. "Hey, I never asked you—you can swim, right?"

"Yeah, but not very well." Carrie Ann kept one hand on the rock. Somehow it seemed harder to stay afloat here than it had in the ocean. Tentatively, she lowered her face into the water, then let herself sink until her head was covered. Maybe this cold water would help her headache. Maybe she wouldn't drink so much wine again.

She floated close to the rocks, keeping her arms and legs in motion, watching Chuckie dive and resurface under the little waterfall on the other side of the pool. That looked like fun, she thought, but decided she was too tired for any more adventure today. She groped along the rocks for a way to climb out.

"Come in my pool, Mommy," Rorie said. Carrie Ann hoisted herself up and crawled the few feet to the smaller pool. The water was cool but not as chilly as the big pool. No wonder Rorie had not hesitated to get in.

"I think your pool is too small for two people," she told Rorie. "I'll stay here and watch you."

The rocks were warm. Carrie Ann found one, conveniently flat, where she could see both Rorie and Chuckie. She stretched out in the sun.

"What, had enough already?" Chuckie's head, streaming water, appeared at the edge of the pool.

"I think when I had enough was last night. I think I might have a hangover. I never had one before. I'm not much of a drinker."

Chuckie laughed. "You ladies had a good time, huh." He pulled himself from the pool and stretched out beside her. His arms looked very strong, the muscles curving hard under smooth brown skin.

Carrie Ann's own skin was soft from the water. She rested her chin on her arms, the sun on her back, watching Rorie carefully stack rocks in a pile. Chuckie lay so close that she could hear him breathe.

She wondered if he would make a move. He certainly had seemed interested last night. Did she want him to be interested? He was very nice, and he was very good with Rorie. Cute, too.

But there was Michael. A little smile came to her face, thinking about him, and about seeing him this afternoon.

"After this, I like take you folks to meet my grandpa," Chuckie said. "That's where I live, you know. We can have lunch there, too."

Drawn back into the present, Carrie Ann turned on her side to face Chuckie. "Is it very far away? I need to get back this afternoon, you know. Things to do."

"Not far, only Upper Paia. Why, what you gotta do this afternoon?"

"Just help Jerilyn with some stuff." She decided to change the subject. "So you live with your grandpa?"

"Yeah, I mostly grew up with him and Grandma, and that's where I went after I came back from Nam. Then Grandma died, and the old man needed somebody to stay with him. That's why I'm still there. He's a good old guy. Worked plantation all his life and still lives in his house the plantation gave him. I think they're waiting for him to die before they tear it down. Hardly any plantation houses left. Everybody moved to Kahului already."

"Is this the grandpa who used to take care of the yard for Emily's family?"

"No, that was my mom's dad. Auntie Nani's husband. This grandpa worked at the mill in Paia."

Rorie screamed, scrambling to the edge of her pool. Chuckie was up and had her in his arms before Carrie Ann could even lift herself out of her prone position.

"What is it, baby?" Chuckie asked the child, who clung to him.

"Something touched my toe."

Still holding her, Chuckie squatted to peer into the pool. "I see it—right there, see? It's an opae, a shrimp. It lives here in the pool. It won't hurt you. In fact, it should be scared of you, because you might want to eat that opae. It's ono, you know."

Rorie frowned, staring at the tiny creature. "It doesn't look very ono. It looks like a bug."

Carrie Ann agreed. She had never seen a shrimp that wasn't fried in batter.

"I'm hungry," Rorie announced. "But I don't want to eat that 'pie' thing."

"Okay, we go. Next time we come here, we bring some food—and we make sure we come when Mommy doesn't have a headache." Chuckie smiled at Carrie Ann.

Chuckie folded their clothes into a bundle and took Rorie's hand for the hike back up the hill. Still in damp swimsuits, they climbed into the Jeep and headed down to the highway. Carrie Ann closed her eyes and leaned back in her seat. As long as it wasn't hitting her in the eyes, the sun felt good, its heat and the warm breeze drying her swimsuit and hair. In the back seat, Rorie sang one of her little songs.

Chuckie's house was at the end of a narrow lane above Paia, in an area Carrie Ann had never visited before. Giant trees grew in a red-dirt yard, shading a small wooden house. Geraniums bright with orange flowers surrounded the house, and behind it, cane waved green in the breeze. On a rickety front porch, an old man in a white T-shirt and khaki shorts sat on a sagging couch. He stood to greet them, smiling. Self-conscious, Carrie Ann pulled her T-shirt over her bikini, then stepped down from the Jeep and slipped into her shorts.

"Come inside, come inside." The old man's face was brown and wrinkled, several teeth were missing, and he had the twinkliest eyes Carrie Ann had ever seen. As usual, she had no idea what race he might be. Chuckie, she recalled, had described himself as Hawaiian-Chinese, so his grandfather must be some similar combination.

The old man had been expecting them. The table against one wall in the small, cluttered front room was laid with food. There was a plate piled with pineapple chunks, a bowl of noodles flecked with green onions, and thin-sliced meat threaded onto wooden skewers. Chuckie and his grandpa—whom he called Tutu—served Carrie Ann and Rorie, and they settled around the little table.

The food was delicious, the meat and noodles savory with soy sauce, and the pineapple sweet. Carrie Ann found her energy reviving as she ate. Her stomach had been in no mood for food this morning. Rorie slurped noodles and chewed meat enthusiastically.

Chuckie's grandpa was full of questions about their trip to the pool and chuckled at the story of Rorie's adventure with the opae. Like Chuckie, he gave her his full attention, and Rorie loved it.

Chuckie and Tutu would not let Carrie Ann help with the cleaning up when they had finished eating, so she sat back and looked around the room, which was filled with a collection of photographs and trinkets. Doilies, reddened by the dust that seemed to tint everything in the house, covered tables and shelves, and on them sat souvenir ashtrays, plastic flowers, carved tikis, various china cups and plates, and clusters of framed pictures. A younger Chuckie smiled from one frame, a graduate's cap on his head, and in another, he wore an Army uniform.

The house itself, aside from the dust, did not seem to be in very good shape. Paint was chipped, the ceiling stained, and here and there light peeked through the walls. The place smelled stale, as if its cloudy windows had been closed for all the years the people in the photographs had lived here.

But there must have been love here too, Carrie Ann thought. What a big family Chuckie had—cousins and aunts and uncles captured here in black and white, smiling in their graduation robes and wedding gowns. She envied him that extended family, those trips to his uncle's place to swim in the pool on golden summer days, and the doting grandfather, who insisted that they take the leftover pineapple and stood waving as they drove away.

She had not known her own grandparents. All had been dead by the time she was old enough to know them, and her parents were cast adrift in the world with only each other for company. Maybe that was why they were still together in what seemed to Carrie Ann a marriage that held no love or excitement. Hard to imagine what it would've been like to live in a family like Chuckie's, she thought as she pulled on a clean pair of jeans later that afternoon. No wonder he was such a sweetheart, growing up surrounded by love. No wonder he was so good with Rorie. He had given her a big hug when he dropped them off, and Rorie had hugged him back. He was so nice to them both that Carrie Ann felt a little guilty.

"I'm sorry I was such a drag today," she had told him as he turned to take her hand. "The pool was beautiful, and your grandpa was sweet. And the food was really good."

"That's okay, I had hangovers before. Next time we go someplace, we make sure we don't do it after you go party in Lahaina. Or maybe I take you there sometime, and we party together. How you like that?"

"Cool. That would be great. I had fun today, and Rorie loved it." She had disengaged her hand from his and backed away, not wanting to get too committed here. After all, who knew where things would go with Michael this afternoon?

But Chuckie was persistent. He stepped closer and kissed her on the mouth, his lips full and soft and warm, a sweet, rather brotherly kiss, but pleasant enough that Carrie Ann almost leaned in for more. Instead, Chuckie backed away, climbed into the Jeep, and drove off while Rorie waved goodbye.

Carrie Ann contemplated her image in the mirror. This was very interesting, she thought with a self-satisfied smile. Never in her life had she had two potential boyfriends at the same time. She leaned closer to the mirror. Her freckles were coming out with all the sun, which didn't thrill her. On the other hand, the rest of her skin was a nice golden brown, and her hair was blonder than ever. Her nipples were outlined under the purple T-shirt she had chosen for her motorcycle ride with Michael. Even after those months of nursing Rorie, her breasts didn't look too bad, she thought. Maybe she should start wearing a bra, riding on these bumpy country roads. But not today. Today, she wanted to be as sexy as possible. She squeezed her thighs together in the tight jeans, feeling a tingle just thinking of Michael.

Rorie was already happily engaged, painting watercolors with Alexis in the little cottage at the back of the O'Connors' yard. There had been time for naps, which meant Rorie was in a good mood, and Carrie Ann was considerably less hung over than earlier in the day. Now all she had to do was get out of here without drawing attention to herself. She cocked an ear toward the kitchen. No one there. Jerilyn might be in her room, reading. She could hear Stevie's guitar in the basement, and she was pretty sure Johnny was down there with him, fooling with the equipment, no doubt.

Trying to appear casual, she slipped quietly out the back door and down the driveway, stopping to pick a sweet-scented ginger blossom to tuck behind her ear. She felt bubbly with excitement and a heightened awareness of her body—of the warm afternoon air and the jeans tight between her legs. This must be how it felt to be horny, she thought, surprised at herself. In the years since she had lost her virginity to Rorie's dad, right out of high school, she'd had plenty of sex. And a lot of it had been fun. But never had she experienced desire like this. Always before, she had surrendered to the guy's urging, or simply gone along because it seemed to be the thing to do.

With Michael, something different was happening. She stood at the end of the driveway, waiting anxiously for the sound of his motorcycle. God, what if he had forgotten? What if he was leading her on? She didn't care what Johnny thought. She had never been more drawn to a man in all her twenty-three years.

Ah, here he came, roaring up the dirt road past Auntie Nani's place. Engine idling, Michael took one hand off the handlebars to grasp her face and pull her toward him. His kiss was hard, his tongue probing. After a moment, he drew away and gestured to the back of the bike. Carrie Ann was finding it hard to breathe.

"Let's go, baby. We got some riding to do."

She straddled the bike and wrapped her arms around his waist, pressing her body tightly against his, remembering rides with Jack on his bike back in El Paso, the time she saw her mother at a stoplight and had to quickly turn her face away so her mother wouldn't recognize her. Her mother hated motorcycles, but Carrie Ann loved them. She inhaled, seeking Michael's scent, as he turned the motorcycle and headed to the paved road, then uphill toward Makawao. The bike sped along a winding two-lane road, past acres of green pasture, placid brown cows, over a narrow bridge above a stream where Carrie Ann could see white ducks floating on calm water. She had ridden this road before, on a shopping trip with Jerilyn in Johnny's truck, but she could see much more from the back of Michael's bike. What a beautiful place. What a beautiful day. The bike thrummed between her thighs. She held Michael tighter.

The bike idled briefly at the intersection of the little country town of Makawao, then turned up a steeper road. More pastures, these with sleek horses grazing. A right turn and they were on yet another road through emerald grasslands with scattered herds of cattle. In the distance, the West Maui Mountains were tinged with blue, across a green isthmus bordered by the sea. This was a part of Maui she had not seen before. Everything was different. Everywhere she went here was different from where she had been before. The little towns of Wailuku, Paia, and Makawao, with their old-fashioned buildings and quiet streets, the beach at Hookipa all sand and blue ocean, the green jungle in the valleys of rainy Haiku. What an amazingly beautiful island.

The road led up the side of Haleakala, through acres of vast ranchland, and then through forests whose trees she recognized as eucalyptus, with their silvery leaves and sharp scent. The air turned chilly, and Carrie Ann wished she had brought a jacket. Michael turned off the ascending highway onto one that was more level, winding through farm fields of green vegetables and bright flowers. They headed downhill again, and spectacular views of the island and ocean spread out below them.

By the time they returned to the familiar roads of Haiku, Carrie Ann felt as if she'd had a tour of an island she never had visited, a whole new place to learn about. Michael turned off the highway into a pineapple field, nimbly skirting ruts in the red-dirt roads.

He stopped at the far end of the field, where windblown trees and tall grass stretched to the edge of a cliff. Stiff from the long ride, Carrie Ann climbed off the bike. Michael opened one of the saddlebags and pulled out an army blanket and a thermos.

"Come on, let's check out the view." Taking her hand, he led the way across the grass to a place where several trees and a couple of large rocks clustered to form a windbreak. Michael spread out the army blanket and flopped down, pulling Carrie Ann with him. "What do you think? Pretty nice, huh?" He gestured toward the cliff edge, a few yards away from them, and the ocean that stretched to a far horizon. Down below, waves broke in cascades of lacey white foam on a shoreline of black rock.

"Wow. This is far out. Thank you, Michael, for taking me on such a trippy ride and showing me all this beautiful stuff."

"Yeah, this island is something else. Too bad you got stuck with those old futs. I can't believe they haven't taken you to look around the island." Michael twisted the top off the thermos and drank, then handed it to Carrie Ann. "Here, try this—fresh carrot juice. Made it myself this morning. Man, I love this stuff. I go through thirty pounds of carrots a month."

Tentatively, Carrie Ann tasted the juice and found it earthy and surprisingly sweet. She'd never thought of carrots as sweet. She took a deeper drink.

Michael pulled a plastic bag from his jacket pocket. He took a stem of marijuana from the bag, and a cigarette paper, and began to delicately dismember the bud and drop bits of pot onto the paper. "Yeah, old Johnny and Jerilyn—what a pair. Ozzie and Harriet with long hair."

"Well, at least they gave me a place to stay. I know they're kinda straight—it's funny, since they smoke pot and have a band and everything—but that's how they are."

Michael shrugged. "Yeah, I guess so. Man, old Johnny sure hates me."

"I don't get it. Why does he hate you?"

"Oh, he thinks I ripped him off on a pot deal a couple years ago. It's total bullshit—I don't know where he gets that idea." Michael paused to lick the edge of the cigarette paper. "He got what he paid for. But what the hell, that's the way he is; nothing I can do about it." He twisted the ends of the joint, struck a match, and took the first hit, then handed the joint to Carrie Ann. Exhaling, he laughed. "What's he going to do when he hears that Pineapple Jam is moving in with me? I'm going to be a rock-and-roll manager, baby, and we'll give those guys of Johnny's some competition."

"Pineapple Jam? That group we heard in Lahaina last night?"

"Yeah, they're moving in next week. I'm going to whip them into shape, and we're gonna leave Blend and old Johnny in the dust. I know they're not that hot right now, but when they have me as keyboard player, lead singer, and manager, you watch—Pineapple Jam is going to be sweet."

"I didn't know you were a singer."

"Yeah, I spent most of the time I was supposed to be in college hanging out in Washington Square Park in New York. The folk scene was really happening then, and I got to be pretty good at singing and not too bad on the guitar. Plus, I had all those piano lessons when I was a kid. My grandmother forced me to practice every day, and I have to admit it comes in handy." He took another sip of carrot juice and another drag on the joint. "I thought about kicking Timothy out and taking over as lead guitarist, but I figure adding the keyboard would give us an edge. Yep, old Johnny is in for a surprise."

Michael stretched out his long legs, reclined to lean on one elbow, and turned to look at Carrie Ann. "Anyway, who wants to talk about old Johnny? What have you been up to lately?"

Carrie Ann passed the joint back to Michael. "Lots of sewing. I just finished embroidering a banana tree on one of Johnny's shirts. And I help Jerilyn with the house and the cooking, and Rorie takes up a lot of my time."

"I guess it's a pretty big deal, being a mom."

"Yeah. But she's a groovy kid. She doesn't cause much trouble."

"She looks a lot like you—pretty." Michael leaned closer and lifted Carrie Ann's hair from her neck. Suddenly, she was self-conscious about how messy she must look, after all the wind on the back of the bike. But Michael seemed not to mind. He kissed her neck gently, under the ear, then turned her face and put his mouth on hers.

Her breath came faster as her tongue met Michael's. Pent-up passion surged through Carrie Ann. Michael pressed himself against her, his whole body long and hard. He smelled delicious.

For a moment she was distracted by a rush of paranoia—could anyone see them here? But Michael reassured her, and his hands moving softly on her breasts quickly dispelled any thought of the outside world.

They helped each other skin out of their jeans and T-shirts, then made love as the warm breeze and the golden rays of late afternoon sun played on their bodies. Carrie Ann had never experienced such ecstasy. Finally, the incredible pleasure reached a crescendo and she felt herself melting from within, clinging to Michael as he climaxed with a cry.

They lay damp and unmoving for a while. Finally, Michael groaned and lifted himself on his elbows to look down at Carrie Ann. "Am I too heavy?"

She didn't want to let him go. "Do you think we can turn over sideways without coming apart?"

"We can try."

It didn't work. Michael slipped out of her, and she felt a great wave of loss. She kept her topmost leg hooked over his hip and pulled herself closer. Michael's hand moved down to stroke her, and she moaned. My God, could they do it again? Carrie Ann opened her eyes as Michael began to move against her. Reality returned in an unwelcome flash.

"Oh, no. Michael, Michael—I can't. I have to go home."

"Huh?" His eyes remained closed, and his fingers continued their play. Carrie Ann forced herself to keep her eyes open, not to sink back into the sensual paradise that was a world away from the life that waited for her at home.

"Michael, the sun is going down. I promised Alexis I would get back, because Rorie gets freaked out if I'm not home when it gets dark."

"It's not dark yet. Come on, baby, this is too good . . . ."

She couldn't resist. Michael was right. It was too good. Carrie Ann's body responded to his hand, and her mind had to follow. Their lovemaking was even more intense the second time, and by the time they finished, the sun was sinking in pink splendor behind the West Maui Mountains. Carrie Ann returned once again to reality.

"Michael, now I really have to go," she said. "Rorie can't handle me being away after dark, and I don't want her to bum out Alexis like she did Jerilyn last night."

Michael opened his eyes, frowning. "Well, can't Alexis keep her busy?"

"She's had her all afternoon, and I don't know how long she can keep her occupied, especially after dark. I don't want her to start crying and freaking out, and then Jerilyn and Johnny might hear her and realize I was gone. I, uh, kinda snuck out today, you know."

Michael sighed. "Damn. You're hot, baby. I could do this all night. But, I guess it's gonna get cold here pretty soon anyway." He pushed himself into a sitting position and helped Carrie Ann sit up. He pulled her to him for a kiss, then stood up and stretched.

"Oh, man. That was outta sight. Next time we'll have to go to my place. The view's great here, but my bed's more comfortable."

Next time. Carrie Ann clung to the implied promise all the way home.

Twilight masked her return, and soon she was at Alexis's front door. Warm light glowed through the screen, and inside she could see Alexis and Rorie sitting on the floor, stringing beads.

"Hello. I'm home." She stepped inside.

"Hi, Mommy." Rorie glanced up, calm and casual. "Look what I'm making, Mommy. Alexis showed me how."

"Looks like you had a good time. Everything go okay?" she asked Alexis.

"Yup. No problems. Little munchkin has been darling."

"Are you ready to go down to get some dinner?" Carrie Ann asked her daughter.

Rorie frowned. "I'm not finished with my necklace, Mommy. You go. I'll come down later."

Alexis laughed. "Well, so much for the nighttime boohoos. Go ahead, Carrie Ann, if you want to. I can bring her down in a while if you want to go see what's happening with dinner."

Hmph. Wouldn't you know it? Briefly, Carrie Ann imagined herself catching up with Michael, pulling him off his bike and into the bushes. But there was no way. Disappointed, she turned to leave. Might as well go see about dinner.

THE ISLAND DECIDES

"Hey, Carrie Ann," Alexis called as she closed the screen door behind her. "How did it go with you?" Carrie Ann paused on the step. She smiled, remembering.

"Great. Absolutely outta sight." She turned and headed down to the main house, down to deal with dinner and dishes and a reality that had returned all too quickly. It was no match for the reality she'd just experienced, so beautiful, so intense. She knew the old reality would change now, somehow, forever.

Chapter Twelve

She had a secret life now. And Alexis had become her ally, a girlfriend who was only too happy to aid and abet Carrie Ann in her romantic adventure.

Alexis and Rorie had hit it off, and to Carrie Ann's surprise and delight, Alexis was cool with Rorie hanging out at her house. Carrie Ann used the phone there to call Michael, and Alexis took messages from Michael about when he would be waiting at the far end of the driveway. Twice, Alexis dropped Carrie Ann at the top of Michael's road and picked her up on the way back from a town trip.

And in between those brief, sweet, intensely exciting times with Michael, he lived in her mind. She heard his voice, the phrases that he used, the things he had said the last time they met; she savored them as she went through her day. Washing dishes at Jerilyn's sink, bathing Rorie, swaying in the corner of the basement while Blend rehearsed, she felt his presence, shaping her perceptions and guiding her thoughts. She wrote Mimi and Kathryn to tell them about her romance; she smiled and thought of Michael while her mother rambled on during her weekly calls from Texas.

Carrie Ann had never had a boyfriend who inhabited her thoughts this way. He knew so much of life. She had so much to learn. She was like a student in his presence, soaking up knowledge of yoga and eastern religions, of how four-wheel drive worked, of what grains to combine to produce a perfect protein. She loved his voice, a deep bass, singing folk songs as he strummed his guitar.

And she loved his house. Like the O'Connors', it was old, built up off the ground, with high ceilings and big windows and a yard full of trees planted generations ago. Most of the interior was filled with furniture not unlike the O'Connors', secondhand couches and big pillows. The kitchen table was scarred, none of its chairs matched, and the refrigerator was an ancient model that stood off the floor on little legs.

But Michael's room was filled with beautiful things, antiques he had shipped from the East Coast. He'd bought the house last year, he told her, with his inheritance from the grandmother who'd helped raise him, the previous owner of these antiques. An earlier inheritance from his father had enabled him to leave his job at the family's book publishing company and move to Maui three years ago. Never again would he work for someone else, he said.

Things were a little crazy around the place the first time he took her home with him, because Pineapple Jam was moving in—or at least three of them were. The drummer, a big Hawaiian guy, lived in Haiku town with his family, behind the little store where everyone shopped for things that couldn't wait for the next trip to Paia or Kahului. The other three would live in the downstairs area at Michael's, a roomy space even bigger than the studio and storage rooms under the O'Connors' house. The band would practice in the shed out back, and they were busily stringing electric lines and tacking egg cartons to the shed walls to improve the acoustics.

Michael gave her a tour of the place one afternoon. The original owners had been a Hawaiian family that had lived here for years, Michael told her. When the last of the old folks died, the single surviving son had preferred to remain in Los Angeles. That was right after Michael's inheritance came in, and he'd ended up with five acres, half already planted in banana trees, and an old house where the previous inhabitants had raised several generations. The upstairs had a big kitchen and living room, three bedrooms, and a bath. Michael said he thought the family might have used the downstairs area as a sort of dormitory for some of the kids—there had been army-cot frames there when he bought it. In a room attached to the back of the house were a toilet and shower for the band to use.

She saw the boys occasionally on her trips down to Michael's or heard their hammering as they put up partitions to make little rooms for themselves downstairs. But Michael's bedroom, at the far back of the old house, was blissfully private.

The sex was wonderful. She couldn't wait to get down to Michael's, and on those days when he picked her up, he turned his bike straight back down the road to his place. When he touched her, she trembled. Each time they were together, her desire for him rose again and again, and his desire matched hers. Their visits were hot, sweaty, and ecstatic.

But he never mentioned the possibility of her coming to stay. Well before sunset, her personal witching hour, he dropped her at the top of the O'Connors' road and zoomed back down to his own place.

And then there were the other women. Carrie Ann had no idea if Michael was making it with anyone else, but he certainly had followers, women who attended his yoga classes. They called, they waved from street corners when Michael took her for rides through Paia and Makawao, and once one of them showed up at his house as Alexis pulled up to take Carrie Ann home. She fretted all the way back to the O'Connors'. Alexis just shook her head. "We warned you, darling, remember? That night at the Blue Lagoon? He's not a one-woman man."

Frowning, Carrie Ann shut up, but she couldn't stop thinking about that chick traipsing down Michael's steep driveway, and his welcoming grin as he stood on the back porch.

Hiding her frequent absences was becoming a problem. Jerilyn had grown used to having her around, and it was awkward when Carrie Ann began, apparently, to spend a lot of time with Alexis. Finally, seeing the hurt look on Jerilyn's face one day as she was heading out the back door, Carrie Ann stopped and plunked herself down at the kitchen table.

"Jerilyn, I have to talk to you about something."

Jerilyn glanced at her and continued to remove clean dishes from the drainer and stow them in the cupboard above. "Oh yeah? About what?"

Carrie Ann hesitated. "It's kind of a secret. I mean, I don't want you to tell Johnny, and I know he is your old man, so I feel kind of weird about asking you not to tell him."

Jerilyn stopped what she was doing and leaned against the counter, arms folded. "Well, I don't have to tell him everything that happens."

"Okay." There was no turning back. "I've been dating Michael. That's where I go when I disappear in the afternoon."

Jerilyn closed the silverware drawer and came to sit with Carrie Ann at the table. "No shit. When did this get started?"

"After that time I went to Lahaina with Alexis and Emily. We saw him there, and he asked me to go for a ride the next day."

"Wow, what a trip. What do you guys do together?" She grinned. "Or do I even have to ask?"

Carrie Ann's cheeks heated up. "Well, we do go on motorcycle rides too."

"And what about Chuckie? He's been coming around a lot, and you've gone out with him a few times too. What's going on there?"

"I know, it's amazing, isn't it. Two guys at once. But I haven't been getting it on with Chuckie. He's really sweet, and I like him a lot, but I don't think I could make it with two guys at once. And, omigod, Jerilyn, this is something else with Michael. I have never had a relationship like this. He is amazing."

Jerilyn cocked one eyebrow. "Oh yeah? He's certainly a babe, no question about that. But he's not really the domestic type, I don't think, so I wouldn't get too carried away with this, honey."

Carrie Ann sighed. "I know. He doesn't seem like he's ready to settle down, especially with somebody who already has a kid. But I tell you, Jerilyn, we really have something going. It's never been like this for me, and I think it's pretty far out for him too."

"Well, guard your heart. And what about Rorie? You haven't been asking me to babysit a lot, so where has she been in all this?"

"Amazingly enough, she and Alexis have become great buddies, and Alexis has been taking care of her and teaching her all kinds of art stuff. They're up there right now, eating popcorn and doing watercolors, if you can imagine the mess."

"That really is amazing! I never would have thought that Alexis would be good with kids, and she's not exactly the kind of person to do a lot of favors for someone."

"She's been helping me a lot. I'm trying to pay her back by doing that embroidery on her jacket." She added hastily, "And so have you! I mean, you do a lot of babysitting for me, and I really appreciate it."

"That's okay, you do a lot around here, and I appreciate your help too, so we're even. And I like having Rorie around—little kids are fun." Jerilyn shook her head. "Well, looks like you have it all worked out, at least for as long as it lasts with Michael. I wouldn't count on him being real stable or real faithful."

"I know. But I think this might be something different. Maybe he's ready for a change, ready to settle down a little bit."

Jerilyn laughed and got up to resume her kitchen work. "Good luck. I won't tell Johnny, although I have a feeling you're going to show up one of these days with a broken heart."

But Michael's greeting, a passionate kiss before she climbed onto the back of the bike, reassured Carrie Ann. Whatever Jerilyn thought, whatever his history with other ladies, Carrie Ann knew this was different.

And she was glad she had told Jerilyn. Riding down the hill with her body pressed tightly against Michael's back, she hummed an old song from her childhood, a song about a secret love. Someday, maybe, she would be able to tell the world about her secret love. Not that anyone else could ever truly know what she shared with Michael. She pitied all those people walking around in their ordinary, everyday lives, without this wonderful glow at the center of their beings.

"Hey, baby, want to go to the beach?" Michael asked a couple of hours later, as he stepped out of the shower. Carrie Ann stopped combing her hair and turned to look at him.

"You mean right now? Where, Hookipa?"

"No, I mean for the day, to Makena. You haven't been there, right? We could leave early some morning, take a picnic lunch, spend the day. It's great—you don't even need a bathing suit, everybody runs around bare-ass naked, getting their butts sunburned. Ever go skinny-dipping? It's a gas."

"I don't know if I can get away for a whole day, because I don't know if either Jerilyn or Alexis is up for taking care of Rorie all day. I'm afraid she might freak out if I leave her for that long anyway, no matter who she stays with." She hesitated, hoping Michael would suggest taking Rorie along with them.

Instead, he hung up his towel and went to pull on his jeans. Carrie Ann wondered uneasily if she had pushed it too far. Somehow, she had to keep these two parts of her life going without either screwing up the other.

Michael did not mention the beach again until he dropped her at the end of the driveway. With the motorcycle's engine still rumbling at a low idle, he leaned to kiss her goodbye and then spoke. "See what you can do about the babysitter bit. Give me a call tomorrow—I'll be home from class by noon—and maybe we can go the next day."

Disappointed, Carrie Ann gave him another kiss, then waved goodbye and turned to head down the driveway. She didn't know how she was going to get either Jerilyn or Alexis to take Rorie for a whole day. Maybe she could offer to make one of them a new dress as a trade.

The sound of Michael's motorcycle had just faded in the distance when she heard the rumble of another vehicle and looked back to see Johnny's truck turning into the driveway. Without pausing to think, she stepped off the road and into the bushes, moving back until she was certain she would not be seen. It would not do for Johnny to find her here on the driveway when surely he had passed Michael riding down the road.

Chapter Thirteen

Carrie Ann settled herself onto the back of Michael's bike and gave him an excited squeeze. This was the day! It had all worked out, and they were off to Makena. Jerilyn and Alexis, cooperating for once, had agreed to take turns keeping an eye on Rorie. In exchange, Carrie Ann would make each a dress, a more-than-fair trade in her mind, because she had recently come up with a simple design composed of nothing more than three rectangles of cloth and some elastic. She could do both dresses in a few hours, she was quite sure, a small price to pay for this great adventure with Michael.

He headed toward Paia and pulled into the gas station where Johnny always stopped. The old Japanese man who owned the place sat grinning in his greasy overalls, as usual, sipping a Coke and joking with a customer who was laboring to remove some part from a rusty old truck. It took only a minute to fill the bike, and then they were back aboard and waiting to pull out onto the highway. Impulsively, Carrie Ann leaned forward to give Michael a kiss on the ear, then settled onto her seat and turned her head to rest on his back.

Her smile faded as her eyes met Chuckie's shocked face. He was in his Jeep, slowing to make a turn at the intersection heading up to his place. She had not seen him for a few days, since the time he had come to take her and Rorie on another trip to the mountain pools. Chuckie had no idea that she was seeing Michael. Shit. Well, he certainly knew now. Self-conscious, she sat up straight and waved tentatively, but Chuckie looked away. He made a quick left turn and headed up the hill without looking back. Michael revved his engine and took off toward Wailuku.

Now what, she wondered. That one brief moment had taken the glow from the day. She worried for a while about Chuckie. He was such a sweetheart, and she did not mean to hurt him. Would he stop coming around? Would he tell Johnny? Bummer. Having more than one man in your life was certainly complicated. Carrie Ann sighed and decided she would try to forget about this and enjoy the day. Here in her arms was Michael, and if she had to make a choice, this was where she would choose to be.

The drive took them through familiar territory, past the hotel in Kahului where she had stayed her first night here, and into Wailuku. Carrie Ann had not been there for weeks, but its sights were indelibly engraved on her mind. There was the Kress store, where she had eaten lunch with Rick, the old white church, and, in the shade behind it, the little green Legal Aid office. There was the old stone courthouse building, where the judge had made his decision and she had been reunited with her child. She realized she hadn't heard from David lately; the social worker's office was right down that street.

But from here on out, it was all new territory. It had been too dark to see anything when she rode this way going to Lahaina with Alexis and Emily. Now she gazed across cane fields that covered the isthmus from the foothills of the West Maui Mountains to Haleakala. Ahead, the blue ocean awaited them. The bike turned off the highway onto a road that ran parallel to the shore through wetlands where long-legged birds preened. They entered a dusty forest with a few old houses scattered among its trees and, here and there, a tall new building. The road was narrow but paved for most of the way. Then the paving ended, and Michael slowed his bike to negotiate his way between ruts and rocks. The farther they went, the more rugged the terrain and the more it seemed they were driving over an endless washboard. On the other side of a barbed-wire fence, trees with dark twisted limbs and feathery leaves grew amid rough rock walls, and here and there stood a tall cactus.

"Ranchers brought this stuff here," Michael explained as they rested in the shade of a tree and shared a bottle of carrot juice pulled from the bike's saddlebags. "The cactus, and these trees, for their cattle—the trees are mesquite, but here they call it kiawe. And the cactus holds water when there's a drought. Lots of droughts around here. This is the dry side of the island. Just like Texas, huh?"

But this desert, if you could call it that, was nothing like her home, Carrie Ann thought as they got back on the road. Her desert was sere and brown, with low-blown shrubs and bare tumbleweeds rolling over sand. Even in the summer heat, this place had trees, spare but green. And across the way was not more brown dirt, but sapphire ocean.

Michael slowed and turned down a still narrower dirt road into the kiawe forest. The sea was no longer visible here, blocked by the kiawe, but the road led toward the ocean. Michael maneuvered around deep ruts, then pulled up his bike at the edge of a beach.

"This is it," he said. "We call it Big Beach."

It was indeed big, and almost empty of people, a broad swath of golden sand that stretched from a dark hill at the near end to a destination she could not discern in the other direction. They settled their stuff in the shade of a kiawe, and Michael undressed. Carrie Ann took off her outer clothes—she had worn a bikini underneath—then hesitated and glanced around. "You sure it's okay to swim naked?"

"Sure it is, I do it all the time. Chances are anybody you see down here is going to be as bare-bottomed as you are, and the cops never come near this place, or at least they haven't been around much since the time they cleaned up and kicked out all the scumbags. The mayor got uptight about things when the hepatitis epidemic was bad and sent the cops to tear up all the shacks and chase the hippies away. You can still see some of their junk in the bushes, and I think a few of them are creeping back in, but it's a lot quieter than six months ago.

Anyway, baby, let's go! Get those clothes off and get in the water!" Michael turned and raced naked down to dive headfirst into a wave that was beginning to curl over into foam.

Carrie Ann looked around one more time. She could see perhaps a dozen people in the water or on the sand, some so far down the beach that she couldn't tell whether they were male or female. Most of them seemed to be naked, and the few who weren't paid no attention to the others. Carrie Ann untied her top.

The sand was hot on bare feet. No wonder Michael had run. It was a relief to step on wet sand and feel cold water swirl up around her ankles. Carrie Ann stood for a moment, watching the waves. They were breaking close to shore, piling onto the sand in a rush of bubbles that drained quickly back to meet the next incoming wave. But they did not seem to be big waves, just frequent, and Carrie Ann thought she could handle them. Out beyond the break, Michael swam a smooth backstroke. When he saw her, he stopped to tread water and wait for her. Carrie Ann paddled out, enjoying the novel sensation of cool water flowing over her entire body, touching her in places usually protected by a swimsuit. She swam directly into Michael's arms and wrapped her legs around his waist, using her arms to keep afloat.

"Hey baby, pretty sexy, huh?" Michael continued to tread water but slipped one hand below the water to caress her. Carrie Ann arched her back, resting her upper body in the water and opening her thighs wider. Every inch of her body responded to Michael's hand and the ocean's touch. "Mmmm. I think we need to go back on shore for a while," Michael said.

Michael helped her through the shore break, and they held hands as they trotted over the hot sand to the shady spot where they had left their stuff. "Put your sandals back on, we're going for a little walk, and you don't want to step on a kiawe thorn," Michael said as he pulled towels from the saddlebags. Carrie Ann wrapped one around her and followed Michael to a place where kiawe trees clustered in such a way as to block the view from every direction. Michael scanned the sand for thorny branches, spread their towels, helped her to the ground, and dropped to his knees.

Wild sex in the wilderness, Carrie Ann thought as she slipped into a place where thought did not exist, where only sensation and pleasure filled the universe.

Sometime later, still breathing hard, Michael rested on his elbows. "Man, that was good. Whew. Hey, are you okay? You aren't lying on any kiawe thorns or anything, are you?"

"Well, now that I'm thinking about it, this sand is kind of hard. But don't move yet." She tightened her thighs to hold him close, reluctant as always to let him go.

Still, the ground was hard, and after a moment Michael pulled loose and they stood. Aware of her surroundings again, Carrie Ann peered through the bushes, wondering what ears might have been listening to their lovemaking. But she saw no one as they found their way back through the trees to the beach.

They ate the lunch Michael had brought and stretched out in the shade, not quite touching. Carrie Ann reached over to stroke Michael's flat belly. Replete, she closed her eyes and dozed off.

When she awoke, Michael was gone. She sat up to look around. There he was, bobbing on the top of a wave as it swelled into shore. Carrie Ann sat watching for a minute, sipping the last of the carrot juice. She squinted at the sky; the sun was dazzling and had moved directly overhead. She had better not stay out too long, or she would burn lobster red, especially in those places the bikini usually hid. But maybe she would join Michael for a quick swim.

She moved quickly over the hot sand and into the water, just as it rose with the arrival of a new wave. She waded out and began to paddle. She wished she could swim more gracefully, but she was not confident enough to try the head-in-water stroke Jerilyn had been teaching her, so this awkward dog paddle would have to do. Her heart pounded as a wave rose, nearing the shore, but she paddled rapidly and managed to keep her head high as she swam through its crest.

On the other side of the wave, Michael drifted easily, bobbing on the ocean surface. She swam toward him.

"Hey, good waves, huh? How are you doing, can you handle this?"

"Okay, as long as it doesn't get any bigger."

"When a swell comes, make sure you don't get in front of the break, and all you have to do is sort of jump it—use your legs like you're doing jumping jacks. And use your arms too, of course. You'll figure it out. Look out, here comes one!"

Carrie Ann swiveled in the water to look toward the horizon, and sure enough, here came the kind of swell that looked like it might turn out to be a big one. Following Michael, she paddled into the swell, then kicked frantically to lift her body and keep her head above the water.

Breathing hard, she laughed as the wave lifted them, then dropped them as it passed, leaving them in its trough. This was fun!

The waves kept coming, and Carrie Ann managed to keep her head above most of them by remaining in constant motion. The sun glinted brightly on the water, and a gentle breeze cooled her face. She had never been this far out in the water before, and it was interesting to look back at the land from this perspective, to see the beach backed by green kiawe forest and behind that, the sloping mountain disappearing into cloud cover.

The waves seemed to come in groups, with a period of lull between them, when Carrie Ann practiced her floating, letting her arms and legs relax while she faced up into the sky. She had no idea how long they had been out there, but she was running out of energy.

"Here comes another set," Michael said when she suggested going in. "Let's wait till the set is over and it will be easier to get in."

By the time this set had calmed, Carrie Ann knew she had to go in. She wasn't used to this much swimming.

"Want to race?" Michael didn't wait to hear her answer, just headed to shore with powerful strokes. Carrie Ann wished she could swim that well, but at least she could get from one place to the other, even if only with her slow dog paddle. Michael made it to shore and stood waiting for her on the wet sand.

She was almost there when the next set came. She wouldn't have realized it if Michael hadn't pointed, shouting, "Carrie Ann, look behind you! Dive under it!"

She turned to see a wave swelling toward her, rising as it came, while the water around her seemed to sink, and her with it. She didn't know what to do. Michael yelled again. "Turn around and dive down under it! Go deep!"

Filling her lungs, she did as he said. Her feet did not touch bottom here, so she went as deep as she could. Above her, the ocean surged, tugging at her limbs, slowing her movement. She kept her eyes squeezed tight, and held her breath until she could wait no longer, then opened her eyes to find the light. The salt stung; she had never opened her eyes under the water before. She burst through the surface and gasped for air, shook water from her eyes, and looked to the sea. Yes, here came another swell.

"Swim out past the break!" Michael shouted. Keeping her eyes on the wave, Carrie Ann tried to do what Michael had said, despite her fear of swimming into that enormous and growing mountain of water. These waves were the biggest of the day, and she had to swim hard to keep her head above water. She reached the wave's peak as it curled over into white foam, and quickly took a deep breath when she saw that she was not going to clear the break. Foam broke over her head; she tried to stay afloat until she could get back up for air.

She was in a trough, between waves, but she could see that there was another one coming. Michael yelled again. The sound of the crashing waves muffled his voice. "Swim out farther!" She obeyed, though she was exhausted. At least if she got beyond the break, she would be able to rest.

The water was calmer on the other side of the break, though she was still frightened and alert to the changing sea. It had been exciting to be in this deep, moving water when Michael was out here with her, but now it was just plain scary.

At last, the set died down, and Michael, still watching from the shore, yelled, "Okay, come on in, you have a couple of minutes." She swam as fast as she could. But she was not fast enough. The first wave hit when she was still a good twenty yards from land. With only time for one deep breath, she found herself underwater, sand blasting her skin as the wave turned and twisted her body. She bounced against the bottom as the powerful surge deposited her on the beach. Gasping, she tried to stand but slipped to her knees. A few yards up the beach, Michael stood with a terrible look on his face. That look frightened her even more, and she turned her head to see yet another wave looming over her. She sucked in air and tried to flatten herself as much as possible as she dove under the wave.

This time, when the wave finally released her, she was even closer to dry sand, but she was unable to stand. On hands and knees, she raised one arm to Michael. Tall as he was, these waves dwarfed him as well. But he had to help her. Why did he stand there, frowning? Another wave was on the way.

At last, Michael stepped forward, still looking doubtful. In a moment, he was in up to his waist in swirling water, her hand firmly in his strong grasp, pulling her to safety. He dragged her out of the water and onto the sand, where she collapsed, still panting.

"I thought I wasn't going to make it," she said when she could speak. "You saved my life, Michael."

"I guess I did, huh? I was afraid I was going to get swept out there with you. You're okay though, right? No broken bones? That's the last thing I need, to bring home another injured chick to Johnny's house."

Carrie Ann's shoulder was beginning to sting, and her knee hurt. She sat up carefully and inspected herself. She was a bit scratched up here and there, and the shoulder was bleeding a little. She would have some bruises later. But she was lucky not to have broken her neck, she guessed. She had not realized how strong the ocean could be. She reached up to touch a sore spot on her head and realized that her hair was matted and full of sand. She groaned. What a mess. She'd had enough of the ocean for one day.

An hour later, they pulled up to the road that led down to the O'Connor's place. The motor quieted to an idle, and Michael looked over his shoulder. "Do you think you can walk, or do you want me to drive you to the house?"

Carrie Ann sighed. She put one foot on the ground and swung her leg stiffly over the bike. "I guess I'd better walk, although I don't think Johnny is home. It will probably do me good to move." She leaned forward to give Michael a kiss. "Thanks for taking me, it was great, until I got caught in the waves."

"Yeah, sorry about that. Well, I better get out of here. Go home and take a nice hot shower, and you'll feel better. See you later." She backed away, and he turned the bike and was off with a roar.

Carrie Ann headed down the road and found that she was limping slightly. That knee did hurt. She would have to ask Jerilyn if she knew any home remedies for bruises.

Rounding the curve into the yard, she was shocked to find Johnny's truck parked in the driveway. She really didn't want him to see her looking like this. And where was Rorie, and did Johnny realize that Carrie Ann had not been around? She had to get a shower before he saw her. She must look awful, covered with sand

and all windblown from the bike. It would have been easy if she still lived out in the old shack, but there were no towels and no clean clothes out there, so she would have to get to her room. If she could make it through the back door and straight into her own room, there was the bathroom and everything she needed to clean herself up and make a cautious entrance later. Quietly, she climbed the back steps.

But as she stepped inside, she glanced toward the open kitchen door and met Johnny's eyes. He did not look happy. She stopped, uncertain about what to do next.

Johnny answered that question, craning his neck to peer around the doorway. "Carrie Ann. Get your little butt in here."

Hesitant, she limped into the kitchen. Johnny sat in his usual seat, and next to him sat Jerilyn, with Rorie on her lap, teary eyed. When she saw her mother, she stretched out her arms, begging to be held. Carrie Ann lifted her from Jerilyn's lap.

"So, what's the trip, Miss Emerson?" Johnny's tone was biting. Jerilyn looked down at her hands.

"What do you mean?" Carrie Ann asked.

"I mean, where the fuck have you been? I decide to come home for lunch and find my old lady taking care of your kid, again, and you nowhere to be found. Then I find out the reason you're not here is that you're out with that asshole Michael Wharton. So, I ask again Miss Emerson—what's the trip? You're out having a fling with somebody I don't want in my house, while you're living here practically scot-free, and you're leaving your kid for somebody else to take care of, which I believe already got you into trouble once. Sounds pretty uncool to me, and I don't like it."

Carrie Ann didn't know what to say. Rorie clung tightly, her face buried in Carrie Ann's sandy hair.

Jerilyn stood up, looking anxious. "Carrie Ann, let me take Rorie outside, okay? This is freaking her out." Speechless, Carrie Ann handed Rorie back to Jerilyn. Rorie, who did not want to let go of her mother, let loose with screams which Jerilyn tried to soothe as she walked rapidly out the back door.

Carrie Ann turned back to face Johnny, who was frowning as he carefully rolled a joint. He twisted the ends, then dropped it into his dope can and looked up at her.

"I think it's time for you to move on, Carrie Ann," he said. "I think we did our best to give you a good start here on Maui, and I don't know that you really appreciated it. But I know that I've had enough, and I'm tired of having Jerilyn cover for you so you can go out and get laid. Therefore, you are going to have to find another place to live. I want you out of here as soon as possible."

Carrie Ann blinked. She could not take this in. Where would she go? She knew that Johnny was not going to change his mind. When he decided to kick Allison out, she had been gone the next day. But Allison had someplace to go, back to her parents' house. Carrie Ann had nowhere. She couldn't leave Maui, and she hardly knew anyone. And what would David the social worker say if she moved out of the household that had met his approval?

Johnny reached into his can, pulled out the joint, and lit it. He did not offer her a toke.

Carrie Ann still could think of no response. She turned slowly and walked out the back door, following the sound of Rorie's cries up the path to Alexis's house.

Chapter Fourteen

Limping to spare her sore knee, Carrie Ann picked her way gingerly along the driveway, wishing she had waited until the sun was higher before leaving the O'Connors'. She had been fine, crossing the lawn, but the driveway through the gulch was dark and slippery. Not much farther, and she would be out in the open again and able to walk on the level edge of the road.

Maybe she shouldn't be doing this. But what else could she do? Yesterday, when she arrived at Alexis's front door after the confrontation with Johnny, Jerilyn had handed Rorie to Carrie Ann, barely making eye contact. She told Carrie Ann she was sorry, this was Johnny's idea and not hers, but there was nothing she could do to change his mind. "And he's pissed off at me for helping you get together with Michael," Jerilyn said, as she left. "I gotta get back and see if I can calm him down." Carrie Ann groaned, overcome with guilt. "I'm so sorry, Jerilyn, I never meant for you to get in trouble for helping me," she said. Clutching her sniffling daughter, she watched Jerilyn leave, wondering if this meant an end to their friendship.

Carrie Ann and Alexis soothed Rorie as best they could. Alexis was mortified; Rorie had been at her house around lunchtime, playing in the yard, when she stubbed her toe on a rock. Instead of coming to Alexis for comfort, she went crying down to the main house and ran smack dab into Johnny, who of course wanted to know where the hell this kid's mother had gone to.

So that was it. Carrie Ann wondered if Johnny might have been looking for a good excuse to tell her to leave anyway, but whatever his trip was, it still came down to one thing. She had to move.

THE ISLAND DECIDES

Kevin, confused by all this conflict, went down to the house to practice. Alexis made tuna sandwiches for dinner and tried to help Carrie Ann figure out what to do next. But there weren't many options. Briefly, she and Alexis considered whether Carrie Ann and Rorie might move into one of the empty shacks at Guava Gulch, but the thought made her shudder. She couldn't imagine living down there herself, never mind taking Rorie back to that place. Panic rose; where else was there? She couldn't afford a place by herself and knew almost no one. They had no choice but to stay on Maui, and Carrie Ann had to find a roof to shelter herself and her child; Johnny had said "as soon as possible."

She waited at Alexis's house until the kitchen light at the O'Connors' house went dark, and she could hear the band begin to play. Now everyone would be downstairs, and she would not have to face them. She crept in the back door, with Rorie asleep in her arms, and into her room. At least for tonight, it was her room.

Though Carrie Ann was exhausted after lying awake most of the night, she dragged herself out of bed before sunrise, grabbed a banana and some crackers from the kitchen to keep Rorie occupied for a while, and took her up to the cottage. Kevin, fortunately an early riser, was plunking on his unplugged bass—did he never get tired of playing? He said he would keep an eye on Rorie until Alexis woke up.

Now here she was, walking to Michael's house. She had thought it out carefully. He had that big house and three guys moving in downstairs. He needed a woman to run the place, and she knew she could do it. And what could be better, anyway, than for them to live together? She loved him, and she was sure he must love her, or they couldn't have had such great sex. Maybe this was meant to be! Maybe this was God's way of bringing the two of them together. She had hoped it would happen, and now maybe it would, sooner than she expected.

Only one problem. And this one brought her back to earth time and time again. Carrie Ann did not come alone. Carrie Ann brought a child with her, and Michael had given no indication that he was at all interested in having a child in his life. Plus, there was the law, as represented by David. He was much nicer than her San Francisco social worker, but he was pretty straight. What would he think of her living with Michael? Surely she would be hearing from him soon, and she had to have her act together by then, whether with Michael or somewhere else. Except, there was nowhere else. And she really, really wanted this to work out with Michael.

Why did this have to happen to her? She finally had found her old man, or at least she hoped she had, but he had to be willing to accept her child—after all, that child was a big part of her need to find a man. Rorie might never know her real father, but she deserved to have a father figure in her life. Carrie Ann had no idea how that would work with Michael, but she was about to find out. Once she was past that roadblock, she would figure out how to deal with the social worker.

The sun was warm on her face as she limped down Michael's road. Her knee hurt even more after the twenty-minute walk from the O'Connors' house. This was the first time she had walked it; always before she had been on Michael's bike or in Alexis's VW. The driveway was steep, and she was glad she could walk on the narrow concrete strips, cracked with age, that ran along the side of Michael's valley.

She rounded a bend in the driveway and peered over the trees to see if there was any life around the house. It looked quiet. It was early yet, and they might have been up late playing music last night.

But the back door was open, and Michael was sitting at the table with a cup of coffee. She knocked gently, and he looked up from the book he was reading.

"Carrie Ann—where'd you come from? Come on in. Want some coffee?"

"Actually, I'll take some water. It's kind of a long walk from the O'Connors' place." The sink was full of dirty dishes, but she managed to find a clean glass at the back of a cupboard.

She drank most of the glass before sitting at the table. Michael leaned back in his chair, arms folded and long legs stretched in front of him, watching her.

"So what's the trip?"

She didn't know where to begin. Now that she was here, with Michael looking so detached, anxiety filled her. She forced herself to inhale deeply and sit up straight.

"Michael, Johnny says I can't live with them anymore."

Michael frowned. "Why not?"

"He was there when I got home yesterday, and he was really pissed off that I had gone out with you and left Rorie behind. Actually, I think he was more uptight about me being with you than about Rorie—or, maybe not, I don't know. Anyway, he said I had to leave as soon as possible."

"Now what?"

This was where things got really scary. Carrie Ann took another deep breath. "Well, I was thinking . . . I was wondering, what if I came to live here?" Michael's frown grew deeper, and Carrie Ann talked faster. "I can be so helpful, Michael. I can cook, and I know how to clean and take care of things, and now you have all these guys living downstairs and no chicks around, you're gonna need somebody to take care of the house. And, well, I was thinking, we really have something going between us, don't you think? I mean, like yesterday—that was incredible, in the woods there—and then you saved my life, Michael! I wouldn't even be alive today if you hadn't been there to help me. So it's like we have this kind of bond, you know. This could be great, Michael. What do you think?"

He didn't say anything. He was still frowning. He got up to walk to the stove and refilled his coffee cup. Carrie Ann clenched her hands in her lap and watched and waited. Michael took his time adding honey to his coffee. Finally, he sat back down and sipped from the cup.

"And what about Rorie?" he asked.

"Well, she is my kid. She has to come with me."

"Hmm. And what about the state welfare people, aren't they kind of keeping an eye on you? I don't want social workers sniffing around here."

"David, the social worker, came to visit a couple of times when I first moved into the O'Connors', but he seems pretty cool. I could tell him I'm your housekeeper. I don't think they're going to be bugging me, as long as I stay out of trouble."

Michael sighed. "I don't know, Carrie Ann, I'm not really the domestic type. And I'm not really into kids."

"I could keep her out of the way, Michael. She's not a noisy kid, and she doesn't make a big mess or anything. She goes to bed early, and she's been listening to rock-and-roll her whole life, so she doesn't like wake up and cry or something when she hears the band practice. We could have the room over in the front corner. It only needs to be cleaned out, and I can do that."

Michael frowned again. "That's my antique storage room. For some stuff I'm not using right now, but I don't want to get rid of."

"We could move it to the other room, where you keep your piano. You could have a music room with beautiful antiques in it. There's space in there if everything was organized better."

"I've been planning to keep the upstairs for me—that's why I made the guys build their rooms downstairs."

Carrie Ann dropped her eyes, blinking back tears. This was not going well. She should have known. Now what would she do? Maybe she could go back and beg Johnny to let her stay. She really hadn't even tried yesterday, just accepted his edict and walked away. Maybe he had cooled down.

Then Michael surprised her. "I'll think about it," he said. "I don't know, Carrie Ann. I don't know if I'm into having an old lady, never mind the kid. But I like you, and I want to help, since the friendly neighborhood asshole jerked the rug out from under you. Let me think about it." He took a slug from his coffee cup and stood. "I have to go teach a class in a couple of hours. If you want to wait, I can give you a ride. You don't want to do that walk twice in one morning, and the second time uphill, right?"

Carrie Ann nodded and dabbed at her eyes with a Kleenex she had found in the back pocket of her jeans.

Michael reached down and cupped her breast in his hand. "How about we get a little, baby? You liked that yesterday, huh?"

Michael squeezed her breast gently, and she stood, letting him pull her to him. That familiar surge of yearning and pleasure began in her crotch and swept through her body, and she opened her mouth and widened her legs and pressed herself against him.

Carrie Ann smiled as she rinsed a frying pan and found a place to wedge it between the overcrowded dish drainer and the windowsill. There—a quick wipe of the counter, and the kitchen looked a hundred percent better than it had when she got here this morning. This was the first time she had washed dishes at Michael's, and she doubted it would be the last. She had the distinct impression that Michael was more kindly disposed to her moving in than he had been an hour ago. Their lovemaking kept getting better. How could anybody not want to be able to do that every day? She hung up the dish rag and went back to his bedroom.

Michael was dressing for his yoga class. He stood in front of a full-length mirror set in an intricately carved dark-wood frame as he tied a pale-blue band around his forehead. What a beautiful body he had, Carrie Ann thought, watching him pull his long blond hair into a rubber band at the back and tighten the drawstring on his baggy white pants. Michael leaned forward to smooth an eyebrow, turned sideways to take one last look at himself, adjusted the gathers on his pants, and reached for his jacket. "Okay, let's hit the road."

"Wow, I've never seen you dressed for a yoga class before."

"We don't usually get together on those days. And something else you hadn't seen—the inside of my VW van. I don't like to get all cleaned up for class and then ride a bike and get messed up." He glanced over at the sink as they passed through the kitchen. "The kitchen looks nice," he said. Carrie Ann had hoped for a more enthusiastic response, but at least he had noticed.

His van was slow to start—"I don't drive it enough, I like the bike better"—but eventually it chugged its way up the steep driveway and onto the road that led to the O'Connors'.

The closer they got, the more uptight Carrie Ann became. She was afraid to ask Michael again about moving in, but she hated to go back without an answer. To her relief, he pulled off the road across from the O'Connors' driveway and turned to face her. Carrie Ann sat very still, waiting for him to say something.

"Okay, Carrie Ann, I have thought about it, and here's my offer. We can try this out for a while and see what happens. You can come down and set up the front bedroom for you and Rorie. You gotta keep her out of my stuff. I don't want her messing up my antiques, so we'll move them to the piano room, like you said. And I want you to keep your stuff in that room too; I'm not into rearranging things in my room right now. But that's just the material part." He looked away. "I like you, Carrie Ann, but I don't really want an old lady. I don't want somebody on my back all the time, expecting me to be something or do something I don't want to do. The deal is, if you want to come live at my place, you do your thing, and I do mine."

Carrie Ann was silent. Exactly what did that mean? She hardly knew how to think about it. She'd only ever lived with one man,

Rorie's dad, and that had been as part of a houseful of people. Besides, it hadn't lasted long.

But she wanted to live with Michael, and if it had to start like this, that was the way it would be. A wave of optimism lifted her spirits. She knew she could change his mind and find a place in his life.

She smiled. "Thank you, Michael. I'll do my best to make you happy that I'm there. I promise Rorie won't be a problem. She really is a good kid. And I forgot to mention—you know I get food stamps and welfare, right? So you don't have to support me or anything."

"Great." He smiled back at her. "That helps. But here's another thing. I won't expect you to pay rent, but you're in charge of the house, okay? You said you want to do that kind of stuff, and the guys sure aren't going to, so I guess that's your job."

"Oh, I will, Michael. I promise I'll keep everything clean, and I'll cook and maybe even plant some vegetables. I really learned a lot from Jerilyn the last couple of months." Thinking of Jerilyn sobered her. "I guess I better get down there and start packing. I don't have much stuff. Alexis could probably fit it all into her Bug. Wow, this is cool." She leaned across the seat and kissed him. "So I can come down today? I could start cleaning up that front room and help you move stuff. What time do you get home from yoga class?"

Michael's smile faded. "Today, huh. I guess so. If we're going to do it, no use waiting around. And it sounds like Johnny wants you gone." He shook his head. "I hope this works out. This is a test, now, a probation kind of thing, okay? We're just trying this."

"I know, I know, Michael. If it doesn't work out, I'll go look for another place to live."

But she would make sure that it did work out, she thought, waving goodbye as Michael steered the van back onto the road. Excited and energized, she turned down the O'Connors' driveway to go and pack for her new life.

"Don't worry, Kathryn, it's going to be okay. This could be what I've been waiting for. I wish you could meet Michael, he is so cool. Maybe I can start learning yoga. I never made it to any of his classes before, because the only time we were ever together we—well, we had other things to do." She giggled and glanced over at Alexis, who was sitting by the window sewing beads onto a leather vest. Rorie lay on the floor next to her, scribbling vigorously in a coloring book.

"I hope you know what you're getting into, honey," Kathryn replied, her voice sounding very far away over the long-distance line. "Living with a man is hard enough but living with a rock band is something else."

"I know, Kathryn, I've been hanging around with you guys for years, and lately with Blend. I know what it's like—lots of noise and lots of work. But it's fun, too, and Michael's house is really groovy. The guys are downstairs, and we'll be upstairs. It'll be like we have our own place, me and Michael and Rorie. There's even a garden, but it's kind of neglected, and I want to get it all weeded and planted. Oh, I wish you could come and visit, Kathryn, and meet my friends here and see how beautiful this place is. Maybe when I get a little more settled you could come and stay with Michael and me."

"Take it easy, honey, first you have to get used to living with Michael and have him get used to living with you and Rorie. He's never had a kid, huh?"

Carrie Ann frowned. Actually, she never had thought to ask him that. "Not that I know of. But you know how lovable Rorie is, and she's really no trouble. I'm sure he's gonna love it. I'm going to make sure he does! I feel like I really know how to run a house, Kathryn, after all the great training I've had from you and now Jerilyn. It's going to be outta sight."

Kathryn sighed. "I wish I could be there, or else that they would let you come back home."

"I know, I miss everybody, and especially you. But there must be a reason this all happened, Kathryn. Maybe it's karma— it was meant to happen so I would be able to meet Michael."

"I hope it works out, honey. I'll call Mimi when she gets home from work tonight and let her know what's going on, and you keep in touch, hear? I'm glad you got that post office box, and we can reach you no matter where you live."

"Okay, thanks, Kathryn. Love to everybody. I'll talk to you soon."

Carrie Ann hung up the phone and turned to grin at Alexis, who responded with a sideways look and an arched eyebrow.

"I hope you're not getting too hung up on Michael. You know, we did warn you about him. He's not exactly husband material."

"We'll see. Anyway, it's like a great weight has come off me. It was really a bummer, having to keep up this whole front. Now I can live my life, and not have to worry about Johnny O'Connor freaking out."

Rorie looked up from her coloring. "What did Uncle Johnny do, Mommy? I didn't see him freak out. But he was kind of mad."

"He was mad," Carrie Ann replied. "And that's what I mean by freaking out. That's why you and I are going to move down to Michael's house, because Uncle Johnny is mad at Mommy. But Mommy is a big girl, and Uncle Johnny can't tell her what to do anymore."

"Now is Michael gonna tell Mommy what to do?"

Alexis and Carrie Ann laughed.

"He better not try!" Alexis said. "And Mommy better not let him."

"Don't worry, it'll be okay." It seemed to Carrie Ann that she had to keep reassuring everyone, but she herself had no doubts. A bubbly surge of optimism filled her, and she jumped to her feet. "I'm ready—are you ready, Alexis? Your back seat and trunk are both stuffed full of our junk, so whenever you're up for it . . .."

They were settled into the Volkswagen, with Rorie perched on Carrie Ann's lap, when Tom the drummer appeared. That's right, Carrie Ann thought—this was Saturday morning, and Tom was off from his job at the chicken farm. He leaned on the door and bent down to look in Carrie Ann's open window.

"Hey, Carrie Ann, hey girl, what's this I hear? You're moving out?"

"Yeah, Tom, old Johnny freaked on me yesterday. But everything is working out groovy. I'm going down to Michael Wharton's." She smiled. "Sorry. I'm moving in with your rival band—Pineapple Jam."

Tom snorted. "Shit, I ain't worried about that. But I sure will miss seeing you around, foxy lady. And you too, little chickadee." He reached in to pat Rorie's cheek.

Suddenly, Carrie Ann was filled with sadness at the thought of leaving this place, where she had found her footing in a period of confusion and dislocation. She reached up to plant a quick kiss on Tom's bearded face. Alexis started the Volkswagen, and Carrie Ann and Rorie waved goodbye to Tom as the Bug turned onto the driveway. Carrie Ann looked up at the kitchen window. There was no sign of Jerilyn. Carrie Ann regretted her lack of courage. She had not even gone into the kitchen this morning, just stuffed her belongings into pillowcases and hauled it all down to Alexis's car. She should have gone looking for Jerilyn to say goodbye. Jerilyn had been her friend and had even helped her spend time with Michael. Jerilyn couldn't help it if her old man was uptight. Carrie Ann blinked away tears as they rode down the hill to Michael's house, and hugged Rorie for comfort. I will get hold of Jerilyn soon, she promised herself.

And for the first time since Michael had said she could move in, she worried that she might be giving up something that she would later regret having lost.

Chapter Fifteen

Rorie dipped an old toothbrush in the bucket of soapy water at her mother's feet and applied herself to a corner of the woodwork.

"Look, Mommy, I got off lots of dirt."

"Good girl! Thank you for helping." Carrie Ann dipped her own rag in the bucket, then reached as high as she could on the door frame. Rorie's participation in the cleaning session probably wouldn't last long, she thought, and might not accomplish much, but how cool to be doing this mother-and-daughter thing in their new home. Carrie Ann was feeling very domestic. Already this morning she had started a batch of bread, now rising under a clean dish towel on the kitchen table. Breakfast was done and the dishes washed, and downstairs the guys were jamming. Michael was with them, and she assumed he was singing, though she could not hear him through the noise of drums and electric guitars.

And now Carrie Ann was cleaning the woodwork in the room where Rorie slept. Actually, it was kind of Carrie Ann's room too, with all her stuff stashed in here. Her stuff, but not herself, she thought with a satisfied smile. She'd been nervous, at first, not sure whether she would be sleeping with Michael or whether the rule about keeping her things in Rorie's room also meant he wanted her to sleep in there. But, limp and satiated after sex the first night, she had simply dozed off beside him, and without discussion both seemed to take for granted that she would continue to sleep in Michael's bed.

She would have to figure out a way to get some furniture for Rorie's room. Their things were stored in a stack of cardboard boxes covered with a piece of fabric. Two single mattresses and an old bedside stand had been stored there when she moved in last week, and Michael had let her keep a nice floor lamp and some brocade-covered cushions when they moved the rest of his stuff to the third bedroom. Carrie Ann had bought a couple of Indian bedspreads at a store in Paia and filled an empty juice bottle with croton cuttings that Michael said would root and grow into new plants. Set on a little shelf attached to the wall in one corner of the room, the crotons' colorful leaves gave the room a bright tropical look and reminded her of the time she had first seen such leaves outside her hotel room window in Kahului.

Not so long ago, she thought. And now here she was, no longer feeling stranded on a strange island but as if she herself were beginning to put out roots. She hummed along with the tune Pineapple Jam was playing downstairs. They weren't as good as Blend, and certainly not as good as Red Dog, but they were not bad, and Michael said he was sure he could shape them up. He really knew a lot about music. One day he had played Mozart for her on the piano in the other room. She was in awe of this ability, having no musical training herself, though she also had no real appreciation for classical music. She could find no underlying structure in all those intricately intertwined notes. Rock-and-roll made more sense to her. Michael said he was bored with this old classical stuff and interested in seeing where he could take a rock band, especially with him singing lead and playing the electric keyboard that should be delivered any day.

Carrie Ann was getting to know the members of the band. There was Weed, who actually kind of looked like a weed, with scrawny limbs, a pockmarked face, and straggly hair. He played bass and was around a lot; she wasn't sure what, if anything, he did to earn a living. Roland, the drummer, and Timothy, the lead guitar player, were construction workers who left early each weekday and stopped to surf on the way home, arriving in time for dinner and then disappearing to play music. They were all sweet to her and to Rorie, if not very helpful around the kitchen. Being the only woman in the household was fun, and Carrie Ann was so energized by her new role that she didn't mind in the least taking care of all these guys. Though they were about her age, she felt motherly toward them. It was as if they were forming a little family here, with Michael as the wise patriarch, Carrie Ann the warm and soothing mother figure, and Rorie the darling baby sister.

The three guys had shared a house in Paia, but the landlord had evicted them in favor of his son and daughter-in-law. Fortunately for them, this had happened at a time when Michael was interested in managing the band, and they had been able to move in downstairs.

One other band member, Keone, lived up in the village behind the store. A big, mellow Hawaiian guy, Keone was married to his high-school sweetheart, Lanihuli. They had a little boy a few months older than Rorie, with another baby on the way. Keone brought Lanihuli and little Jesse down to practice sometimes. The two children played well together, so it looked like Rorie would have a friend, and Carrie Ann liked Lanihuli, placid and smiling in pregnancy.

Things were working out great. Carrie Ann had spent a full month's worth of food stamps stocking the kitchen with everything from spices to whole-wheat flour. She enjoyed the creative aspect of feeding all these people and the praise the guys gave as they wolfed down the food. The three musicians loved Rorie, and Michael at least was tolerating her. Thus far, Rorie had been good about staying out of his room.

Carrie Ann had worried that the move to Michael's might cause Rorie's night terrors to start again. But Rorie seemed upset about the move only on the first morning, when she woke up alone in a new place. Carrie Ann bolted from Michael's bed in response to her crying and thereafter made herself get up at first light to take Rorie into the kitchen for a quiet breakfast while everyone else slept.

Living by a child's schedule was not as easy here as it had been at the O'Connors', where Johnny's job and Stevie's school dictated household hours. Here the band practiced later, and visitors were in and out of the house. Carrie Ann had met more people since moving here than she had living for two months at the O'Connors'. As the band and various visitors sat late around the table in the center of the living room, Carrie Ann's eyes would grow heavy. Long before everyone else was ready to crash, she crept off to sleep. When he came to bed, Michael would rouse her with a hand between her legs, and she would be awake again until near dawn, and time to get up with Rorie. Life at Michael's was exhilarating but exhausting.

Still, she was managing to get a lot done around here, running on a stream of ecstatic energy that made sleep almost irrelevant. She stood back to survey the door frame and dropped her rag into the bucket. That was enough cleaning for today, time to finish the bread and think about lunch, and maybe go down and listen to music later on. As she had with Red Dog and Blend, she liked standing in the corner, moving in time to the music.

The phone rang. Carrie Ann wiped her hands on her shorts and went to answer it.

"Carrie Ann, it's Mimi! How's your new house?"

"Mimi, it's wonderful to hear your voice! My new house is great, and so is the man that comes with it. Did your roommate tell you I called?"

"Yeah, eventually. So what about this guy? Is he The One?"

"I sure hope he is—so far so good. I wish you could come and visit us and meet him."

"Actually, that's why I'm calling. I am coming to visit, with Aunt Bea."

"Far fucking out! When? I can't wait!"

"Pretty soon—in two weeks."

Carrie Ann was thrilled. Could things get any better?

"Where are you going to stay? And how did this come about, anyway?"

"Not sure where we're going to stay—Aunt Bea's taking care of everything, and I get to go along for the ride. Lucky, huh? Aunt Bea wants to look around and see if there's some sort of business thing she can do there. She visited Hawaii once years ago and loved it, and now that she's getting this divorce settlement money, she decided she might as well try something outrageous like moving to Hawaii from Georgia. Crazy, huh?"

"I think it's great, and I am so glad you're coming with her. I really miss you."

"I know, I miss you too. I can't believe I get to visit you over there, in Hawaii of all places. What a trip! Rorie must have grown a lot. How is little Sweet Pea?"

"She's fine. She's right here, helping me scrub woodwork. Want to talk to her?"

Rorie took the phone, and after a few brief replies, returned it to her mother. Carrie Ann and Mimi had a lot to talk about, and when at last she hung up, Carrie Ann felt momentarily lost. She could hardly wait to see Mimi, and two weeks seemed a long time away. She missed her friends in San Francisco. On the other hand, if she were to leave Maui, she would miss the people here. She wondered how Jerilyn was doing without her. Carrie Ann had called after she'd been at Michael's a couple of days and apologized to Jerilyn for leaving without saying goodbye. Jerilyn, in turn, had said how sorry she was about Carrie Ann having to move. Stevie missed playing with Rorie, she said, and, while Johnny was still being hardheaded, everyone else was bummed about how things turned out.

But no matter how sad everyone was, the reality was that Carrie Ann had been kicked out of the house, and it was awkward even to talk with Jerilyn on the phone. At least Alexis was still a friend; she had stopped by to take Carrie Ann and Rorie to the Laundromat and the beach in Paia the other day.

Carrie Ann was punching down the bread dough to prepare for its second rising when the music downstairs stopped. A minute later, she heard the motorcycle roar. Where was Michael going? She peered out the kitchen window in time to see the bike turn up the driveway. Why was he always taking off without coming in to say goodbye or tell her where he was going, she wondered, biting her lip. She sighed, then went back to punching the dough.

Four baking loaves were beginning to scent the kitchen when she heard the motorcycle return. Michael carried a passenger, a red-haired man dressed all in purple. When he got off the bike, she saw that he was even taller than Michael, and he had what appeared to be a small conga drum strapped to his back.

Intrigued, Carrie Ann glanced over at Rorie, who was sitting on the living-room floor playing with a toy truck that Lanihuli had given her. Rorie had created something of an obstacle course with odd boxes and kitchen tools and was trying to force the toy truck through a cardboard cylinder left from a roll of waxed paper.

"Honey, I'm going downstairs to listen to music. You come down too if you want to, okay?"

"Okay," Rorie answered without looking up from her play.

Downstairs, the musicians were tuning up, and the tall newcomer was perched on a stool and beating a soft rhythm on his drum. Carrie Ann went to stand by Michael and put her arm around his waist. He glanced down at her and nodded toward the drummer, who bowed in Carrie Ann's direction. "This is Cameron. He's going to sit in with us. His old lady Clarice and her kid will be down in a while. I'll send her upstairs when she gets here. Hey, how about some coffee and sandwiches or something?"

"The bread will be ready pretty soon, if you can wait."

"Far out." He returned her hug briefly, then disengaged himself and went over to fiddle with a knob on one of the speakers. The band's sound soon filled the little shed, and conversation was impossible. Carrie Ann closed her eyes and let her body follow the beat of the drums for a few minutes, only to be called back to reality by Rorie tugging on her hand, wanting lunch.

She was taking the loaves out of the oven when Cameron's old lady Clarice arrived, with her small son on her hip. Clarice was a delicately beautiful black woman dressed, like her old man, in purple. Even little Kikuyu wore a tie-dyed purple T-shirt over his droopy diaper. Rorie was enthralled with the toddler and began leading him around the living room, trying to teach him the names of various objects.

Clarice settled herself at the kitchen table. Carrie Ann thought she looked tired. Clarice dug through her shoulder bag and pulled out a jar of artichoke hearts and a small package of bacon. "You mind if I cook up some of this bacon on your stove?" she asked.

"Sure, go right ahead. Here's a frying pan," Carrie Ann said. "I'm going to be slicing up this bread as soon as it cools, and I'm making tuna sandwiches, if you want to wait and have a sandwich."

"I think I need to feed Kikuyu—he hasn't had anything to eat for a while, and he must be getting hungry." She popped open the jar of artichoke hearts. "Come here, Kiku honey, Mama's got something for you."

To Carrie Ann's amazement, the baby actually seemed to enjoy eating artichoke hearts. She was not surprised to see Rorie shake her head and back away when Clarice offered her a bite. Carrie Ann couldn't imagine feeding such a thing to a little kid. She shrugged and turned back to mixing mayonnaise into a bowlful of tuna.

By the time the sandwiches and coffee were done, Clarice had fed Kikuyu several crispy strips of bacon. Rorie, who loved bacon, was happy to accept a share. Carrie Ann went downstairs to tell

Michael the food was ready, and a few minutes later the musicians trooped upstairs to help themselves. Carrie Ann handed Michael his sandwich and a cup of coffee.

Her bread was a hit. Michael finished his sandwich and sliced another piece off the loaf Carrie Ann had set on the table.

"Have some more bread, you guys, Carrie Ann just baked it," Michael said, spreading peanut butter on his slice. "Honey, how about getting us a coffee refill?"

Carrie Ann glowed. He had called her "honey," right in front of everybody.

Two joints and another loaf of bread later, Michael led the band downstairs. The music started up again. Carrie Ann surveyed her domain. Both the kitchen and living room tables were littered with coffee cups and plates, breadcrumbs, and smears of honey. On the mattress in the corner, Clarice lay with Kikuyu. She had been nursing him after eating her own lunch and had fallen asleep with her son. In the kitchen, the empty bread pans waited to be washed. The last, lonely loaf remained, and Carrie Ann thought she'd better stash that somewhere if she wanted to have bread for tomorrow.

"Rorie, how about helping Mommy carry coffee cups to the kitchen?"

Rorie looked annoyed. "Oh, okay," she said with exaggerated patience. Still holding her toy truck in one hand, she picked up a mug in the other and headed for the kitchen. Carrie Ann could see that Rorie would not be much help. In fact, it looked like she was on her own here. Gathering dishes from the living-room table, she began to think about what she should cook for dinner.

She was about finished washing dishes when the phone rang. It was Jerilyn.

"Carrie Ann, the social worker called," she said. "I said you weren't here and got his phone number so you can call him back."

Carrie Ann gripped the phone tighter, her heartbeat quickening. "Oh shit. I've been trying not to think about him. Did he say anything about coming to visit?"

"No, but it's been a few weeks, so I wouldn't be surprised if that's what he had in mind. I didn't tell him that you moved, just said you weren't here."

Carrie Ann took a deep breath. "Thanks, Jerilyn. What's the phone number?"

She went back to wiping down the kitchen counters. Of course, she had known this day would come. She really should have called David to tell him she was moving, but she was hoping he would figure she was fine and leave her alone. These people had way too much power in her life. What business was it of theirs if she lived with Michael? It wasn't hurting Rorie, and who knew where it might lead? She was making a place for herself in Michael's life, helping him succeed, and soon, she hoped, he would realize how important she was to him.

Still, the reality was that she had to make this social worker happy if she wanted to keep her child. And, if things didn't work out with Michael, she definitely wanted to be able to take Rorie home to San Francisco. Maui was great, but how could she stay without Michael?

David might not approve of her living with Michael if he knew they were sleeping together. But she did have a separate room and a bed. She had decided when she moved down here that if she had to explain things to David, she would tell him she was working as a housekeeper in lieu of paying rent. It would have to do; what other choice did she have? And she needed to somehow persuade him to visit when things were quiet around here. She couldn't imagine David showing up on a day like this, when the band was raucous downstairs, and the air was thick with marijuana smoke.

She waited for the few moments of quiet when the band took a break, then dragged the phone as far as its cord would allow; it was just long enough to reach into Rorie's room. She shut the door so no one would interrupt, then dialed David's number.

Sure enough, David wanted to do a home visit. And he was not at all happy that she hadn't informed him about moving. "I hope you realize, Carrie Ann, that Judge Yoshioka was pretty upset by what happened to Rorie. If you had family here, it might be different, but you're all alone with her. The judge specifically said he wants me to keep a close eye on you folks. I have to know where you are, and you can't be moving around to new places without letting me know about it, understand?"

"I am sorry, David, I thought it would be okay. I'm sorry I didn't call you. It was kind of sudden, and I've been getting used to this job and getting the place cleaned up."

"So why did you move?"

"Johnny and I weren't getting along," she said, "and then I heard that Michael had a big house and needed a housekeeper, so I applied. I figured it's only for a while, until we can go back to California. I can't get a regular job, with Rorie to take care of, and I don't know where else I could live or how I could afford to rent a place on my own."

"I need to come see the place. I'll be in Haiku tomorrow morning. How does that sound?"

Carrie Ann agreed, trying not to sound relieved. Tomorrow would be perfect. Michael had a yoga class in the morning, Roland and Timothy would be working, and she could ask Weed to stay out of the way.

Now all she had to do was make sure the house looked acceptable. The kitchen was almost clean, though of course she would have to whip it back into shape after dinner. As soon as Clarice and Kikuyu woke up and wandered downstairs, she started on the living room. She made sure there was nothing of hers visible in Michael's room and put Rorie's room in order, with a couple of extra pillows on the bed that was supposed to be hers. There was no time to bake a treat to impress David, but she had that one loaf stashed away.

The place looked as good as it could, she thought the next morning as Michael headed up the driveway. She had cut bright red flowers from the pagoda plants by the front step and filled vases for Rorie's bedroom and for the kitchen table, and now she started a fresh pot of coffee. She dressed Rorie in one of the outfits she had made on Jerilyn's sewing machine, and when she saw David's car come down the drive, Carrie Ann steered her daughter to the round table in the living room and set her up with kid scissors and a magazine someone had left at the Laundromat. Rorie loved cutting out pictures; it would occupy her while Carrie Ann showed David their room, and some bread and honey after that should keep her little mouth too full for any embarrassing four-year-old comments about where Mommy slept.

Before they sat down for coffee and bread, Carrie Ann briefly opened the door to Michael's music room, filled with his antique collection. It seemed to impress David, as did the view of her little vegetable garden from the kitchen window.

"Well, Carrie Ann," David said, spreading butter on a slice of bread, "this is a great old house, and it looks like you're doing a good job as housekeeper. I would like to meet Mr. Wharton. When do you expect him home?"

"I'm not sure. He teaches this yoga class in Paia, and I never know when he'll be back."

David frowned, but his expression changed as he chewed a bite of bread. "Ummm, good bread. Maybe you should go into business as a baker. Well. I must say, I am not as happy about your situation here as I was when you lived at the O'Connors' in a family-type setting. Maybe I can meet Mr. Wharton the next time I visit."

Carrie Ann could do nothing but agree that it would be great for David and Mr. Wharton to get together, though she fervently hoped that would never happen. Michael would not be pleased if he had to deal with a social worker.

"And I think it might be good if you give me a call every week, for an update. If I don't hear from you, I'm going to be wondering what's going on, and I'll have to start making unannounced visits. Keep in touch."

The thought of David showing up without warning gave her chills. God knew what he might walk in on. "I'll call," she promised. "Like every Friday or something, how's that?"

She walked David to his car, smiled and waved as he left, and congratulated herself on getting through this visit, at least. She would deal with the next one when the time came, and if she called him often enough, maybe she'd never have to deal with a visit from David again.

Chapter Sixteen

The sun shone dimly through beige silk drapes at Michael's windows. Carrie Ann forced herself to keep her eyes open and turned over to squint at the clock. She had to get up. Rorie was probably awake, and Mimi and Aunt Bea would be here soon. They had arrived yesterday, gone straight to some big hotel near Lahaina, and today were coming to visit. The thought of seeing Mimi perked her up, even though Carrie Ann would have liked to sleep in. Sitting, she glanced over at Michael. As usual, he slept on the edge of the bed, his back turned to her. He rolled into that position each night after they had sex and remained there until morning. He was not a very cuddly person, Carrie Ann thought wistfully.

Rorie was indeed awake, still sitting on her bed and playing with a Mr. Potato Head toy Carrie Ann's mom had sent her. Carrie Ann had to give her mother credit for that one—Rorie had been playing with this toy for days. Carrie Ann reminded herself once again to write a thank-you letter. Somehow, she never could find time to write letters these days.

The kitchen was still a mess from last night. Carrie Ann had been too stoned and sleepy to deal with the dishes, and as usual, no one else had bothered. She couldn't have it looking like this when Mimi and Aunt Bea came. She'd better get to work.

She dressed herself and Rorie, put a pot of water on the stove for oatmeal, and started cleaning. By the time Michael and the guys appeared one by one looking for coffee, she had the dishes done. And when a sleek white rental car rolled tentatively down the steep driveway, Carrie Ann was already outside, cutting flowers and foliage to make an arrangement for the living-room table.

"Carrie Ann!" Mimi leaned out the passenger window, waving enthusiastically. Carrie Ann set her flowers on the grass and ran to hug her friend. Aunt Bea climbed out of the driver's side and came to offer her own hug. Carrie Ann had met Mimi's aunt only once before, not long after she had moved into Mimi's apartment on Haight Street, when Aunt Bea came to visit and took them out to dinner at a little place in North Beach. Aunt Bea had not changed, except that her platinum-blonde hair had grown longer. There was a family resemblance between the two—both Mimi and her aunt were tall and pretty, with long legs, small waists, and lush breasts. But Mimi's shiny brown hair hung straight and was so long that she had to flip it out of the way when she sat down. Aunt Bea's shoulder-length hair was carefully curled. Her eyes were lined, her lips painted, and her lashes artificially thick. Today she wore a gauzy white gown that looked something like a toga, with gold clasps at the shoulders and a gold belt at her slender waist, with gold sandals on her feet. Carrie Ann was relieved to see that she had not worn her diamonds. That would have been a bit much, around here.

Mimi, on the other hand, had shed her San Francisco silk dresses and stockings and wore a crocheted halter top and cut-off jeans, with no makeup. She reached into the car to pull out her sandals, put them on, and looked around.

"Wow, Carrie Ann, this place is beautiful. What a score!"

"Isn't it great? Come on, I'll show you around. Let me get Rorie down here." She turned to call up the kitchen stairs. Rorie came slowly, peering suspiciously through the stair railing, but let herself be enveloped in Mimi's hugs. Mimi squatted so she was at eye level with Rorie, reminding the child about visits to Golden Gate Park and the time they rode a trolley car, and soon Rorie was smiling. Rorie had not seen Mimi for several months, Carrie Ann realized, a long time in the life of the child. Acquaintance renewed, Rorie tagged along, holding Mimi's hand, as her mother gave the visitors a tour.

"This is my garden—well, it was here before I came, but no one else has been working in it lately. I cleared this space over here, still have a lot to do. And see those little green sprouts? Those are green beans. Rorie helped me plant them, didn't you, honey?"

They walked down toward the lowest point of the property, where water sometimes ran in a narrow stream when there was heavy rain. The previous owners had planted a banana orchard here. "It needs a lot of work," Carrie Ann told them. "The guys in Pineapple Jam—that's Michael's band—were supposed to be weeding around the bananas as part of their contribution to living here, but you know how those rock-and-roll guys are." Mimi joined in her laughter and began to tell her the latest crazy story about Red Dog and Duke's efforts to get them gigs.

A wave of homesickness swept over Carrie Ann as Mimi talked. But she could see that Aunt Bea was mesmerized by the beauty of this place, and Carrie Ann felt a certain proprietary pride about this island she had only recently discovered herself. Wishing again that she could be in two places at once, she grabbed the flowers she had dropped on the lawn and led her guests up the back steps and into the kitchen. Michael stood from his place at the table, gorgeous in a faded blue work shirt that matched his eyes. Carrie Ann took his arm, beaming. When Aunt Bea offered her hand in greeting, he bowed over it, then waved toward the living room.

"Why don't we sit in the living room, ladies? Carrie Ann, maybe we could have coffee in there."

Aunt Bea raised one eyebrow and looked at Carrie Ann.

"I'll help you, Carrie Ann," Mimi said.

"You can make the flower arrangement," Carrie Ann replied, smiling. A few minutes later the two of them set full mugs on the table before Michael and Aunt Bea. Carrie Ann passed out slices of fresh-baked banana bread and scooted Rorie's chair closer to the table so she could eat without dribbling crumbs everywhere.

"Michael has been telling me about this house. Quite an interesting history," Aunt Bea said. "And what are these wonderful red flowers?" She leaned forward to sniff the bouquet. "They smell like—oh, I guess vanilla with cinnamon added, wouldn't you say?"

"Michael says the flowers are called pagoda plant, and they were here when he bought the place. But they don't have any scent. It's that leaf that smells sweet. What's it called, Michael?"

"Laua'e. It's a kind of fern, though it doesn't look much like other ferns," Michael replied.

"Michael knows a lot about plants," Carrie Ann said. "Michael knows all kinds of stuff about Maui."

"And what do you do for a living, Michael?" Aunt Bea asked.

"I have an income," Michael said curtly. Carrie Ann had never dared to ask where Michael got his money. She was a little embarrassed that Aunt Bea had, and Michael did not sound pleased to be asked. But Aunt Bea smiled and went back to admiring the house. After a few more minutes of small talk, Michael drained his coffee cup and stood up.

"I guess I'll take off and let you ladies have a hen party. What are you two going to be doing while you're here?"

"Everything we can fit into five days!" Mimi said.

"We're staying at the Sheraton, and I want to spend some time looking at business opportunities," Bea said. "And we thought we might try to go out to Hana—I hear it's lovely."

"It is that, though it's a long trip, and the road's pretty rough for a nice rental car like that. You'd better start out rested for that drive. Well, have a nice time while you're here. Carrie Ann, are you going to be cooking dinner?"

"We thought we might take Carrie Ann and Rorie with us for the day, and maybe even talk them into spending a few days with us at the hotel," Mimi said.

Carrie Ann looked at Michael. He shrugged. "Sure, whatever works. See you when I see you, Carrie Ann." And he was off, down the back stairs. A moment later, the motorcycle started up.

"Where are we going?" Rorie asked.

"You're going with us, Sweet Pea," Mimi said, grinning as she stood to clear cups from the table. "Carrie Ann, pack up some stuff, and let's hit the road!"

"I think Bea is going to make it into every store on the island before she leaves," Carrie Ann said, shading her eyes against the bright Kaanapali sun to watch her daughter digging in the sand. She stretched out and propped her head against a rolled-up towel so she could keep an eye on Rorie without having to move.

"Yep, my Aunt Bea is one very determined lady," Mimi said. "She's on a mission to figure out what kind of store to open. She used to be a buyer for her friend's boutique in Atlanta, until Uncle Ugly got a promotion and made her quit so she could be a full-time decoration for his executive lifestyle. And of course, there's retail in the blood—Granddaddy had all those stores in Atlanta way back when. I don't know what she's gonna do when it comes to running the thing, though. I can't imagine her sitting in a store all day, and I think she would get bored with the day-to-day management."

"She can always hire someone."

"True." Mimi hoisted her body from her beach towel and sat up. "As long as she finds somebody good and doesn't let herself get ripped off."

"I think your Aunt Bea is too smart to let that happen. How old is she, anyway? She doesn't look that old, except she kind of dresses in that 1950s movie-star way. Anyway, she seems to be pretty hip."

"She's about forty-five, I think. She's lived through a lot, and some of it you wouldn't want to live through—like that creep of a husband. But she and my dad had a really great childhood. Their family owned a farm and raised horses, but they mostly lived in this big house in Atlanta, so they had the best of both worlds. They went to private schools and all that, and their dad owned the furniture stores—they were one of the richest Jewish families in town, even during the Depression. I think Aunt Bea went up to New York for a couple of years when she was younger, did some modeling. And then, of course, she married Uncle Creepo, and they had two kids, my cousins, Ben and Rachel. They're both in college on the East Coast."

"She's really cool. You're lucky to have somebody like that in your family. I've had fun these last two days, and I sure wish you didn't have to go."

"Me too." Mimi stared thoughtfully toward the ocean. Waves foamed against the shore. A scattering of tourists walked the beach or splashed in Kaanapali's turquoise waters. "It's beautiful here. You know what I've been thinking? I really like this place, and I've about had it with those lawyers I work for. What if Aunt Bea really does do this business thing, and she opens a store someplace, maybe in Lahaina? What if I moved over here to run the store with her?"

Carrie Ann sat up straight. "Yes! What a great idea! Oh Mimi, do you think she would go for it?"

Mimi shrugged her sunburned shoulders, winced, and carefully lowered her bikini top's straps. She opened a bottle of suntan lotion and rubbed her arms with coconut-scented cream. "Why not? I've worked as a legal secretary for five years, and I can do bookkeeping, type letters, and keep things organized—what else do you need to run an office? Of course, we'd both be learning the retail business together. And I could spend time in the shop, too. That would be kind of fun. I'm going to talk to her tonight. Maybe she'll have a better idea of what she wants to do when she gets back from visiting stores." She grinned at Carrie Ann. "Wouldn't that be righteous? What a gas, both of us living here. Man, I hope this works out."

"You know, Mimi, I've been wanting to go back to San Francisco since I got here, but with things working out so well with Michael, if you moved here, I might change my mind," Carrie Ann said, returning Mimi's grin.

The sun's heat soon drove them back to the hotel room. This would be the second night Carrie Ann and Rorie had spent here. The first day, Carrie Ann had taken Mimi and Bea on an Upcountry tour, following the routes she'd learned on Michael's motorcycle. She wished, when they drove by the O'Connors' driveway, that she could take her visitors down to meet Jerilyn and Alexis and see where she had begun her life on Maui. But Johnny might be there, so they kept going. Mimi wanted to hear all about the move to Michael's. Aunt Bea listened silently.

From Upcountry, they had driven straight to Kaanapali, winding down the mountainside with its panoramic view of the isthmus that joined Haleakala to West Maui, across the isthmus, and then along the steep cliffs of the Pali. The ride was breathtaking; wherever they looked, the ocean reached from the land's boundary to the world's edge, with the great sunset sky as a backdrop.

Aunt Bea took them out to dinner at the hotel restaurant, the fanciest place Carrie Ann ever had eaten. Carrie Ann and Rorie slept on the sofa bed in the hotel room, listening to the waves murmuring in the darkness, and they all ate breakfast on the balcony overlooking a long white-sand beach. On the horizon, an island floated on an endless ocean. Another side of Maui that she had never seen, Carrie Ann thought.

They set out for a drive the next day, past Haiku on the way to Hana. Michael had been promising to take her to Hana, but they'd not gotten to it yet, partly because he wanted to go on the bike, and that meant there was no room for Rorie. Now Carrie Ann realized that this wasn't the best way to spend the day with a four-year-old, anyway—the road's deep curves along jungle-clad cliffs made Rorie carsick. Bea and Mimi were very nice about it, but Carrie Ann felt guilty when they had to turn around before they were even halfway to Hana.

As long as they were driving by, they stopped off to see how things were going at the house. Carrie Ann grabbed a couple of clean sundresses for herself and Rorie while Bea and Mimi watched the band set up to rehearse on the front porch. Then they headed for the little towns of Kahului and Wailuku, where Bea seemed determined to check out the contents of every store on Market Street. She stopped often to talk with the store owners. By afternoon, Rorie was cranky, and Mimi and Carrie Ann were happy to be dropped off at the hotel with nothing to do but go down to the beach while Aunt Bea explored Lahaina.

Now they'd had enough sun, especially Rorie, who was looking decidedly pink. They trudged back through the sand, rinsed off under the cold outdoor shower, and went back to the room.

Aunt Bea arrived as the sun was setting. She carried little white cartons of Chinese food, still hot after the short drive from Lahaina, and a cold bottle of pink Chablis. They dined on fried rice, beef broccoli, and lemon chicken, sitting on the balcony as the clouds grew pink and silver waves lapped the shore. Rorie finished her dinner and wandered in to sit on the carpet and play with the Tinker Toys Willie had sent with Mimi.

"My goodness, I was hungry," Aunt Bea said at last, pushing her paper plate to one side and propping her feet up on the balcony railing. "That was certainly a busy day."

"So did you learn anything useful?" Mimi asked.

Aunt Bea nodded. "Yes, I think I did. For one thing, Lahaina is definitely the place to be. We got a pretty good look at Makawao and Paia the other day, and I don't see much potential there. Wailuku is busy—though I think Kahului is going to kill it—but they are both bread-and-butter sort of places, where the locals shop. Somehow they don't seem like towns where a newcomer like me could get a foothold. But Lahaina—well, I can see all sorts of opportunities over here. I think this tourism thing's going to grow and grow, so the question becomes, what do you sell to tourists?"

"What do you think that will be?" Mimi asked.

Aunt Bea frowned. "That's the part I'm not sure about. I'm accepting suggestions, if anyone has one."

"Michael says people always need to eat and wear clothes," Carrie Ann said.

"And what does Carrie Ann say?" Bea asked.

"Uh, well, I hadn't really thought about it. I guess Michael is right; he usually is pretty on top of things."

"That may be," Aunt Bea said. "But I would like to see Carrie Ann think for herself. Seems to me the whole time we've been together, practically everything you've had to say has started out, 'Michael says.' I'm a bit worried about you, honey, giving up all your power to a man."

"What do you mean?" Carrie Ann laughed nervously. "I don't know that I have any power, anyway."

"Well now, that's exactly what I mean. You girls are awfully young—I know it doesn't seem that way to you, but you are. And by the time you get to my age, I hope you've not had to learn the hard way, as I did, to save something of yourself for yourself, because you never know when you will have no one else to depend on. It's all very well to want a man. Heaven knows I certainly did, and all my friends did, and still do. But I hate to see you submerge yourself, become sort of an ego sponge soaking up the overflow from some man's psyche. You got to walk that lonesome valley by yourself, girl, so you better be ready to hike."

"I don't really do that well on my own," Carrie Ann said. "I feel like I'm marking time, waiting for a man who wants me to share his trip. Isn't it a woman's job to help a man succeed? Now I've found Michael, for the first time I think I've found somebody worth following. I really love him, and I think I can be his lady. But how can you be someone's lady and not—what did you say? Give up your power?"

Bea shrugged. "That's a tough question, honey. A lot of it depends on the man. My husband certainly wasn't interested in sharing power, and he would do just about anything to get me back under his thumb when I tried to get out. Michael looks to me like somebody who wants to be the boss, and he does seem to attract followers." Bea laughed. "I bet you didn't even notice this. When we stopped off at the house this morning? The band was playing out in the yard, and we stayed to listen awhile."

Mystified, Carrie Ann nodded.

"Did you see what that one skinny little guy was doing during the break?"

"You mean Weed? Kind of wild hair and bad skin?"

"Yeah, that's the one. There was that one time when they were trying to set up the speakers, and one of the musicians was standing up there by himself, fooling around on his guitar. I didn't notice what the other guys were doing, but Weed was following Michael around, copying his every move. Michael walked to the other side of the lawn to listen from a different place, and Weed walked to the other side of the lawn. Michael crossed his arms and stroked his chin, and Weed crossed his arms and stroked his chin. Then Michael took his shirt off and tossed it over his shoulder, and I swear, Weed took his shirt off and tossed it over his shoulder!" Bea laughed again. "I tell you, it was amazing. That man certainly has charisma."

Carrie Ann didn't know whether to be proud or embarrassed. She knew Michael was a leader, someone to whom people were drawn. Other women eyed him all the time, and men came over just to hang out and hear what he had to say. But somehow, the idea of Weed mimicking him like that seemed slightly ridiculous. A phrase came to her mind, one she had heard her father use: Big fish in a small pond.

Bea leaned over to pour herself another glass of Chablis. "I don't mean to put down your sweetheart, honey, but I know men. Michael doesn't look to me like a good long-term bet. If I were you, I'd spend some of my energy trying to build up some independence for myself. Who else do you have that you could call on, right here on Maui, if something went wrong?"

This line of discussion was starting to bother Carrie Ann. Who was Aunt Bea to say whether Michael was a good old man for her, on the basis of a couple of brief meetings?

"I could call Alexis, or . . ." Her voice trailed off as she ran through a list of names in her mind. She was no longer welcome at Johnny and Jerilyn's house, she hadn't heard from Chuckie since that day he saw her with Michael, she had no idea how to get hold of Emily, and she would just as soon not have to call either her lawyer, Rick, or David, the social worker. Maybe she could walk up to Lanihuli's house in an emergency. But now that she thought about it, there really wasn't anyone else.

"Sounds to me like you need to get out some," Mimi said. "Maybe if you didn't stay down at Michael's all the time, went out and met some more people, that would be good."

Now Mimi was picking on her. "You don't know how hard it is when you have a kid, Mimi," Carrie Ann defended herself. "You can't just go places, you have to either take your kid or find somebody to watch her."

"That's true. I'm sorry, I should know what it's like, after seeing you for the past few years doing it all by yourself. But at least in San Francisco, you had friends."

"On the other hand, I couldn't find a man there, right? You know that's what I've always wanted—what I need—to find the right man to be with. And Michael is wonderful. I wish you could get to know him better. He is so cool, and I have learned so much being with him. I think he's really happy to have me around, too. That house looks a hundred percent better since I've been there. I don't know what he would be doing without me, because those musicians aren't much help. And as for friends—well, I guess you're probably right. I do need to make some new friends."

"Mommy!" Rorie came out to the balcony, rubbing one eye and dragging her blanket behind her.

"Looks like somebody's sleepy," Bea observed, sipping her wine.

Carrie Ann was relieved to have an excuse to get up and leave the balcony for a while. She pulled the sofa bed open and helped Rorie into her nightgown. How on earth had the conversation gotten off on this tack? First they were talking about Aunt Bea's business plans, and the next thing she knew, everybody was critiquing Carrie Ann's life and relationship. She knew they meant well, but they did not understand, either her dreams or Michael's good points.

The tooth-brushing ritual was more trying than usual tonight, because Rorie was tired and sunburned. Finally, Carrie Ann picked up her clean but cranky child and carried her out to the balcony.

"Goodnight, sweetheart," Bea said, stretching up to accept a kiss. "Where did you get that pretty nightgown?"

"My mommy made it," Rorie said.

"You made that, Carrie Ann? Even the appliqué?"

"Yes, while we were living at the O'Connors'. Jerilyn had a sewing machine, and I really got a lot done. Well, I better get this baby into bed."

When she returned a few minutes later, Mimi and Bea were deep in conversation. Carrie Ann hesitated—was this private? But Mimi turned to her, and said, "Hey, Carrie Ann, Aunt Bea likes my idea about coming out here to help her. Cool, huh?"

Carrie Ann grinned. "Far out! Oh, I can't wait. When do you all think you'll be here?"

"It's going to be a while," Aunt Bea said. "I have an appointment with a real estate agent in the morning, and we'll see what the rental market is like. Then I have to figure out what to sell in this fabulous new store. And I'm wondering, Carrie Ann, if you might have given me an idea."

"Me? What?"

"A store selling children's clothing. In all the stores we've looked at the past couple of days, have you seen anything that features kids' stuff? And what do grandparents pick up on their vacation trips for their grandkids? And what do little visiting tourists want to wear? Something cute and Hawaiian. Carrie Ann, where'd you get the idea for that nightgown?"

Carrie Ann shrugged. "I wanted to decorate it. I had a little bit of pink fabric, and I remembered seeing plumeria flowers that were about that same color." She stopped and thought about it for a moment. "Actually, the flowers I had in mind were the first plumerias I ever saw. I remember thinking that they looked like the kind of flowers that Rorie draws. So I cut out a few and stitched them on."

"Honey, I think we might have found you a way to get some independence. Mimi tells me you're a pretty good seamstress, and you've made a lot of original stuff. I don't know if this is all going to work out, and I still have a lot of planning to do about exactly what to carry in the store. But I'm hoping you will do some sewing for me, at least, and in the long run, who knows—we might be doing our own manufacturing. I can see you as Designer-in-Chief!"

Aunt Bea filled their glasses with the last of the pink Chablis and lifted hers. "I propose a toast. To us—independent women of the world!"

Giggling, Carrie Ann and Mimi clicked glasses with Aunt Bea, drank deeply, and settled back under a starry sky to plan a bright future.

Chapter Seventeen

Rorie played on the grass outside the back door, crawling on her knees as she rolled her toy truck across the lawn. Carrie Ann knew she was lucky; Rorie was able to entertain herself a lot of the time. Pretty amazing for a four-year-old. Babysitting Jesse a few times had shown her how lucky she was to have such a self-sufficient and undemanding child. Maybe because Rorie had spent most of her life as an only child living among adults, she had learned to play on her own. And the way she loved toy trucks, she'd probably grow up to be a mechanic or something.

There couldn't be a more beautiful place for a child to play. Michael had rallied the boys to work in the yard while they were off with Mimi and Bea, and the watermelon scent of fresh-cut grass was everywhere. The sun was warm on Carrie Ann's skin. She stopped for a moment to watch a golden butterfly hover among pagoda flowers. Next to the crimson blossoms, a stalk of bananas was turning yellow. The breeze stirred the banana tree's green leaves against a clear blue sky. More and more, this lovely place felt like home. She smiled, glad to have seen Mimi and excited about her and Aunt Bea coming back to stay, but really happy to be home with Michael.

She walked over to the other side of the yard to see how he was doing with the van. Weed was with him, both of them poking around inside the van's engine.

Michael stood straight and wiped his greasy hands on a rag. "Okay, that ought to do it. Let's see if it'll start up."

He climbed onto the front seat and turned the key. The engine sputtered to life, and Weed cheered and began to gather up the tools.

"Does this mean I can go to the Laundromat and the grocery store?" Carrie Ann asked.

"If I can get it to start again." Michael turned the engine off, and then on again. "Right on. Looks like a laundry day to me."

An hour later, she and Rorie were chugging up the driveway, pillowcases stuffed with laundry on the back seat. On the highway, she settled into a steady cruise and headed for Paia.

As they pulled into town, she slowed the van. A crowd of longhairs clustered in front of the little courthouse at the edge of town. She recognized several people—there was Clarice, Cameron the drummer's old lady, with her little boy on her hip. And there was Sundance! Standing on the top step, next to a pudgy little man in a suit, she was frowning and shaking her finger at Rick Stinson. Carrie Ann was intrigued, but she didn't want Rorie to see Sundance. She made a left onto Baldwin Avenue and drove up the hill to the Laundromat.

She parked and unloaded her bags of dirty clothes. Soon she had five machines going and could relax at a table against the front window. Too bad she hadn't brought her book; at least she had thought to bring paper and crayons to keep Rorie busy. She glanced out the window, then tensed as she recognized Johnny's truck pulling into the Laundromat parking lot.

Through the Laundromat's back door, she heard the truck door slam, and then the truck reversed, and she saw it head back down the highway. Jerilyn came in the door with a full basket of laundry and a box of detergent. She stopped when she saw Carrie Ann and looked surprised. But then Jerilyn broke into a broad smile, and Carrie Ann smiled back.

"Auntie Jerilyn!" Rorie dropped her crayon and scrambled down from the bench to run to Jerilyn's side. Jerilyn set her laundry basket on the floor and hugged Rorie, then stood up to meet Carrie Ann and gave her a hug too.

She was so happy to see Jerilyn again, Carrie Ann realized, a wave of fondness filling her as Jerilyn tossed her laundry into a machine, slammed the door, and inserted the requisite quarters. They had the Laundromat to themselves today and lots of time with nothing to do but wait for their clothes to get clean and catch up on each other's lives.

Things at the O'Connors' were fine, Jerilyn told her, with no big changes since Carrie Ann had left. "But I do miss you, and we have to get together. Johnny isn't really mad at you, you know. He can't stand Michael. It's this guy thing they have going. I wish I had a car, I would come and get you, and we could go to the beach or something."

"Maybe I could come and get you—did you see the van outside? That's Michael's, and he lets me use it. Maybe next time I'm going somewhere, I could call and see if you can come with me. You might want to go shopping, or to the library or something, right?"

"Good idea. We could have a girls' day out, and let these old guys have their feud or whatever it is. Forget about them. Tell me what's been going on in your life."

That took a while, especially with Rorie chiming in. Soon the first of Carrie Ann's machines finished its cycle. As she stood to transfer damp clothing into a dryer, Johnny's truck pulled into the parking lot. A moment later Johnny himself appeared at the door. Behind him was Clarice, clutching a bag of laundry with one hand and Kikuyu's grubby little fist with the other.

Somehow, having Clarice there made seeing Johnny a little more comfortable. After an awkward moment, he stepped forward and gave Carrie Ann a peck on the cheek, then gestured toward Clarice. "I found Clarice walking up the hill," he explained. "Kind of a tough hike, with laundry and old Kikuyu there to drag along."

"I saw you down at the courthouse, Clarice," Carrie Ann said. "What's going on down there?"

"Antone's hearing on the building permit thing. It's not looking good. Rick's trying to talk him into giving up, and that would mean we'll have to move."

"I didn't know you lived down in the Gulch," Carrie Ann said. "I thought you lived up in Makawao."

Clarice snorted and began to throw laundry into an empty machine. "I did live up there, with that fool Cameron, but not anymore. He got kind of rough with me one night, and I'm not putting up with that. I grabbed my baby and got out of there. No man is gonna mess with me."

"Wow. So you're living down at the Gulch, just you and Kikuyu?" Jerilyn asked.

"Yeah. I'd about had it with his drumming anyway. That man never stops from dawn 'til dark. Only problem is, it looks like they're going to close down Guava Gulch, and we'll have to find somewhere to live. And my car died, so I don't know how I'm going to house hunt." She looked gloomy, but then brightened. "I did hear that Cameron might be leaving, though, and his landlord likes me better than he ever liked Cameron. Maybe I could rent his place when he's gone."

"Cameron's leaving?" Johnny grinned. "Is anybody taking up a collection to help him buy his ticket? I'd be happy to contribute."

That got a laugh, though Carrie Ann didn't know enough about Cameron to be sure why everyone seemed to be happy that he was leaving.

Jerilyn loaded her damp laundry back into her basket—she liked to hang it out to dry on the line at home—and Johnny hauled it to the truck. Jerilyn gave Rorie and Carrie Ann goodbye hugs, promising to call, and the O'Connors were gone.

Carrie Ann practically had to drag Rorie away when it was time to leave. She was having fun with Kikuyu, crawling on the floor around the Laundromat and getting filthy. But they still had to stop at Horiuchi Market and get home in time to fix dinner. Carrie Ann was planning a tuna casserole, although the guys were probably getting pretty tired of tuna. Still, she thought as she carefully counted out food stamps to Mrs. Horiuchi, tuna was cheap, and it cost a lot to feed all these people. Besides the six who lived at Michael's house, three downstairs and three up, you never could tell who would show up for dinner. Michael had given her twenty dollars when she left the house, but she had used some of that to pay for the washers and dryers. No one had brought home any food while she was gone with Mimi and Aunt Bea, so this was an expensive shopping trip.

She thought about money as she drove home. Aunt Bea's lecture had stuck with her and seeing Clarice on her own reinforced the message. Not that she thought Michael ever would "get rough" with her, as Clarice put it. And not that she thought there was any chance they were going to be splitting up. But it would be nice to have a sewing machine and use it to make some money. She really missed being able to use Jerilyn's machine, and she'd need one if Aunt Bea did open her store. She would have to figure out how she could get one. Maybe Michael would have an idea where she could look for a secondhand machine. How she would pay for it was another matter. Maybe she should stash a little from her next welfare check.

A strange car sat at the bottom of the driveway, and when Carrie Ann reached the top of the stairs, arms loaded with grocery bags, she found half a dozen people clustered around the kitchen table. One of them was Allison. Carrie Ann hadn't seen her since the day Allison's father had arrived to pick her up after Johnny kicked her out of the O'Connors' house. She wasn't particularly pleased to see her now, sitting next to Michael. On the other side of Michael sat a stranger, an older man with a big nose and a dark mustache. Weed was there, sitting close to a chick who was almost as scrawny as him. And, of all people, Cameron, who was tapping lightly on a set of bongo drums, eyes closed as he swayed to his own beat.

Michael and Weed went down to get the laundry, and Carrie Ann pulled milk and eggs from her grocery bags and put them into the refrigerator. Rorie stood open-mouthed in the kitchen, watching Cameron play his drums.

"I'm going to dump this laundry in your room," Michael said as he came in the back door. "We're getting ready to drop acid. This is Brian." He nodded toward the mustached man. "He brought us some Sunshine, good shit."

Acid. Carrie Ann hadn't even been around any of that stuff for months. She knew she had seen and experienced amazing things on acid, but the thought of the drug coursing through her system made her shiver with distaste. She had no desire to feel that acid taint in her throat, as if she'd sucked on an aspirin, or to experience the unpredictable and sometimes terrifying distortions of reality, and the long, grinding comedown. Her trips had been vivid and overwhelming while she was high, but she could never quite recall what had happened once she came down. She knew some part of her had sensed realities beyond what she could have known in any other way, but there had been too many bad times with LSD. And she had an uneasy feeling that, for every insight she'd had while high, there had been a cost, as if she'd been somehow stealing from the future.

Carrie Ann began to put away canned goods. The skinny chick, introduced to her as Semilla, tried to help, mostly getting in the way. It was such a novelty to have someone else help that Carrie Ann was not sure she liked the idea. This was, after all, her kitchen. And there sat Allison, laughing as she gazed up at Michael. What the hell was she doing here? Had all these people come in the car parked down in the yard?

They had, she learned as the conversation continued around the kitchen table. Brian, it seemed, had called Michael to say that he had this acid. Michael's place was a better setting for a trip than Brian's shack in Makawao town. Could he come down with some people who wanted to drop? And one of them just happened to be Allison. What a coincidence, Carrie Ann thought. She wondered if it had been Allison's idea to come down here. And shouldn't Allison be in school today?

Brian pulled a medicine bottle out of his pocket and made a ceremony of handing a tab to each person around the table. They all swallowed their pills, smiling, and sat back to sip coffee and wait. It would be perhaps half an hour before they started to rush. When Brian offered her a tab, Carrie Ann ducked her head. "I have to keep an eye on my little girl, and I'm not really in the mood today. Thanks anyway."

No one seemed to mind that, though Carrie Ann was certain she saw Allison smirk. She poured herself a cup of coffee, and pulled a chair up to the table, making sure it was closer to Michael than Allison's.

"What's been happening with you, Allison?" Carrie Ann asked. "Still living with your folks?"

Allison shrugged and twirled a strand of auburn hair around one finger. "Yeah, what the hell. I try to spend as little time as possible there, but you know how the law is. My probation officer keeps reminding me I have to stay in school and live at home until I'm eighteen. That's less than a year. I guess I can stand it till then, as long as I get out of that place and get stoned often enough."

"I saw Johnny and Jerilyn at the Laundromat today."

Allison examined her fingernails, frowning. "Well, that must have been a thrill. Good old Johnny. I hear he kicked you out, too."

"Yeah. But it's just as well." Carrie Ann leaned closer to Michael and put her arm through his. "I'm much happier living down here with Michael."

Allison raised one eyebrow. "Yeah, looks like you got a real cozy scene going on here."

"Now ladies, behave," Michael said, smiling as he packed buds into a Zigzag paper. Carrie Ann thought he looked unpardonably smug, sitting there between two chicks. She sniffed and sat back in her chair. She could not be bothered to compete with this teenager; after all, she was the one sharing Michael's bed and keeping his kitchen.

Michael lit the joint and passed it around, and the conversation at the table resumed, a mixture of gossip and far-out stories. Weed, sitting up straighter than usual in an apparent attempt to impress Semilla, told them a story he'd heard from someone who'd been up in Haleakala crater and swore that he had seen flying saucers. "He said there were these green and blue lights that landed up on the rim, and then these little creatures got out and walked along the edge of the crater, all lined up in a single row. He was scared shitless that they were gonna come down and get him, but they just hung out for a while and then got back in their ships and left."

"Hey, I met a guy out in Hana who saw something like that," Brian said. "He said there was a bunch of them, all in line and marching along the coast on the edge of a cliff."

"That sounds like the night marchers," Allison said. "I think they're supposed to be these old Hawaiian warriors, and you don't want to get in their way."

That began a discussion of spooky Hawaiian stories, which led to Michael getting up to look for a book on Hawaiian myths he had somewhere back in his roomful of treasures, and Allison getting up to dig through the record collection in the living room in search of a Hawaiian album she remembered seeing last time she was here. With the record on the turntable, Allison danced around the living room, her movements reminding Carrie Ann of Chuckie's phrase: psychedelic hula. Cameron's bongo rhythm changed to match the song on the record. Michael reappeared with his book, and he and Brian paged through it, looking at pictures. Weed and Semilla disappeared out the back door. Carrie Ann was starting to experience a little contact high—a phenomenon she had noticed before when she was around acid trippers. Perhaps their LSD-soaked brains put out some sort of powerful vibe, or maybe it was simply that she was picking up on their mood, but it was something. She was sure she had seen hallucinations one time, turquoise paisley designs that crawled slowly over the sink's porcelain surface as she washed dishes while Duke and the members of Red Dog were peaking on acid.

She closed her eyes, wondering if she would see paisley on her eyelids.

"Mommy!" Rorie came whining into the kitchen, dragging her blanket. "I'm hungry. I want something to eat."

Michael looked displeased. "Carrie Ann, you're gonna have to keep her out of the way. I don't want somebody getting bummed out by one of her tantrums."

Carrie Ann flushed. Michael had never said anything about Rorie's behavior before. Why did it have to be now, with Allison swanning around the living room, and Brian and Cameron listening in? And Rorie didn't really have tantrums, just normal four-year-old tears. All she needed was some food.

"Don't worry, she'll be fine." Carrie Ann handed Rorie a cracker to keep her quiet while she made a peanut butter sandwich. "Let's go outside and play, honey," she said, and went to gather up her book, Rorie's toys, and an old bedspread. It would be a long day, Carrie Ann thought. Acid trips went on for hours. At least it was beautiful today, and they could hang out in the shade until sunset.

But the acid droppers had a similar idea. They had, after all, come down here so they could trip in a natural setting. So, while Carrie Ann tried to concentrate on her novel under a mango tree in one corner of the yard, when she glanced up she would see Weed and

Semilla wandering around, holding hands and stopping to stare at various flowers. Michael sat in the lotus position under a banana tree, ignoring Brian, who propped himself against a nearby palm tree and carried on some sort of monologue. Cameron took off his purple T-shirt and sat on the porch steps to play his drums in the sun. Allison, also topless, continued her gyrations on the porch. When Rorie left her toys and ran to the porch steps to dance along, Carrie Ann decided that was the limit. She strode to her daughter, picked her up, and headed away from the house into the trees at the edge of the yard. Rorie protested but calmed down when Carrie Ann let her play in the tiny stream trickling along the bottom of the gulch.

Eventually, the drumming stopped. Carrie Ann peered through the bushes and found the yard quiet and empty. She gathered the lilikoi and guavas she had found along the stream, and they headed back to their shady spot. Carrie Ann read to Rorie until she fell asleep, then napped herself. When she woke, Rorie still slept next to her. She looked around the yard. No one was in sight.

She found them all in the living room, with a Ravi Shankar raga on the record player. Weed and Semilla sprawled on the couch, their bodies intertwined. Cameron sat against one wall, staring into space, still tapping with one finger on his bongo drums. Brian lay on his back, gazing up at the ceiling. He turned to look at Carrie Ann; his pupils were dilated so much that his eyes seemed black. His face took on a look of wonder. "Wow," he said. "I can see your aura. It's so bright!"

Michael, sitting cross-legged in one corner, turned his head slowly to look at Carrie Ann and gave her a remote smile, then turned his attention back to a nearby wall. Allison, sitting unfortunately close to Michael, giggled. Carrie Ann attempted a smile. She wasn't quite sure what she should do, the only straight person in a house full of stoned-out acid freaks. Maybe she would make some tea. They might like that.

By the time she had served everyone cups of peppermint tea, Rorie had awakened from her nap and was in the kitchen, complaining again about being hungry. Carrie Ann knew none of the others would want to eat, and Roland and Timothy would not be home until late. They were working on some carpentry job in Lahaina and liked to eat and go drinking with the other guys after work. She made grilled cheese sandwiches for herself and Rorie and took their food into Rorie's room. She wished there was something to do—a television would be nice right now—but she and Rorie would have to get by with reading and drawing pictures quietly, staying out of the living room and out of everyone's way. It was dark already; Rorie would be asleep soon, and Carrie Ann could relax and quit worrying about her bringing everyone down.

But even after Rorie had crashed, and Carrie Ann went back into the living room, it seemed strange to sit around while everyone else was tripping, their consciousness in some other dimension that they all seemed to share, beyond Carrie Ann's reality. She felt gauche and exposed, as if they could see through her, as if they were all in some sort of telepathic contact and could look into her mind as well as each other's, but she could not look into theirs. After a while, she took her book into Michael's room and lay down to read.

She was thinking of turning off the light when she heard strange thumping noises coming from the living room. She knelt and reached to push the drape away from the window. From here, she could see across the back of the house and into the windows on one side of the living room. Cameron was crawling around on the floor as if he were looking for something. Every so often, he would stop and pound his fist on the floor. As she watched, he began to sob and shake, and soon he was lying on the floor, writhing and moaning as if he were in pain or fighting off some sort of demon. Carrie Ann could see Brian and Michael, sitting on chairs at the table, gazing at

Cameron as he rolled around on the floor. They did not seem to be concerned, so she watched for a while and then lay down again.

Sometime later, after she had dozed off, Michael came in and stretched out beside her. She turned to him, but he held her off with one hand and lay flat on his back. Rebuffed, Carrie Ann rearranged herself and tried to go back to sleep.

A few minutes later, she heard voices outside the window. She could not discern exactly what they were saying, but she recognized the voices as Weed and Semilla, and she heard her name and Michael's. It sounded as if the two outside were calling to them, and she sat up, thinking she should go check it out. Michael's hand shot out to grasp her forearm, restraining her. She relaxed and lay down again. In a while, Weed and Semilla stopped calling.

Carrie Ann drifted off, only to be wakened by the sound of Rorie crying. It was a regular nighttime cry, not the unnerving screams of her night terrors, but Carrie Ann knew she had to do something about this immediately, or everyone would be bummed out. She rolled out of bed and stumbled to the door. The bathroom light was on. Weed and Semilla stood naked next to the toilet. Seeing her pause at the open door, they looked utterly blown away, stunned by her presence and guilty about whatever it was they had been doing. Carrie Ann was embarrassed. She did not stick around to see what made them look so ashamed. But she wondered, as she comforted Rorie, what on earth had been going on here tonight. All these people had come down here hoping the beautiful setting of Michael's place would put them on a good trip, but thus far it seemed to her the vibes had been very weird. She was glad she had chosen not to drop. She curled up with Rorie, and eventually both slept.

The house was quiet the next morning. Brian and Cameron lay crashed on cushions in the living room. Michael was in his room. Allison, Weed, and Semilla were nowhere to be seen. Carrie Ann fed Rorie, made a pot of coffee, and went outside to work in the garden. She was halfway through weeding the carrot patch when Allison and Roland came out the basement door and went upstairs to the kitchen, with Roland's hand resting familiarly on Allison's hip. Carrie Ann sat back on her heels and smiled. Very interesting. She liked that, seeing Allison with a handsome surfer dude. If Allison was with someone else, that meant she would not be hitting on Michael.

Still, Carrie Ann wished she didn't have to go into the house and find Allison sitting at the table again. And she really did not look forward to seeing Weed and Semilla. Would they remember that weird moment last night? And what about Cameron? He'd certainly freaked out. She was glad Rorie had gone to sleep before things got so strange. Rorie did not seem to realize that there had been anything unusual about yesterday's gathering. She had plenty of energy this morning, running back and forth between the house and the garden while chanting "Faster, faster, faster!"

Carrie Ann knelt again in the garden and dug at a weed with a particularly deep root. Maybe, if she stayed out here long enough, the people in her house would go away, and she wouldn't have to see them today at all.

Chapter Eighteen

The sun was hot, here by the side of the road. Carrie Ann moved back into the shade of trees that edged the Hana Highway. She didn't want to be too far back, but she thought she was visible to drivers anyway, in her red dress.

Here came a truck, a rusty, rattletrap-looking thing. It slowed, and the driver beckoned. Carrie Ann recognized the driver, with his bushy gray mustache. She had met him one time with Johnny when they stopped at a pig farm. The old guy had met them at the gate, surrounded by a passel of yapping dogs, and sold Johnny a couple of used tires for his truck.

"Where you like go?" he asked, pulling his tight T-shirt lower over a big belly.

"Paia."

"Hop in. I take you there."

She climbed onto the seat and settled down for the ride. She hoped her food stamps would be in her post office box today. She really needed to do some shopping. They were down to tuna and brown rice for dinner tonight, and she didn't even have enough flour to make a batch of bread. Thank goodness for the avocados ripening on the tree outside and guavas she'd been making into juice.

"So, where you living?" the old man asked.

"Down in the gulch back there, where I was standing by the driveway."

"Didn't I see you one time before?"

"Yes," she replied. "I met you one time with Johnny O'Connor."

"He your boyfriend?"

She laughed. "No, he's married. My boyfriend is named Michael."

"And what you got under that short dress? I hear you hippie girls no like wear underpants."

Carrie Ann gulped. How the hell was she supposed to answer that? She edged over on her seat, trying put distance between herself and this old man.

He reached over and flipped up the skirt of her dress. He grinned.

"Oh shoots. You get underpants. How about bra? You get bra?"

"I want you to stop this truck right now. I need to get out." Carrie Ann put as much conviction into her voice as she could.

The old man shrugged and pulled the truck to the side of the road. Carrie Ann wasted no time getting out and backed away from the dust his tires kicked up as the old man gunned his engine and drove away without looking back.

Now what? He had put her out on an open stretch of road between pineapple fields, too far to walk back to where she might find a phone. Who would she call anyway? Alexis was the only person she could think of. Could she remember that phone number? She had decided to hitchhike because the van was broken down again, and Michael had taken off somewhere on his motorcycle. Maybe she should have caught a ride with Roland and Timothy when they went to work, but then she would've had to drag Rorie along. Semilla, though always willing to watch Rorie, was not an early riser, so Carrie Ann had waited and then set out to hitchhike. She'd never imagined she would run into something like this lecherous old man on a quick trip to buy groceries.

There was nothing she could do now except try to get a better ride. She wished there were trees along this stretch of the highway, because it wasn't getting any cooler as the day moved on. She shaded her eyes to watch the road. A car appeared, and she stared at it intently. It was against the law to actually stick out your thumb to hitchhike, so people who wanted to catch a ride would stand by the side of the road and wait. This car did not slow down. Nor did the next two.

But the fourth car was a familiar one. It was Chuckie's cherished silver Jeep. Carrie Ann's chest tightened with anxiety. She was really relieved to see him slow down and to know she would have a ride with someone she knew and trusted. But she had not spoken to Chuckie in more than a month, since that day at the service station.

She climbed in, and they sat looking at each other for a minute before Chuckie slowly pulled back onto the highway. He kept his eyes on the road as he drove.

"So, how you been?" he asked.

"Just great. How have you been?"

"Okay. I hear you living down at Michael's place."

"Yeah."

"I guess that means, you and me, we cannot go out together anymore."

"No, I guess not. I like you for a friend, Chuckie, but Michael is my old man now."

He surprised her by turning to flash his brilliant smile, and she remembered how sweet Chuckie was and, for a moment, regretted that she could not see more of him.

"When you get tired of Michael, you call me up," he said. "I take you out."

The vibe seemed to lighten, and she relaxed. She had been dreading seeing Chuckie all these weeks, and now he was being so nice. For the rest of the ride into Paia, they carried on a comfortable conversation, talking about Rorie, Chuckie's grandpa, and the fish Chuckie had caught yesterday. By the time he dropped her off at the post office, she knew she had regained a friend and did not hesitate when Chuckie leaned over to kiss her goodbye. She stood on the sidewalk, a bit wistful as she watched him head uphill toward his grandpa's house.

The food stamps were in. She walked across the street to Horiuchi Market and bought peanut butter, cheese, powdered milk, and a small bag of flour. She did not want to be too loaded down with groceries when she was hitchhiking. But she was lucky getting a ride back, going all the way from Paia with a long-haired couple who lived out in Hana.

Michael's motorcycle was there when she got to the bottom of the driveway. He was in the kitchen, cutting up a pineapple.

"Did you get peanut butter?" he asked as she entered the back door, breathing hard after her hike from the highway.

"Yes, I did."

"Good, because I got bread, but I didn't know we were out of peanut butter." He helped himself, smeared guava jelly onto a second piece of bread, and sat at the table with his sandwich and a couple of spears of pineapple. "Man, that's a sweet pineapple. Little, but sweet—that's the ratoon crop, they're always sweet."

"The what?"

"Ratoon crop. That's the second batch that comes up after they've harvested the main crop."

Carrie Ann finished making sandwiches for herself and Rorie and started cutting the crusts off Rorie's bread.

"Hey, Michael, this weird guy picked me up today." She described the old man, his rusty truck, and the farm where she had first seen him.

Michael appeared unconcerned. "That's old Moniz. He's harmless. Just a dirty old man."

"Well, it was really gross, having him touch me like that. When do you think the van is going to be fixed? I don't like hitchhiking very much."

Michael frowned. "I'm doing my best, Carrie Ann. I spent the whole morning digging this part out of a car at the junkyard, and Weed and I are gonna work on it. Lighten up, okay?"

"I'm not on your case, I'm only asking . . ."

"Get off my back." Michael took another bite of his sandwich and turned his attention to the newspaper he had brought home.

Carrie Ann stood for a moment, then turned to go downstairs and call Rorie from the yard to eat her sandwich. She was halfway out the door when the phone rang. She looked at Michael, who didn't move, just raised his eyebrows and looked back at her. She went to answer the phone.

When she picked it up, she was glad she had. It was Mimi.

"Carrie Ann! I'm so excited! It's happening—we're moving to Maui!"

"Mimi, how cool! When? Did your aunt get a store? Where are you going to live?"

"I should be there in about three weeks. The timing worked out just right for me to give notice on the job, and then I'll have a week to clean up the apartment. I know someone looking for a place, so I'm going to sublet it. I want to hang onto this place for a while, in case things don't work out.

"Anyway, Aunt Bea will be there next week, looking for a place to stay. I think she's planning on living right in Lahaina town. She says the real estate dude found her three good store locations, and she's sure that at least one of them will work out. It's happening, baby—we're going to live on the same island!"

Mimi's call lifted Carrie Ann's mood. But she still brooded about Michael. She had not meant to get on his case, but he seemed on the defensive. She wished he would take a little more responsibility for her and for running the house. Sure, he'd gone shopping, but he had not bothered to ask her what they needed and instead bought only a loaf of bread and a bag full of carrots for juice. And it had been scary, that trip with the old man. You would think it would mean something to Michael, that she had been frightened. What if the old man had been a rapist or something? She hoped she wouldn't have to hitchhike again soon.

She had to give him credit. Michael worked on the van all afternoon and had it going by dinnertime. Carrie Ann decided to thank him with the best dinner she could come up with (even though it was tuna, again), and once she had Rorie in bed she took a shower and rubbed herself all over with sweet-smelling coconut oil. Conscious of the sensual touch of the evening air on her damp skin, she closed the bedroom door behind her and dropped her towel to the floor. Michael looked up from the book he was reading, and she gave him a smile.

"Want a backrub?" she asked, stretching herself seductively across the bed to stroke his thigh.

Michael set his book on the bedside table. He didn't say anything, but smiled back at her, stripped off his shorts and T-shirt, and lay face down on the bed. Carrie Ann straddled him and leaned forward to slide her breasts over his back. She poured coconut oil into her palm and kneaded his shoulders. After a minute, Michael rolled over, and as she guided him home, she knew that everything was all right again between them.

Carrie Ann was in a cheerful mood as she steered along the Pali's curves on the way to Lahaina. Her little household was shaping up. Semilla actually was turning out to be fairly helpful since she had moved in. Weed had scrounged enough scrap lumber, old windows, and roofing tin to build a tree house down near the streambed, and the two were settled there in domestic bliss. Neither seemed to have any memory of the night Carrie Ann had surprised them in the bathroom.

With Semilla on hand as a babysitter, Carrie Ann had been able to go riding with Michael a few times without having to worry about what to do with Rorie. She and Michael got along well most of the time, and when they didn't, sex always smoothed things out again. Of course, there was that one time when she and Rorie came home from a beach trip with Alexis and Emily to find no one around except him and Allison, sitting innocently at the kitchen table. She had no idea how long Allison had been there; now that she was seeing Roland, Allison had an excuse to come down whenever she wanted. Carrie Ann suspected that Roland was exactly that, an excuse to get close to Michael. But it was Carrie Ann, not Allison, who slept in Michael's bed.

In the distance, Carrie Ann could see the masts of sailboats. They were almost at Lahaina. She fumbled in her purse for the piece of paper where she had written directions to Aunt Bea's house.

It was on the ocean side of Front Street, an old house painted white with green trim and a faded red tin roof. The lawn needed mowing, and vines crawled over the porch roof. Heavy clusters of coconuts hung under the fronds of two palm trees in one corner of the yard. The front door and all the windows were open, and the strains of "Yellow Submarine" drifted through the screens.

"Carrie Ann!" Mimi, dressed in a bikini, greeted her with a big hug and knelt to kiss Rorie. "Sorry, I'm probably stinky from all this cleaning—no one had lived here for a while, and the place is a mess. I just started painting. My room is going to be lavender!"

Bea came to greet them, gorgeous as usual in pink hot pants and a halter top.

"Hey, Bea, I like your house," Carrie Ann said as they embraced. "Do you have a store yet?"

"Isn't it wonderful? I love this place. And yes, I do have a store. In fact, we're going down this afternoon to sign the final papers, and you can come along if you want."

"Come see the house, Carrie Ann and Rorie. It is so groovy," Mimi said.

THE ISLAND DECIDES

The house had been the home of a mid-level plantation manager, Mimi explained. After the man died a year ago, his wife had decided to leave for the mainland, and the house sat vacant, with most of its furniture left behind, slightly shabby but perfectly usable. The layout was something like a capital H, with a big living room at the center and wide French doors opening to a view of the Lahaina shoreline and ocean. Two bedrooms made up one side of the H, with a bedroom and kitchen on the other. Everywhere, tall windows opened to the breeze, and fancy molding edged the ceiling.

Carrie Ann changed into her bikini and pitched in to help Mimi paint. Bea enlisted Rorie to carry things to her bedroom as she unpacked them from boxes stacked in the living room. Bea had chosen the largest bedroom, with an ocean view. But Mimi had an ocean view too, and a French door that opened onto the back porch, steps from the beach.

They ate lunch on the back porch, then got ready to head down Front Street to the business district. Bea dressed for the occasion in a sundress that showed off her newly acquired tan, the girls threw T-shirts and shorts over their bikinis, and they all piled into Bea's car.

Lahaina was a quiet little town, bigger than Paia but otherwise similar, with old-fashioned one- or two-story buildings. Corrugated iron awnings extended over the sidewalks, providing shade against Lahaina's fierce afternoon sun. Some of the second stories obviously were living quarters, and some had little balconies. Carrie Ann saw a fish market, some mom-and-pop grocery stores and restaurants, and what looked like a small movie theater. Across the street, a railing edged the shoreline, and gentle waves lapped against a narrow beach. Aunt Bea pulled over to park in front of a shop with wide windows. A dog dozed by the open door. Two young women sat on the balcony, watching the sparse traffic on the street below.

Inside, they found a couple of elderly men waiting for them in an empty store whose walls were lined with simple wooden shelves.

A counter ran the length of the room, and a door behind it led into a tiny office. While Bea talked with the old men, Carrie Ann and Rorie followed Mimi through the office, where an old roll-top desk sat against one wall, and out the back door. Behind the building was a tiny courtyard. Someone had filled the little space with greenery and flowers planted in everything from tin cans to concrete pots. A tree with glossy green leaves grew in one corner, its branches shading much of the area. A narrow staircase, of the same weather-beaten wood as the rest of the building, led to a small landing and a door into the second story.

"Wow, this is trippy," Mimi said. "I can't believe I get to work here. I wonder if we'll be able to use this little backyard. What a nice place to take a break or eat lunch. And the ocean is right across the street! This sure beats working in downtown San Francisco."

"Did Bea decide what to sell?"

"Yep. She should pay you royalties for helping her come up with the idea—it's going to be children's clothes. I hope you've been busily stitching away, because we're gonna need inventory."

"Actually, I haven't done anything. Taking care of the house and Rorie seem to keep me busy all the time, and I don't have a sewing machine anyway. I was thinking I should try to get one, but I haven't done anything about it."

"Well, Bea does have some stuff coming in on the barge next week, so by the time we get the place fixed up we'll have something to sell. But you should go for it, Carrie Ann. You could make yourself some money."

Aunt Bea appeared, with a signed lease in one hand and a set of keys in the other. The two old men came behind her, smiling as she introduced them. Joe and Fred Galvez were brothers who lived upstairs with their wives. The staircase here led to their apartment, and they would use the gate in one corner of the little garden as their entryway. The old men climbed the steps, to be greeted by one of the young women from the balcony, who smiled down at the newcomers before closing the door.

"Is that one of the wives? She seems awfully young," Mimi said.

"Yes, she is," Bea said. "The real estate agent told me the two old men ran this store by themselves for years, and business has been good enough in the past couple of years that they could afford to import some young wives from their hometown in the Philippines. I guess they decided it's time to retire and enjoy living with their sweet young things." Bea smiled and looked around the little garden area. "I hope we'll be good neighbors. They'll keep taking care of the plants, but they said we could come out and enjoy this garden anytime. Well, girls, we'd better get back to the house. I have some carpenters coming in here tomorrow, and pretty soon Mimi and I will have to get down here and start being shopkeepers. But today, I suggest we finish up our work at the house and hit the water."

They managed to get a little more work done before giving in to the temptation of the beach in Bea's new backyard. The water was cool in the Lahaina heat. Rorie showed off her swimming skills as the three adults relaxed, drifting in the calm water.

As the sun sank toward the ocean, Mimi and Carrie Ann moved furniture back into place in Mimi's room. In the kitchen, Aunt Bea fried chicken, and Rorie tore up lettuce leaves for salad. Mimi and Carrie Ann cleaned their paintbrushes, then poured themselves glasses of pink Chablis and put plates on the old table left on the back lanai by the former occupants of the house. Mimi brought a cushion from the rattan couch in the living room for Rorie's chair, and they all sat down to the feast Bea had somehow pulled together in the midst of moving in. Rorie gobbled her food, then asked, "Mommy, can I go play on the beach?"

Carrie Ann surveyed the shoreline. The sun lay low on the horizon, and the sea was quiet, the beach empty. "You may if you'll stay right in front of the house, where we can see you." Rorie climbed down from her chair and headed to the beach.

Carrie Ann watched as Rorie squatted to peer at something on the sand, then scraped up the last of her potato salad. "Wow, that chicken was good—thank you, Bea. How nice to eat someone else's cooking."

"Are you still doing all the cooking and washing the dishes?" Mimi asked her.

"Most of the cooking, but Weed has a new girlfriend, you know, Semilla, and she helps out with the dishes. Which is great, because none of the guys do, that's for sure."

"I still say you're selling yourself short, Carrie Ann," Bea said. "The amount of work you do around that place, Michael should be paying you in addition to giving you a free room—and I guess it's not even free room and board, right? Because you buy the groceries with your food stamps, is that right?"

"Well, yeah, I guess I do buy a lot of the food. But my food stamps wouldn't be enough to feed everybody. Michael buys food, and the two construction guys bring stuff home. They sure eat a lot though."

"Where do you see this relationship going?" Bea asked.

Flustered by this forthright question, Carrie Ann paused. It was one thing to fantasize in her own mind about a future as Michael's old lady and maybe someday his wife, and another thing altogether to tell someone else about that fantasy. "I'm hoping it will be long term and maybe even permanent," she said finally.

For a moment, Bea said nothing, sipping her wine and gazing out to the pink glow on the horizon. Then she set the glass down and refilled it. "You know my story, right, Carrie Ann? I'm sure Mimi has told you about my horrible husband."

"A little bit."

"I have a few years on you girls, and besides my own experience, which was bad enough, I have a lot of women friends who've been through the same and worse. Have you ever heard of a consciousness-raising group? No? Well, my consciousness-raising group was what finally woke me up and gave me the guts to leave Harry and get a divorce. And that was the best thing I've ever done for myself." She lifted her glass, and Mimi and Carrie Ann raised theirs to clink in a toast to Bea's freedom.

Bea took a sip, then continued. "Consciousness-raising groups are a big deal back in Atlanta. You get together a group of women, and everyone sits in a circle and shares their thoughts and feelings about whatever the topic is for that evening—love, men, money, beauty, children, growing old—you name it, we talked it over. Everybody gets a turn, you can pass if you want, and nobody interrupts while you're talking. No questions, no comments. By the time you make it all the way around the circle, I swear it's miraculous. It's like you can actually sense the consciousness level rising. You find out you're not the only one who's had these thoughts and these experiences, and you begin to get some perspective on your own life." Bea paused, swirling her wine in a glass that reflected the sunset's glow.

"So that's what happened to me. Can you believe I left after that time he held a gun to my head, and then I let him talk me into coming back again? It took a lot of support from my women friends for me to really leave and really stay away, but dammit, I did it. No man will ever treat me the way Harry did, ever again. I will go to my grave single rather than have a man push me around like that. And I'm glad I had a good lawyer and was able to come away with some money to start over. God knows I earned it." Bea set her glass on the table and leaned forward, her gaze earnest. "But that's where I worry about you, Carrie Ann."

Carrie Ann turned her gaze from the shoreline, where Rorie was silhouetted against the sunset glow, and blinked, surprised. "You're worried about me?"

Bea nodded. "I don't know how Michael treats you, though I thought he seemed a little high-handed when I first met him. But here you are, spending your youth and energy and beauty on this man who really doesn't seem to appreciate it very much. And if you two break up and you have to move, then what? What would you take with you?" Bea shook her head and sat back in her chair. "The only way you would get anything of his—all those antiques and his 'income,' whatever that may be—is if you're married. But he sure doesn't seem to me like the marrying kind. And I don't think he would make much of a husband, even if he did marry you." Bea took a deep breath and a sip of wine. Carrie Ann and Mimi exchanged glances. Bea was certainly wound up tonight.

"Sorry to talk so much," she continued, smiling a bit sheepishly. "I don't mean to lecture, but I had to say this stuff. I can't have you girls making the same mistakes I made, and all my friends made, and not at least share with you what I've learned in life."

"Well, thank you, Bea," Carrie Ann swallowed a sip of her own wine, taken aback by the intensity of Bea's lecture. She wished the phrase "not the marrying kind" would quit popping up. "Thank you for caring about me. I'm glad you got out of that terrible marriage. I don't think Michael would ever do anything like hold a gun to my head." She paused for a moment, biting her lip. "But I do have to admit, you're right about his not appreciating me very much." She told the story of hitchhiking to Paia and being groped by Old Man Moniz, and of Michael's response. It was good to share a story that had replayed in her mind again and again. For the first time, she admitted to herself how hurt she had been by Michael's indifference to her safety.

"Oh my God," Bea said, rolling her eyes. "Listen, Carrie Ann, you are always welcome here if things don't work out with Michael. We have that extra bedroom and you and little Rorie could move right in." Carrie Ann glanced down toward the shore, where Rorie was kneeling on the beach, using her hands to bulldoze sand into some sort of structure.

"And, speaking of little Rorie," Bea went on, "you have to think about her welfare, as well as your own. I understand it's a difficult situation, and you can't pull up roots and move back to San Francisco. Don't you have some social worker who's keeping an eye on things? What does he think about this arrangement with Michael?"

"He knows about it, but I wouldn't say he was really happy about it," Carrie Ann admitted.

"I can bet you he would be a lot happier if you were living over here with Mimi and me, making clothes and helping out in the store," Bea said. "It would give you a chance to get on your feet and either go back to San Francisco with a few bucks in your pocket or maybe even to stay here and find a place of your own, if that's what you decide. Think about it. I'm really sincere in this, Carrie Ann. You're a talented and promising young woman, and I know you and Mimi are great friends. You let me know if you change your mind."

"Okay, thank you, I will. I really want to make it work with Michael, but it's good to have friends and a backup plan." Carrie Ann looked toward the shore. A red glow lined the horizon. "I better call Rorie in before we can't see her anymore." She got up and left Bea and Mimi at the table, feeling guilty relief at how glad she was for an excuse to leave this challenging discussion. Why did everyone have to pick on her about Michael?

"I guess it's time to head for home," Carrie Ann said, as she helped Rorie dust sand off her feet. "It's been such a great day. I'm happy you got that store with the beautiful little garden, and I know it's gonna be a great success. And I love your house!" She lifted Rorie, and the child snuggled against her, wrapping her arms around Carrie Ann's neck. "Bea, thanks for the great dinner. I promise I'll think about what you said, and I promise I'll get some sewing done for your store. I have some really cool ideas that I can't wait to try as soon as my check comes and I can find a sewing machine."

Bea stroked Rorie's head and gave Carrie Ann a quick kiss, Mimi helped her gather her belongings, and they stepped out into the warm Lahaina night.

"Bea really means it, you know," Mimi said as she watched Carrie Ann settle Rorie on the back seat and cover her with a blanket. "She mentioned it earlier. I think she's kind of worried about you, and I have to agree that you could do better than what's going on at Michael's house. I know he's a babe, but maybe not the one for you. Heck, he's not good enough for you! He doesn't deserve you!"

Carrie Ann turned to face Mimi, torn between loyalty to Michael and a nagging sense that Mimi and her aunt might be right. She hugged her friend. "Mimi, I can't tell you how glad I am that you are on the same island with me. It's like God knew I needed a friend, and not only did he send you, he sent Aunt Bea and jobs for us both!"

Teary-eyed but giggling, they said good-night, and Carrie Ann steered the van out onto the road and headed for home.

The stars were sharp and clear over the ocean, and few cars traveled the cliffside highway tonight. Carrie Ann took her time and enjoyed the beauty of the drive. So clear, that sky. If only her mind held such clarity; if only her thoughts would settle and let her see the way forward. Bea and Mimi had a point, she knew that. When she'd driven over this morning, she'd been happy about her life at Michael's, sure she could make it work. But there was another side. It wasn't only that Michael expected her to do so much around the house, or that he was a bit dictatorial in his ways. The real problem was that he was detached, lacking in affection, uncaring about her feelings. Was she only a convenience for him? She remembered that silly joke from her childhood days, walking home from school with a girlfriend who told her the definition of a housewife: "Someone you screw on the bed and she does your housework for you." Was that all she was to Michael?

It would be cool living with Mimi again, and Bea was a trip, older and wiser for sure, but casual and fun to be around. She liked her pink Chablis, but Carrie Ann couldn't see any signs that Bea might have a drinking problem like her mother did. David probably would like to see her living with two women rather than with Michael, even though he didn't know what was really happening. And, yes, it would be great to make her own money and not have to rely on an inadequate welfare check and food stamps. She knew she was creative and hard-working, and maybe she could go somewhere with her clothing designs. With Bea as a partner, someone who knew about business, there was no telling what might happen.

But against all those arguments and the vague sense of dissatisfaction she had to admit she'd experienced for weeks was one major factor: Michael. Tall, handsome, sexy—oh my God, was he sexy. Any arguments against him were lost to the part of her that began to tremble and breathe hard the minute he laid a hand on her. She couldn't wait to get home to him tonight. It was like that every day, waiting for night to fall and those secret hours in the darkness of his room.

This incredible sex had to mean as much to Michael as it did to her, she was sure of it. But their relationship was more than romantic. Carrie Ann knew she could help Michael make Pineapple Jam famous. Already, she supported him and his band with her cooking and housekeeping, but she knew she could do more to help Michael succeed. Wasn't it the most important role any woman could play, to help her man succeed? The band was sounding much better these days, now that Michael had his keyboard and could keep them on track. He was talking about setting up a concert soon, and Carrie Ann had been working on poster designs. She looked forward to being behind the scenes, helping put on concerts here and, who knew, maybe flying to the other islands someday or even, perhaps, to the mainland. Maybe she could introduce Michael to Duke, who knew everyone in the California rock-and-roll scene. She was excited at the prospect of being the one with the crucial connection that helped Pineapple Jam make it big.

As she pulled the van into its usual parking spot, she saw that a strange car sat in the driveway, and the house was lit up. Wondering who the company might be, Carrie Ann lifted the sleeping Rorie and went up the back stairs, hoping the noisy conversation inside would not wake her. Fortunately, Rorie was sound asleep and did not stir as Carrie Ann tucked her in. She was glad of that, because among the crowd sitting around the cluttered living room table was Allison. Carrie Ann did not want to spend time quieting Rorie when the teen queen was sitting right next to Carrie Ann's old man.

She brought a chair from the kitchen and managed to squeeze in on the other side of Michael's chair, laying a possessive hand on his knee and leaning over to kiss him as she settled at the table. Two empty gallon wine bottles and one still half full were on the table. Carrie Ann poured herself some wine and looked around. In addition to the regulars—the guys from downstairs and Weed and Semilla—there was a man she didn't know, and he was not the usual sort who came down this driveway. He looked very straight, with short hair and a button-down-collar shirt.

"Carrie Ann, this is Peter the Pecker Checker." Everyone around the table laughed and cheered, and Allison leaned over to put her arm around his shoulders. "Peter works for the Department of Health," Michael continued. "He lives in Honolulu, and he comes over here every month to run the VD clinic."

Peter made a clumsy bow, nearly bumping his horn-rimmed glasses on the table. He pushed his hair back from his forehead and grinned at Carrie Ann, bloodshot eyes magnified by the glasses' thick lens. "How about a joke? Do you like jokes, pretty lady?"

"Well, sure," Carrie Ann said, and wondered why everyone started laughing again, even before Peter had told his joke. They all seemed to be very drunk, and stoned too, judging by the number of roaches in the ashtray on the table.

"Okay. Here goes. This guy gets out of the VD hospital, see, and he goes to hire a hooker, 'cause he's horny. So after they have sex a few times, he tells her he hasn't had sex in three months because he's been in the VD hospital. So then the hooker says, "How's the food in there, anyway? 'Cause I'm going there tomorrow!"

Carrie Ann smiled, but everyone else around the table exploded with laughter. "Tell us another one, Peter!" Weed cried. "He knows lots of jokes, Carrie Ann."

"Okay, okay. How's this one. What two things in the air can make a woman pregnant?"

There were a lot of rowdy guesses, none of which made much sense.

"Okay, okay. Her feet! Get it? Her feet!"

That started another round of laughter and table pounding. Carrie Ann got it, but somehow Peter's jokes didn't seem to strike her as funny as they did everyone else. She drained her wine glass and filled it again, then reached for a half-smoked joint. It looked as if she had some catching up to do.

Chapter Nineteen

Carrie Ann could hardly wait. They had finally set the date for Pineapple Jam's first concert, two weeks from now. It would be in the gym, up above Paia, where Michael taught yoga. The boys were practicing late into the night, and Carrie Ann was busily turning out posters. She had hand-stitched herself a new dress for the concert, from an old embroidered-linen tablecloth, wishing with every stitch that she'd found time to look for a sewing machine. But that could wait; at least she had a new dress for the concert, edged with fringe that she knew would swing and sway when she danced.

She still had to figure out what to do with Rorie that night. She stopped coloring the psychedelic swirl that spelled out the concert time on her latest poster, and looked up at her daughter, sitting across the table drawing her own poster on flimsy typing paper. Already, Rorie's posters covered one side of the refrigerator. Carrie Ann sighed. Having a child was such a full-time thing. Every waking moment, she either had to keep Rorie amused and out of trouble, or make sure she was where someone else would look after her. The night of the concert, everyone would want to be there, except probably the O'Connor household. And she knew she couldn't ask Jerilyn to watch Rorie. Oh well, something would come up. She would think of something.

She heard footsteps on the back porch. The door opened, and Allison stuck her head around the corner.

"Oh. Hi. I thought Michael might be up here," Allison said.

"No, he's out." Carrie Ann was not about to share any more information than that; it was none of Allison's business where Michael was. Besides, she wasn't really sure herself. As usual, he had ridden off on his motorcycle without telling her where he was going. But that was also none of Allison's business.

"Well, I'll wait." Allison came in and sat at the kitchen table. "What are you folks doing?"

"We're making posters, for my mommy's concert," Rorie said.

"It's not Mommy's concert, honey, it's Michael's band's concert," Carrie Ann said.

"I'd like to make a poster," Allison said. "Can I have a piece of paper?"

Reluctantly, Carrie Ann handed Allison a sheet of poster paper. They didn't have much in the way of art supplies, but Carrie Ann had been able to make some pretty nice posters, she thought. She hoped Allison wouldn't get the idea that she was part of this whole project.

In the distance, Carrie Ann heard Michael's motorcycle. She tensed, knowing the weird vibes that always came down whenever she, Michael, and Allison were in a room together. How did Allison get here, anyway? Carrie Ann wished Roland were home. At least when he was here, she was less likely to flirt with Michael.

The motorcycle roared up to the house, slowed to an idle, and cut off. Michael's footsteps came up the back stairs.

"Hey girls, howzit. I see everybody is busy being creative." Michael shrugged out of his leather jacket and tossed it on the back of the chair.

"Look at my poster, Michael," Rorie said, holding up her sheet full of scribbles.

"Yeah, great," Michael said, opening the fridge. He pulled out the jug of guava juice Carrie Ann had made this morning and took a swig, straight from the jug.

"Michael!" Carrie Ann protested. "Use a glass, please."

"Yes, Mother," Michael said, shooting an amused glance at Allison, who smiled back. Carrie Ann's jaw tightened.

"Well, little schoolgirl, what are you doing out here on a weekday?"

"Oh, I felt like getting out of town, so I caught a ride with one of the kids who lives out this way."

"Right on. So, are you ready to rock out?"

"Can't wait. It's gonna be bitchin'."

"We're really sounding good, especially since we got those new speakers. This is gonna be a great concert."

Allison set her crayon down and pushed her half-finished poster toward Rorie. "Hey, I got to hit the road. Here, Rorie, wanna finish my poster?" Rorie examined Allison's poster critically, perhaps wondering whether it was worthy of her efforts. Allison stood up, then hesitated, gripping the back of her chair. Finally, she spoke.

"Michael, can I talk to you outside?" Allison's words came rapidly, as if she did not have the breath to take her time.

Michael looked puzzled but followed Allison out the back door.

Carrie Ann sat for a moment without moving. Then she stood up and walked to the kitchen window, trying to step quietly on the kitchen's squeaky wooden floorboards. From the window, she could see Allison and Michael out behind the shed. Allison was doing all the talking, while Michael stood with his arms folded. Then Michael spoke briefly while Allison nodded, and Allison left to hike up the driveway. Michael stood looking after her, then turned and went into the shed.

Carrie Ann went back to her chair and her poster. Outside, she heard the roar of the Rototiller. Apparently, Michael was going to work on the garden. It was the first time he had shown any interest in the garden in weeks, and while she was glad he was finally getting around to tilling the area she had asked him to clear, she wondered why he had decided to do this now, instead of coming back into the house after Allison left.

THE ISLAND DECIDES

By the time he did come in, dripping sweat and spattered with bits of dirt, Carrie Ann had put the posters away and was starting on dinner. She glanced at him as he opened the fridge and helped himself to another drink of guava juice. No way was she going to say anything about the juice, not after that last time. And she knew she should keep her mouth shut about Allison. But she couldn't help herself.

"So, what is Allison up to? She didn't stay long. Why did she come down here today?"

Michael shrugged. "She wanted to know how to get hold of somebody."

"Oh really? Like who?"

Michael shot her a sideways look, then reached for a dish towel and used it to wipe the sweat off his face.

"Peter the Pecker Checker."

"Why on earth does Allison want to get hold of him?"

Michael shrugged again. "Who knows. Maybe she likes his jokes. Or maybe she thinks she has VD." He tossed the dish towel back onto its hook, turned on his heel, and walked out of the kitchen. A few minutes later, she heard the sound of the shower.

That was the end of that conversation; Carrie Ann did not ask again. The mystery deepened a few days later when Peter himself showed up. He did not stay to party, just sat down to smoke a quick joint, then stood outside talking with Michael before getting into his car to head up the driveway. Carrie Ann could not resist peeking out the window again, and she was pretty sure she saw Michael give Peter a baggie, probably some buds from his latest score.

But there were plenty of other things to occupy her mind: bread to be baked, meals to be cooked, laundry to haul into Paia. Carrie Ann was eager to get some seeds into the ground Michael had tilled. There were always weeds to be pulled. And of course, the usual crowd gathered daily around the living room table, smoking cigarettes and dope, drinking coffee, and generally making a mess.

Michael had not come to bed. Carrie Ann rolled over to glance out the window. The moon was full tonight, and Michael and the others had decided to hike down to the ocean. Carrie Ann was too exhausted to even think about such a thing, and of course she couldn't leave Rorie, so she had headed to bed about the time they left on their hike. She sat up to peer at the clock on his bedside table. One a.m. How could that be? She'd been in bed by ten. They couldn't still be out hiking.

She got up, pulled on her robe, and went out into the moonlit living room. Someone was crashed on the single mattress that lay against one wall, a friend of a friend who had showed up around dinner time, still here. Great. She checked the kitchen. No one there, and when she looked down toward the stream, where Weed and Semilla lived, she saw no flicker of light. From the back porch, she leaned out to look for Michael's motorcycle. It was not there. She must have been deep asleep to miss the familiar growl of its engine when he started up. Where had he gone?

Back in bed, she lay flat, running over the possibilities in her mind. Unfortunately, there were so many that she knew nothing about. What did Michael do when he was out, which was frequently? What was going on between him and Allison, with her coming around so often? The vibes had been weird when she was here the other day.

Carrie Ann turned onto one side and closed her eyes. In a few hours, she had to be up, no matter what Michael was doing. But her stomach hurt, and her heart did too.

When she opened her eyes, morning light poured through the window. Still no Michael. His jacket was not hanging on its usual hook. He had not come home.

She pulled herself out of bed and headed for the bathroom, then gently opened the door to Rorie's room. She was awake and in a good mood. Rorie gave her mother a big smile and held up her coloring book. "Look, Mommy. A jungle with monkeys and snakes."

"And a butterfly too," Carrie Ann said, reaching into Rorie's box for shorts and a T-shirt. "You're a good artist. You know how to choose just the right colors."

Rorie tipped her head, regarding her work, then nodded. "That's why my posters are so pretty," she said.

"We'll make some more after breakfast, okay? And then Auntie Lanihuli is coming to get you to play with Jesse, remember?"

"Umm-hmm." Rorie lifted her arms so Carrie Ann could pull her T-shirt on. "We're going to play on the swings Jesse's daddy made."

In the kitchen, Carrie Ann started the coffee and put water on to boil for oatmeal, half listening to Rorie chatter on about Jesse's toys.

Today, she had planned to finish up a few more posters and take them to the stores between here and Makawao, cajoling storekeepers to put one up. Somehow that idea was suddenly a bit less appealing. What the hell? Did Michael think it was okay to go out and be gone all night without even telling her? And where was he? Maybe it was time for her to go hang out in Lahaina for a while with Mimi and Bea. Maybe he needed to experience life without her around to cook and clean and entertain his friends, not to mention the fabulous times they had in bed. Was that not enough for him?

Surely he would realize how important she was to his life if she wasn't around for a few days. Mimi had promised to come and get her anytime, and it would be fun to be on the beach for a couple of days with good women friends. Rorie would love it.

But she would have to see what happened when Michael came home. Would he be open about it? "Sorry, honey, but I took so-and-so home and decided I didn't want to chance coming home on the bike at night, so I crashed at his place. Remember that night

I almost hit a cow in the middle of the Hana Highway?" Or what if he had in fact hit something this time—should she be calling the hospital? She shook her head and decided to get on with her day and see what happened.

They were finishing up their oatmeal when the bike came down the driveway. Carrie Ann froze as she heard Michael climb the stairs. He gave her a brief smile. "Hey, baby, how's it going?" He tossed his jacket over a chair and went to pour himself a cup of coffee.

Carrie Ann tried to compose herself. Her heart was jumping and her shoulders tight. She couldn't help it. She had to ask.

"Where were you last night?"

Michael paused, then dumped a heaping spoonful of sugar into his cup. He stirred the coffee and tossed the spoon into the sink, then turned to Carrie Ann.

"Carrie Ann, the trouble with living with a chick is she thinks she owns the pink slip on you. Well, you don't."

Michael took a sip of his coffee without breaking eye contact, then turned and headed for the bedroom. Carrie Ann sat biting her lip and holding her face steady. Rorie looked at her and frowned.

"Mommy, what's a pink slip?"

"Something to do with cars, honey. Are you pau eating breakfast? We have to get to work, you know. Why don't you go get your paper and colors and get started?"

Carrie Ann gathered the breakfast bowls and walked to the sink, surreptitiously wiping her eyes. She was working her way through last night's pile of dirty dishes when Michael came in, fresh from the shower, and patted her on the butt. She kept her face averted. He leaned down to kiss the back of her neck and said, "Gotta go. See you later," then walked out the door.

She couldn't believe it. She couldn't believe his behavior, and she couldn't believe her own, putting up with this crap. Angrily, she scraped the burnt gunk off the edge of a casserole dish. She should have listened to Mimi and Bea all along. They were right. Michael didn't care about her. She would leave.

As soon as she thought it, she began to second-guess herself. How could she go now, when the concert was coming up, possibly the beginning of a big career for Pineapple Jam? How could she let go of her own investment in their success, not to mention her investment in her relationship with Michael? Maybe she should stick around until the concert. Maybe seeing her dance in her new dress would charm him. Maybe she could ask people how they heard about the dance and find that it was her posters that had brought them there. Maybe she could, somehow, get him to realize that he needed her, that he wanted her, and only her.

Yes, that was it. She would do her best to look sexy and fun, twirling in her new concert dress, then take off into the night with Mimi and leave Michael wondering if she would ever return. It would serve him right to worry for a change. Then, if she came home, and he still seemed to dismiss her importance in his life, she would really leave. Even now, hurt and angry as she was, she could hardly believe she was contemplating such a move.

The phone rang, and she wiped her hands and went to answer. It was her social worker, David, and he was not happy. He had heard about the day Alexis took Rorie to town and lost her.

"I'm so sorry, Carrie Ann, it was only for a few minutes," Alexis had said when she returned with the half-asleep Rorie. Alexis and Rorie missed seeing each other, now that they no longer lived next door, and that day Alexis had asked if she could take Rorie along while she ran a quick errand in Kahului.

"We were at the shopping center, and I really needed to pee," Alexis said after Carrie Ann had settled Rorie on her bed and shut the door. "Rorie insisted she didn't need to go, so I left her standing outside the stall while I went. Then, of all things, I guess she went over to look out the door, and she spotted that foster family. You know, the people she stayed with before?"

Carrie Ann nodded, dread rising in her chest.

"Then she ran out of the restroom to catch up with them, and when I came out of the stall, she was gone," Alexis said. "I was freaked out, of course! She just disappeared. Then I saw Chuckie, and he helped me look, and we found her with that family. I guess he knows them, so he went up to them with me and acted like he was helping me take care of her, and we had just lost track for a minute. "

Carrie Ann closed her eyes and took a deep breath, memories of the last time a friend had managed to lose her daughter echoing in her mind. Today, Rorie was home and safe. That was what mattered. But this might be the next worst thing that could happen, Rorie's former foster parents seeing her running loose, without supervision.

"How did they react when you showed up? And how was Rorie?" she asked Alexis. "She was really attached to them, you know. I've always been afraid of running into them someday."

"Well, she did seem pretty clingy. The lady had picked her up, and they looked worried, trying to figure out where she came from and at the same time all smiley and happy to see her. It was lucky Chuckie was there, because you know how she loves him, so when he held out his arms, she went to him right away. He introduced me, and we stood around talking story for a couple minutes, then we sort of wandered off together. The people were nice—Linda and Kimo, right? They had this little girl with them who seemed happy to see Rorie. I think it was okay, but I'm really sorry I didn't keep her with me. I never thought she might run off like that!"

Carrie Ann was grateful to Chuckie for his presence of mind. He'd recognized the De Silva family's name when she told him her story, back when they first met, and he must have known they would be only too happy to report Carrie Ann if they thought she'd lost

Rorie again. There was nothing she could do but keep her fingers crossed and hope they wouldn't.

Then came this phone call. They had indeed reported her. Carrie Ann had never heard this tone of voice from her soft-spoken social worker.

"Linda was quite disturbed to see Rorie on her own at the shopping center, running around with you nowhere in sight. What are you thinking, Carrie Ann? You can't keep sending your child off with irresponsible people who don't keep track of her. I'm going to have to put this in my monthly report, and I don't think the judge is going to be happy to hear it."

She soothed him as best she could, insisting that it had been a fluke; Rorie had run off only because she recognized the De Silva family, something that could have happened even if Carrie Ann had been there with her.

"Nevertheless," David replied, "Rorie is your kuleana, no one else's, and you have to take that seriously."

"My what?"

"Your kuleana. It's a Hawaiian word that means your responsibility, your very important responsibility. This child has only you to watch out for her. You need to remember that, because, if you don't, the state will take over that kuleana."

She hung up and sank onto Rorie's mattress, her eyes filling with tears, frustrated and fearful. She had tried to be sure her child was in the care of people who were responsible. Alexis had been great so far, and Rorie loved being with her. Alexis wasn't used to going out with a child in tow, that's all; she didn't realize you had to keep hold of a four-year-old all the time.

But Carrie Ann couldn't afford to upset David and Judge Yoshioka. She'd have to keep her daughter close, even if it meant dragging her along on errands that made Rorie tired and cranky. No more leaving her with Semilla, and Alexis would have to come down here if she wanted to hang out with Rorie. Lanihuli seemed like the only safe option, a mother who understood what it took to watch over children and who was glad for a playmate to keep her busy little boy occupied in the safety of a fenced backyard.

As pleased as Lanihuli was to have Rorie over, Carrie Ann was going to owe her a lot of babysitting by the time this concert was over. She had left Rorie with Lanihuli and Jesse several times lately when she went into town to put up posters for the concert. She came home from one trip with her feelings hurt because the saleswoman in a Kahului store had been hostile, almost nasty, when Carrie Ann asked permission to tack up a poster.

But Michael insisted that she keep going. "Publicity is everything," he'd said last night. "If we don't get the word out, we won't have an audience. It's getting to the point where we need to make some money, and this is your part of the operation, babe."

At least he recognized her contribution, and he was right about the money. Weed continued to be unemployed, and Roland and Timothy had finished their job in Lahaina and were lounging around with nothing else to do that would bring in any cash. Today, they had disappeared early in Roland's truck, probably to go surfing. If she didn't want to feed the whole household with her food stamps, she'd better get a move on.

She could hear Weed downstairs, plunking on his bass. Michael had gone off somewhere on his motorcycle. Carrie Ann checked her remaining stash of posters—three left. If she wanted to hit every store in Makawao, she would probably need a few more. This would be a good time to make some, because Lanihuli had come down to pick up Rorie after lunch, and she'd be up at their house for the afternoon.

With no one around to distract her, Carrie Ann produced three more posters in record time. She tucked them into a folder, changed clothes, and went downstairs to tell Weed she was taking the van to Makawao.

But the van would not start. Weed came out and fooled around with the engine, but nothing happened.

"Sorry, Carrie Ann. I guess we'll have to wait for Michael. I don't know what's wrong with it."

"Shit. I was hoping to get these all distributed today. It's only another few days until the concert, and we need some time for people to be able to see them."

"Well, maybe he can fix the van when he gets home, or maybe he'll take you on the bike."

Carrie Ann had her doubts about going anywhere on the bike, even if Michael did get home before store-closing time. The sky was gray, with clouds hanging low and ominous; it suited her mood. She felt weighed down and yet unmoored, oppressed by dread of an uncertain future. She wandered aimlessly around the house, arguing with herself. Out the window, raindrops splashed on leaves. Soon rain was pounding on the metal roof, drowning out the electric bass sounds from downstairs.

It was the first time Carrie Ann had seen such rain since she came to Maui. The weather had been gentle and warm, with just enough quiet rain falling in the night to keep the landscape green. But there'd been nothing like this storm.

She sat watching the pouring rain from the shelter of the front porch. There was an exciting immediacy to the moment, the rain pounding on the roof, streaming from the eaves, and dripping from wet, shiny green leaves. The air smelled fresh and alive; it was cool against her skin. The grass was almost a fluorescent green against the dark gray of the sky.

It rained for about twenty minutes, then gradually slowed to a drizzle and finally stopped. The air was still. Out in the shed, Weed had stopped playing, and the only sound was that of water drops falling from one slick surface to another.

A cup of tea would be nice. She got up to go into the kitchen and fill the kettle, then stopped to listen. Yes, that did sound like Michael's bike, coming down the hill very slowly. She went to the window to look out. It was Michael, with someone on the back of the bike, head down as if to shelter behind him from the rain. Michael pulled carefully under the eaves of the shed and dismounted.

Shit! It was Allison. Carrie Ann sighed and put the kettle on.

Michael stomped up the back steps and came in pulling off his rain-spattered leather jacket. He sat down and took his boots off. Allison followed, her steps slow. She was also soaked, her auburn hair dripping.

"Carrie Ann, how about getting us a couple of towels," Michael said. "Damn, what a downpour. I guess the rainy season has begun."

Wordlessly, Carrie Ann went to dig towels from the hallway closet. She stood waiting for the kettle to whistle, watching as Michael and Allison dried themselves off.

"How about something for Allison to wear, Carrie Ann. Your stuff should fit her, huh?"

Carrie Ann went to look through her cardboard boxes. She found a pair of jeans she didn't much like and an old T-shirt, handed them to Allison silently, and grabbed the kettle from the burner to stop its shrieking.

"You guys want some tea?" she asked grudgingly.

"Yeah, sure, that would be great. I'll be right back, I got to get some dry clothes on." Michael headed for the bedroom, while Allison went to change in the bathroom. A few moments later, she was back, dry but looking rather subdued. Carrie Ann poured three cups of peppermint tea and set one on the table in front of Allison. She stood leaning against the kitchen counter and blew on her own tea to cool it.

When Michael returned, he took his leather jacket from the back of the chair where he had thrown it, dug into one pocket, and pulled out a paper bag from which he dumped two small pill bottles. Carrie Ann moved closer to the table.

"Okay, Carrie Ann, I need your help with Allison here. She's in a little trouble, and we're going to fix it." He held up one of the pill bottles. "These pills contain ergot, but she already took that," he said. "That should probably kill the fetus. And these are antibiotics, to make sure she doesn't get an infection."

Carrie Ann's mouth dropped open, and she nearly spilled her tea. Allison slumped over her teacup, looking glum.

"Michael, what on earth are you talking about? What is this stuff?" Carrie Ann demanded.

Michael sat back in his chair, crossed his legs and folded his arms. His face took on a stern look, as if he would brook no nonsense.

"Allison is pregnant, and we're helping with her abortion."

Carrie Ann looked from Michael to Allison, who pushed her damp hair off her face and focused her attention on the window, where rainwater still dripped from the eaves.

"How are we going to do that? Are you out of your mind?"

"No, Carrie Ann, I am not out of my mind, and I would appreciate some support. This is not really such a big deal. This stuff comes from Peter, he's a health professional, and he assures me everything is very safe, very sterile. It will be over in a couple of hours. Allison needs our help, and I would think you of all people would be willing to help out someone in a tight situation."

"But Michael, I don't know anything about abortions. Isn't it illegal? And hey, Allison." She turned to the girl, who briefly glanced her way before turning back to frown at the window. "I thought you were on the pill. Didn't Jerilyn tell me you were taking the pill? How did you ever get pregnant, anyway?"

"Well, I might have forgotten to take it a few times. And I got pregnant the usual way. Sorry if it's inconvenient for you."

"Now listen, Carrie Ann, let's get on with this," Michael said. "Allison already took the ergot, so this thing is happening. We just have to help her get through it. The ergot causes contractions, the stuff comes rushing out, and it's all over. Simple, clean, and final."

Michael looked pleased with himself. Carrie Ann, on the other hand, was too shocked to speak. Allison stood up without a word. In a minute they heard her retching in the bathroom.

Carrie Ann sat there looking at the pills on the table. She was a little dazed by it all. "This ergot stuff. How do we know she's not going to bleed to death or something? And how much pain is involved?"

Michael waved his hand impatiently. "Hey, this stuff comes from someone in the profession, some contact of Peter's. Would they give us this stuff if they thought anything could go wrong?" He stood and dropped the pill bottles back into the bag. "I'm not debating it anymore. Here's what I want you to do. There's an old shower curtain in the hall closet. Put it over the spare mattress in Rorie's room, and then pick out the oldest, funkiest sheet we have and put that on top of it."

"In Rorie's room?" she asked, dismayed.

"Why not, she's not here, right? The way I heard it, Keone will bring her home after dinner, so we have the rest of the afternoon to get this over with." He set the bag on the table and picked up the wooden box where he kept his stash. "I'm going out and smoke a joint with Weed and make sure he stays out of the way. I'll be back. You go make up the bed."

He walked out the kitchen door. Carrie Ann sat motionless at the table. Allison came out of the bathroom, her face still damp from washing after her vomiting session.

"Are you sure you want to do this?" Carrie Ann asked.

"It's too late, it's already started. I took that stuff when Michael picked me up from school an hour ago. And anyway, I can't have a kid."

"Couldn't you have the kid and give it up for adoption?"

Allison shook her head vehemently. "Not a chance. For one thing, my mom would never let me give it away. She'd make me keep it to learn a lesson or something. No way. I'm not going to be a mother. I've seen you with Rorie. I know what it's like. No thanks, I'll pass."

Carrie Ann looked away. She hadn't realized she was setting such a bad example of motherhood. Finally, she stood up. It seemed to her she should be doing something to stop all this, but she had no idea what that would be. How could Michael expect this of her? But here she was, faced with a reality she never could have foreseen, with no way to change the course of events. She guessed she had better go make up the bed and hunt up some old towels. She'd never been to an abortion before, but she had heard someone describe a spontaneous miscarriage, and she was expecting blood.

Half an hour later, there was still no major change. Michael had come back upstairs, and the three of them sat around the kitchen table, waiting for something to happen.

"Why don't you go for a nice walk up the road," Michael suggested to Allison. "Maybe that will get things moving."

Carrie Ann grimaced. "I don't know about that. How do you feel, Allison?"

Allison looked up from the magazine she was reading and scooped her hair back off her face. "I feel okay, kind of like I have the cramps."

"You better go with her, Carrie Ann," Michael said. Carrie Ann hesitated—why her? She decided it was not worth arguing about.

They walked around the yard a few times, then up the road, which was slippery from the rain. They made it about halfway up the driveway before Allison began to complain. "It's getting worse. Now it's like bad cramps."

They turned to walk back, Allison clutching her belly with one hand and using the other to hold onto guava branches along the road, trying not to slip on the wet driveway. Overhead, lightning flashed, and distant thunder rumbled. The rain had not returned, but the air was humid and heavy. As they descended into the valley, it was as if they entered a pool of vibrations that swirled around them, slowing their movements.

They climbed the back steps, and Allison went straight in to lie down. Carrie Ann went looking for Michael. He was in his room, stretched out on the bed with his eyes closed.

"Michael, wake up, it's happening."

"Huh?" He lifted his head, blinked, then settled back into the pillows. "So, let it happen."

"But what do we do now?"

"I told you—let it happen. She just has to expel it."

Carrie Ann stood in the hallway outside Michael's room. She could hear Allison breathing hard in the room next door and the steady drip of water from the roof onto leaves outside the bathroom window. What the hell was she supposed to do? How had she gotten into this mess? What if Allison bled to death or something? Carrie Ann would be in big trouble, even though she'd been dragged into this trip against her will. Maybe she would go to jail. And surely the court would take Rorie away if word of this got out, even if Allison was fine.

Fuck it. She didn't have to do this. Michael had started it; he could finish it. She'd grab a few clothes and call Mimi. They would go to Lahaina for a few days until this was all over.

"It might take a while," Mimi said when she answered the store phone. "I'm closing up pretty soon, but then I have to drive out to Kaanapali to get Bea. She's golfing. So it probably will be a couple of hours before I can get there," Mimi said. "What's going on? You don't sound good. Is everything okay?"

"I'll tell you all about it later," Carrie Ann replied.

"Is this it? Are you giving up on this guy?"

Carrie Ann sighed. "I don't know. I keep fighting with myself. I love him, Mimi. He's so cool. But some shit is going down that I just can't deal with. I thought if I split for a while, I'd be able to figure things out. And maybe he'll appreciate me more if I'm not around."

"Well, think about this," Mimi said. "I know how you feel about him. But how does he make you feel about yourself? I don't mean the sex, I know that's great. I mean every day, just going about your life. If he's The One, he should make you feel smart and beautiful, like you're really groovy and the best thing that ever happened to him, and he should treat you that way. Is that how it is?"

Trust Mimi to come up with something Carrie Ann could not answer and had to admit was right on. She never felt like she was enough for Michael; lately, she was always on edge, trying hard even just to get his attention. When was the last time he'd told her she was pretty?

She hung up, biting her lip, went into Rorie's room, and pulled the overnight bag from its shelf. Allison was on the bed, clutching her knees to her chest. She groaned, a deep, painful sound. Carrie Ann paused in her packing. That didn't sound good. "Do you want a hot water bottle or something?" she asked.

"Ummm."

Carrie Ann figured that meant yes, so she filled the bottle and gave it to Allison. She went back to stuffing clothing into her overnight bag. Then Allison groaned again, louder, and rolled from side to side as if to escape the pain. It reminded Carrie Ann of her own labor, something she thankfully had managed to forget for more than four years. Allison's groans turned to low, guttural screams, and she clutched her belly. Carrie Ann could hear Michael's keyboard out in the shed, barely audible against the pounding of a rain squall on the roof and the dreadful sounds Allison was making. Shit. How could she leave now? Michael certainly would not be here to help this girl; he hadn't even bothered to check in before heading out to play music.

"Where the hell did Michael go?" Allison asked. Her face glistened with sweat.

"I guess the boy can't take it," Carrie Ann replied as she wiped Allison's forehead with a damp cloth.

"Fucking men," was Allison's response.

"That's exactly what you'd better not do in the future if you want to avoid this kind of trip," Carrie Ann said, trying to lighten up a heavy situation.

"Tell that to Michael," Allison replied and moaned again.

Carrie Ann sat back, contemplating that statement. That bastard. Allison was just a kid, no matter how mature she tried to act. Was this Michael's baby? Maybe from before he started seeing Carrie Ann, back when Allison lived with the O'Connors? Or maybe even since Carrie Ann had moved in here, devoting her life to Michael and his ambitions. She'd have to do the math to figure it out, but there was no time for that. She had been right about the blood.

Carrie Ann cleaned up the mess and offered Allison sips of carrot juice between contractions. She examined each bloody towel before shaking the solid bits into the toilet and tossing the towel to soak in the bathtub. She wondered how she'd know when this was over, what they would do if it kept going on and if the girl on the bed before her seemed to be bleeding to death. Carrie Ann wondered if she'd have to go look for Michael and make him take Allison to the hospital in the van, or even ask Mimi to take her. She couldn't believe how many of these nasty clots Allison was expelling. And yet no matter how hard Carrie Ann looked, none of them resembled the precious fragment she was waiting for.

Then it was there. The fetus was unmistakable: a tiny flesh-colored mannequin in an embryo's curled posture. Carrie Ann slowly picked up the little thing lying on the bloodstained towel between Allison's thighs. It had dark little eye spots; its miniature fingers and toes were distinct. Amazing that it could be so small and yet so perfect.

"Here it is," Carrie Ann said, staring at the little figure in her palm. "Want to see it?"

"No!" Allison squeezed her eyes shut and turned her head away.

Carrie Ann went into the bathroom, half-intending to flush the fetus as she had all the other pieces of matter that had come from Allison's body.

She couldn't do it. Standing there next to the toilet, she knew that this little thing, whatever it might have become, was not sewage.

The sky was dark, and the wind was blowing, though the rain had stopped. Thunder boomed in the distance. Carrie Ann looked out the window, trying to think of where they could bury the fetus. If they put it in the soft dirt of the garden it could be turned up by accident or mangled by the tiller. Maybe Michael could dig a hole somewhere, but thus far he hadn't been much help. He'd probably tell her to flush it.

Finally, she decided that, unless Michael had a better idea, burning would be the best solution. It seemed clean and final, as he said this whole thing should be. She left the fetus wrapped in a tissue on the bathroom counter and checked on Allison, who had calmed down considerably and was bleeding only slightly. Then she went to the top of the back stairs and called down to Michael. There was no answer from the shed. After a minute, Carrie Ann realized there was a note on the kitchen table. "I'm down at Weed's smoking a joint. Back soon."

For a long moment, Carrie Ann stood there, looking at that note. She was going to have to do it herself. She couldn't count on Michael anymore. Not at all, not for anything.

There were newspapers in a pile on the table. Kerosene was in a can on the back porch. Before Carrie Ann went out to the shed to gather some wood scraps, she looked in on Allison again. The girl was sitting up and was sipping juice. Carrie Ann changed her sheet and put a cover over her.

Then she collected the fire-making supplies in a paper bag, went into the bathroom, and picked up the fetus. As she walked across the lawn to the old cistern where they burned trash, the wind and thunder were quiet. A heaviness still lay over everything, as if the air for miles around had settled and concentrated in this valley. Carrie Ann set the fetus on a rock, still wrapped in its tissue. She crumpled papers in a pile on the wet ashes that filled the cistern, added the wood scraps, splashed kerosene over it all, and lit the fire. She wanted a good hot fire.

Overhead, the sky loomed dark and low. Carrie Ann picked up the fetus and unwrapped it. In the fire's light, she looked at the tiny form curled in the palm of her hand, and then she looked up at the sky.

Something was watching. Carrie Ann could feel its presence, observing without judgment. Somehow she knew that this was an event of great gravity and that there would be a price to pay. She had never felt anything with more certainty

The flames were strong enough; the little body disappeared immediately when she dropped it into the fire. Carrie Ann stood watching as the wood scraps burned, thinking about what she would do next, calmly visualizing everything step-by-step. No more arguing with herself. She knew what she wanted.

When the fire burned down to embers, she would go into the house and finish packing—all their clothes and Rorie's toys, the drawings from the refrigerator, the Indian bedspreads, even the potted croton she'd planted from a rooted cutting. It was too late today to call David and tell him she was moving, but she'd do that first thing in the morning. She would leave what remained of the food she'd bought with her food stamps, but she'd take the bread she had baked yesterday. Let Michael get his own damn bread. And he could clean up all those bloody sheets and towels she'd dumped in the bathroom, too.

But before she packed, she would call Lanihuli, just to be sure Rorie was safe and to be sure she stayed there until Carrie Ann and Mimi could pick her up. There was no reason that child ever should come down this driveway again, certainly no reason she should come back to find Allison lying pale and weak in her bed. Carrie Ann yearned to hold her child, to stroke her shining hair, and kiss her dimpled chin. She hadn't seen Rorie since morning, such a long time ago. It seemed to Carrie Ann that nothing mattered more.

In the cistern, the little fire had died away, leaving only fading embers. Carrie Ann took one last look. Then she went back into the house to get her act together.

ACKNOWLEDGEMENTS

The Island Decides, first published in 2013, tells of "early hippie days" on Maui. Newly revised, it is the first in a trilogy of novels about women making their lives on this island loved by so many.

Many people helped and encouraged me over the years I worked on this story. Most of them are Maui folks, but it was in Arkansas that I first began to write about the characters and situations in this novel, at the University of Arkansas creative writing program in Fayetteville. I am grateful to my teachers there, William Harrison and JoAnne Meschery, for introducing me to the basics of writing fiction, and to Elizabeth Engstrom, whose Maui workshop continued the process.

Mahalo nui loa to Madge Walls for her careful and helpful critiques and to my friend, the late Janie Taylor, for her expert job of copyediting. Thanks to early readers Beth Butler, Jane Lovell, Morlee Walters, Benni D'Enbeau, Stephanie Austin, Sue Lipp, Sue Grissom, Joelle Rudin, Kathleen Gilliland, Marsha Cavin, Jennifer Bohlin, Connie Kent, and Kathleen Jensen all of whom offered useful suggestions.

This novel was inspired by my memories of the late 1960s and early 1970s on Maui, but it is fiction. None of these situations, and none of these characters, could possibly match the crazy reality of that time.

Learn more about my other books at https://jillengledow.com. Find out what happens next to Carrie Ann and Rorie in *A Dollar and Love*[1]. And stay tuned: *Rose's War* is next.

---

1. *https://books2read.com/adollarandlove*